Christmas Stories from Louisiana

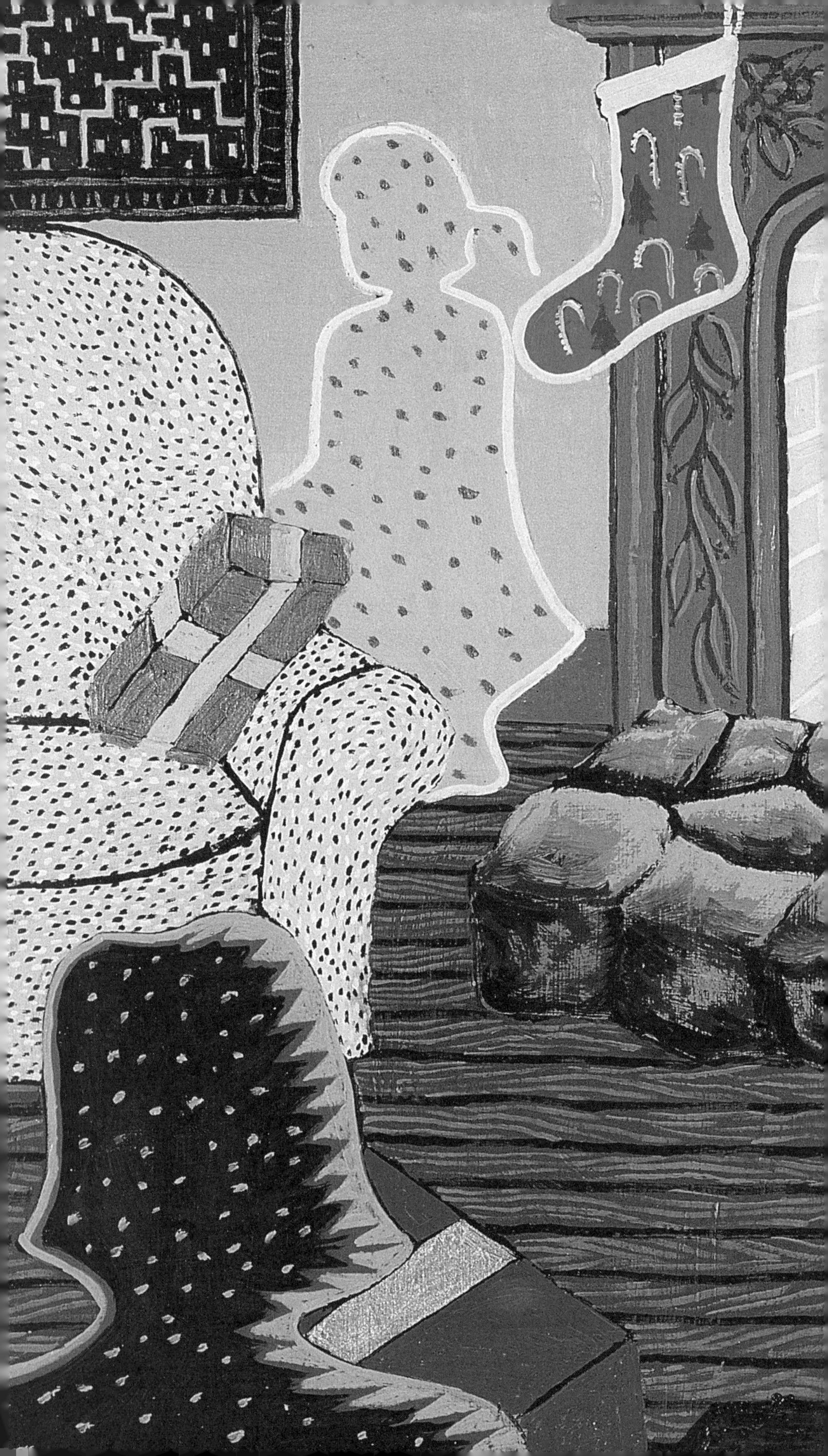

Christmas Stories from Louisiana

Edited by Dorothy Dodge Robbins
and Kenneth Robbins

Illustrations by Francis X. Pavy

UNIVERSITY PRESS OF MISSISSIPPI / JACKSON

www.upress.state.ms.us
The University Press of Mississippi is a member of the Association of American University Presses.

07 06 05 04 03   5 4 3 2 1

"Madame Martel's Christmas Eve" by Kate Chopin previously published in *The Complete Works of Kate Chopin*, ed. Per Seyersted (Louisiana State University Press, 1969); "Snow" from *A Good Scent from a Strange Mountain* by Robert Olen Butler, © 1992 by Robert Olen Butler, reprinted by permission of Henry Holt and Company, LLC; "About Grace" by Kelly Cherry previously published in *First Light* (Cheyenne, WY: Calypso Publications, 1997), all rights reserved, used by permission of Kelly Cherry; "Popcorn for Christmas" by Debra Gray De Noux and O'Neil De Noux originally published in *Romantic Interludes Magazine* (Winter 1994); "Little Miss Sophie" by Alice Dunbar-Nelson appears in *The Goodness of St. Rocque, and Other Stories* (New York: Dodd, Mead, 1895); "The Holy Assumption of Mr. Tinsel" by Patty Friedmann, previously published in *Xavier Review* (Spring 1992); "Won't You Lead Us in 'Jingle Bells'?" by Harnett T. Kane from *Have Pen, Will Travel* (Doubleday and Sons, 1959); "Christmas Gifts" by Ruth McEnery Stuart from *A Golden Wedding and Other Tales* (Harper and Brothers, 1893); the excerpt from *Twelve Years a Slave* by Solomon Northrup (Auburn: Derby and Miller, 1853; reprinted by Louisiana Sate University Press, 1968, ed. by Sue Eakin and Joseph Logsdon); the excerpt from *Children of Strangers* by Lyle Saxon © 1989, used by permission of the licenser, Pelican Publishing Company, Inc.; "A Christmas Story" by Katherine Anne Porter, from *Mademoiselle* (December 1946), reprinted with the permission of The Permissions Company on behalf of Barbara Thompson Davis, Literary Trustee for the Estate of Katherine Anne Porter.

Library of Congress Cataloging-in-Publication Data

Christmas stories from Louisiana / edited by Dorothy Dodge Robbins and Kenneth Robbins.
     p. cm.
  ISBN 1-57806-588-7 (cloth : alk. paper)
   1. Lousiana–Social life and customs–Fiction. 2. Short stories, American–Louisiana. 3. Christmas stories, American. I. Robbins, Dorothy Dodge. II. Robbins, Kenn.
   PS558.L8 C49 2003
   813'010832763–dc21   2003003713

British Library Cataloging-in-Publication Data available

Dedicated to our children, Daniel and Madeline

CONTENTS

INTRODUCTION

Dorothy Dodge Robbins

Christmas is often associated with things Louisiana cannot provide–snow chief among them–and there is a sense of longing in many of these stories from this fair-weather state, parts of which are subtropical, for the ice and cold and white of a winter wonderland up north. But let this be a short-lived envy. Despite the fact that often the grass is still green, the rosebushes still in bloom, and the children still in shorts, no one celebrates the Christmas season quite like the Cajuns, Creoles, and sundry diverse others who populate Louisiana. In this eclectic collection of stories and memoirs from–or inspired by–Louisiana, Christmas is an extravagant *fais do do*, whether celebrated with community around a bonfire on the banks of the Red River or alone at home in front of a flaming log in the fireplace. These stories center around Christmas essentials–snowflakes serving as mere trimming–like the expectant birth of a special baby, the reuniting of family members at holiday homecomings, and the preparation and giving of gifts.

While secular celebrations make their rounds in this anthology, including an appearance by Santa Claus as an unrepentant junk food aficionado in "Like a Bowl Full of Jelly," many of the stories incorporate religious motifs. The selection from Lyle Saxon's *Children of Strangers* explores events surrounding the birth of a son conceived through the union of members of separate cultures. The story conveys the wonder and anticipation of birth set against concerns for the youth of the mother, the humble conditions of the infant's birthplace, and the uncertainty of paternity–each an allusion to the birth over two thousand years ago that marked the first Christmas. It is left, however, to Katherine Anne Porter to bring clarity to both secular and religious issues in her charming piece, "A Christmas Story."

Recollections of family gatherings replete with Christmas cheer and its mirror emotion, holiday depression, are prominent in this anthology. "Trying to Sing" is both a homage to holiday traditions unique to a particular family–including a headless plastic choirboy on the front lawn and a potent fruity concoction in the kitchen–and a bittersweet memoir about the author's final Christmas with her dying grandfather and still-intact family. The chapter from *Requiem for a Year* recounts a young man's lonely introspective Christmas away from home spent in the company of an ailing kitten and the family of his estranged lover. And in "About Grace," the narrator shares a family legend about the repercussions heaped upon her eight-year-old brother when he examined his Christmas gifts a day early.

Gifts are central to the celebration of Christmas, though the best gifts are often those which require no wrapping, as verified by a number of the selections. In Alice Dunbar-Nelson's story "Little Miss Sophie," selfless giving is epitomized by the title character who slaves over a sewing needle in her French Quarter hovel to salvage another person's Christmas dream, embracing in the process the loss of her own. Both haunted by memories of snow, a Jewish lawyer and a Vietnamese waitress exchange conversation in lieu of presents on Christmas Eve in Robert Olen Butler's "Snow." Reversing the traditional pattern of bestowing gifts, the conclusion of "Won't You Lead Us in 'Jingle Bells'?" lightheartedly conveys what happens when giving becomes taking.

There are certain elements traditional to Louisiana literature, like the grotesque and the Gothic, that insinuate themselves into the Christmas spirit down south. "The Holy Assumption of Mr. Tinsel" is a darkly humorous account of what befalls one puppeteer when his local holiday icon becomes too heavy for its strings and closes down a section of the French Quarter. "A Color of Christmas" delivers a greeting card most families would not want to receive from a daughter on death row, but it explains why she won't be home for the holidays this year.

Ghost stories are standard Christmas fare in New Orleans, reputedly the most haunted city in America, and a tad darker than Dickens's London. Two are included for late-night reading pleasure: "Christmas at the Barriloux's," set in a contemporary suburb where the welcoming committee for the new tenants happens to be the old tenants, and "Popcorn for Christmas," in which the city morgue becomes the venue for an after-hours Christmas Eve party crashed by a local police officer. Psychological ghosts, the vestiges of unrequited desire and guilt, also appear in a number of other tales, chief among them Kate Chopin's "Madame Martel's Christmas Eve," in which a widow receives a welcome Christmas Eve vision, not of sugar plums, but of her late beloved husband.

Louisiana's legacy as a slave state also makes its holiday appearance in this collection. Two distinct versions of slave-era plantation celebrations are offered, the first by Ruth McEnery Stuart, whose childhood in Louisiana preceded the emancipation of enslaved peoples. Her "Christmas Gifts" is naively nostalgic in its depiction of congenial relations between masters and slaves. Evoking a far different image of Christmas for the plantation slaves is the account offered by Solomon Northrup, taken from *Twelve Years a Slave.* Solomon's abduction as a free adult in New York landed him in bondage in Louisiana. He recalls the feasting and dancing as being part of only a few days' respite from the constant labor, want, and brutality that characterized the remainder of the year. Taken together the two remembrances are intriguing in their differing perspectives and competing descriptions of plantation life at Christmas time.

This collection of Christmas tales and remembrances represents over two centuries of Louisiana life and lore and crosses over into a third. Though traditional in their explorations of a number of themes associated with the Christmas season, these authors nonetheless reflect Louisiana, whether that particular essence is geographic, cultural, gastronomic, or attitudinal. The settings vary, from a Crescent City back alley to a maximum security cell in Angola to the cotton fields adjacent to the banks of the Cane River, but each contribution is uniquely flavored with Louisiana spice. This holiday reading season, hold the nutmeg and reach for the Tabasco!

Madame Martel's Christmas Eve

Kate Chopin

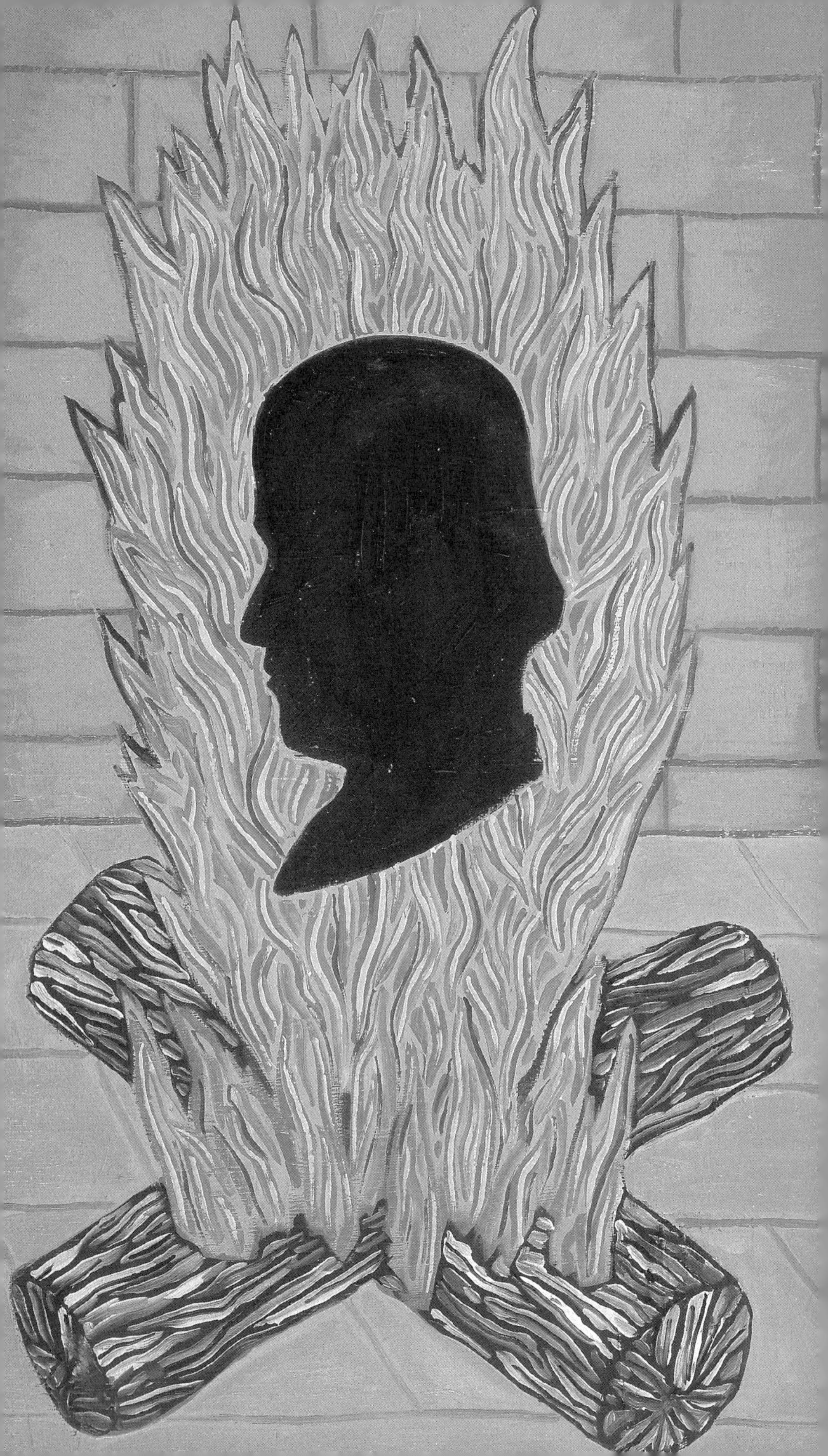

Madame Martel was alone in the house. Even the servants upon one pretext and another had deserted her. She did not care; nothing mattered.

She was a slender, blond woman, dressed in deep mourning. As she sat looking into the fire, holding in her hand an old letter that she had been reading, the naturally sorrowful expression of her face was sharpened by acute and vivid memories. The tears kept welling up to her eyes and she kept wiping them away with a fine, black-bordered cambric handkerchief. Occasionally she would turn to the table beside her and picking up an old ambrotype that lay there amid the pile of letters, she would gaze and gaze with misty eyes upon the picture; choking back the sobs; seeming to hold them in with the black-bordered handkerchief that she pressed to her mouth.

The room in which she sat was cheerful, with its open wood-fire and its fine old-fashioned furniture that betokened taste as well as comfort and wealth. Over the mantel-piece hung the pleasing, handsome portrait of a man in his early prime.

But Madame Martel was alone. Not only the servants were absent but even her children were away. Instead of coming home for Christmas, Gustave had accepted the invitation of a college friend to spend the holidays in Assumption.

He had learned by experience that his mother preferred to be alone at this season and he respected her wishes. Adelaide, his older sister, had of course gone to Iberville to be with her Uncle Achille's family, where there was no end of merrymaking all the year round. And even little Lulu was glad to get away for a few days from the depressing atmosphere which settled upon their home at the approach of Christmas.

Madame Martel was one of those women–not rare among Creoles–who make a luxury of grief. Most people thought it peculiarly touching that she had never abandoned mourning for her husband, who had been dead six years, and that she never intended to lay it aside.

More than one woman had secretly resolved, in the event of a like bereavement, to model her own widowhood upon just such lines. And there were men who felt that death would lose half its sting if, in dying they might bear away with them the assurance of being mourned so faithfully, so persistently as Madame Martel mourned her departed husband.

It was especially at the season of Christmas that she indulged to the utmost in her poignant memories and abandoned herself to a very intoxication of grief. For her husband had possessed a sunny, cheerful temperament–the children resembled him–and it had often seemed to her that he had chiefly welcomed in Christmas the pretext to give rein to his own boyish exuberance of spirit. A thousand recollections crowded upon her. She could see his beaming face; she could hear the clear ring of his laughter, joining the little ones in their glee as every fresh delight of the day unfolded itself.

The room had grown oppressive; for it was really not cold out of doors–hardly cold enough for the fire that was burning there on the hearth. Madame Martel arose and went and poured herself a glass of water. Her throat was parched and her head was beginning to ache. The pitcher was heavy and her thin hand shook a little as she poured the water. She went into her sleeping-room for a fresh, dry handkerchief, and she cooled her face, which was hot and inflamed, with a few puffs of *poudre de riz*.

She was nervous and unstrung. She had been dwelling so persistently on the thought of her husband that she felt as if he must be there in the house. She felt as if the years had rolled backward and given her again her own. If she were to go into the playroom, surely she would find the Christmas tree there, all ablaze, as it was that last Christmas that he was with them. He would be there holding little Lulu in his arms. She could almost hear the ring of voices and the patter of little feet.

Madame Martel, suffocating with memories, threw a little shawl over her shoulders and stepped out upon the gallery, leaving the door ajar. There was a faint moonlight that seemed rather a misty effulgence enveloping the whole landscape. Through the tangle of her garden she could see the lights of the village a little distance away. And there were sounds that reached her: there was music somewhere; and occasional shouts of merriment and laughter; and some one was lustily blowing a horn not far away.

She walked slowly and with a measured tramp, up and down. She lingered a while at the south end of the gallery where there were roses hanging still untouched by the frost, and she stayed there looking before her into the shadowy depths that seemed to picture the gloom of her own existence. Her acute grief of a while before had passed, but a terrible loneliness had settled upon her spirit.

Her husband was forever gone, and now the children even seemed to be slipping out of her life, cut off by want of sympathy. Perhaps it was in the nature of things; she did not know; it was very hard to bear; and her heart suddenly turned savage and hungry within her for human companionship—for some expression of human love.

Little Lulu was not far away: on the other side of the village, about a half mile or so. She was staying there with old and intimate friends of her mother, in a big, hospitable house where there were lots of young people and much good cheer in store for the holidays.

With the thought of Lulu's nearness the desire came to Madame Martel to see the child, to have the little one with her again at home. She would go herself on the instant and fetch Lulu back. She wondered how she could ever have suffered the child to leave her.

Acting at once upon the impulse that moved her, Madame

Martel hastily descended the stairs and walked hurriedly down the path that led between two lines of tall Magnolias to the outer road.

There was quite a bit of desolate road to traverse, but she did not fear. She knew every soul for miles around and was sure of not being molested.

The moon had grown brighter. It was not so misty now and she could see plainly ahead of her and all about her. There was the end of the plank walk a rod or so away. Here was the wedge of a cotton field to pass, still covered with its gaunt, dry stalks to which ragged shreds of cotton clung here and there. Off against the woods a mile away, a railroad train was approaching. She could not hear it yet: she could only see the swiftly moving line of lights against the dark background of forest.

Madame Martel had drawn her black shawl up over her head and she looked like a slim nun moving along through the moonlight. A few stragglers on their way to the station made room for her; and the jest and laughter died on their lips as she passed by. People respected her as a sort of mystery; as something above them, and to be taken very seriously.

Old Uncle Wisdom made a profound bow as he stumbled down from the plank walk to give her the right of way. His wife was with him and he dragged his granddaughter, Tildy, by a willing hand. They were on their way to the station to meet Tildy's "maw" who was coming to spend Christmas with them in the shanty yonder on the rim of the bayou.

Through the open door of a cabin that she passed came the scraping notes of a fiddle, and people were dancing within. The sounds were distressing to her sensitive, musical ear and she hurried by. A big wagon load of people swung into the country road, out for a moonlight drive. In the village proper there was much flitting about; people greeting each other or bidding good-bye in doorways and on steps and galleries. The very air seemed charged with cheerful excitement.

When Madame Martel reached the big house at the far end of town, she made her way at once to the front door and entered, after a faint knock that never could have been heard amid the hubbub that reigned within.

There she stood within the entrance of the big hall that was thronged with people. Lights were hanging from the huge rafters; the whitewashed walls were decorated with cedar branches and mistletoe. Someone was playing a lively air upon the piano, to which no one was paying any attention except two young Convent girls who were waltzing together with much difficulty in one corner.

There were old ladies and gentlemen all seeming to be talking at once. There was a young mother, loath to quit the scene, foolishly striving to put her baby to sleep in the midst of it. A few little darkies were leaning against the whitewashed wall, clinging each to an orange which someone had given them. But above all there was the laughter and voices of children; and just as Madame Martel appeared in the doorway, Lulu, with flaming cheeks and sparkling eyes, was twirling a plate in the middle of the room.

"*Tiens!* Madame Martel!"

If the cry had been *"tiens! un revenant*–a spirit from the other world!"* it could not have had a more instantaneous, depressing effect upon the whole assembly. The piano ceased playing; the Convent girls stopped waltzing; the old people stopped talking and the young ones stopped laughing; only the plate in the middle of the floor seemed not to care and it went on whirling.

But the surprise–the suspense were only momentary. People crowded around Madame Martel with expressions of satisfaction at seeing her and all wanted her to do something: to take off her shawl; to sit down; to look at the baby; to accept a bit of refreshments.

"No, no!" in her gentle, deprecatory voice. She begged they would excuse her–she had only come–it was about Lulu. The child had not seemed entirely well in the morning when she left home. Madame Martel thought that she had better take her back; she hoped that Lulu would be willing to return with her.

A perfect storm of protest! And Lulu the very picture of

despair! The child had approached her mother and clung to her, imploring to be permitted to remain as if begging for very existence.

"Of course your mama will let you stay, now that she sees you are well and amusing yourself," asserted a comfortably fat old lady with a talent for arranging matters. "Your mama would never be so selfish!"

"Selfish!" She had not thought of it as selfish; and she at once felt willing to endure any suffering rather than afflict others with her own selfish desires.

Surely Lulu could remain if she wished to; and she gave the child a passionate embrace as she let her go. But she herself could not be induced to linger for a moment. She would not accept the offer of an escort home. She went as she had come– alone.

Hardly had Madame Martel turned her back than she could hear that they were at it again. The piano began playing and all the noises started up afresh.

The simple and rather natural choice of the child to remain with her young companions, took somewhat the aspect of a tragedy to Madame Martel as she made her way homeward. It was not so much the fact itself as the significance of the fact. She felt as if she had driven love out of her life and she kept repeating to herself: "I have driven love away; I have driven it away." And at the same time she seemed to feel a reproach from her dear, dead husband that she had looked for consolation and hoped for comfort aside from his cherished memory.

She would go back home now to her old letters, to her thoughts, to her tears. How he and he alone had always understood her! It seemed as if he understood her now; as if he were with her now in spirit as she hurried through the night back to her desolate home.

Madame Martel, upon quitting the sitting-room where she had been poring over her old letters, had lowered the light on the table. Now, as she mounted the front stairs, the room appeared to her to be brighter than the flare of the dying embers could have made it; and mechanically approaching the window that opened upon the gallery, she looked in.

She did not scream, or cry out at what she saw. She only gave a gasp that seemed to wrench her whole body and she clutched blindly at the window jamb for support. She saw that the light under its tempered shade had been raised; the embers had fallen into a dull, glowing heap between the andirons. And there before the fire, in her own armchair, sat her husband. How well she knew him!

She could not see his face, but his leg was stretched out toward the fire, his head was bent, and he sat motionless looking at something that he held in his hand.

She closed her eyes; she knew that when she opened them the vision would be gone. With swift retrospection she remembered all the stories she had ever heard of optical illusions: all the tricks that an over-excited brain is apt to play upon one. She realized that she had been nervous, overwrought, and this was the revenge of her senses: disclosing to her this vision of her husband. How familiar to her was the poise of his head, the sweep of arm and set of his shoulder. And when she opened her eyes he would be no longer there; the chair would again be empty. She pressed her fingers for an instant hard upon her eyeballs, then looked again.

The chair was not empty! He was still there but his face was turned now toward the table, completely away from her and a hand rested upon the pile of letters there. How significant the action!

Madame Martel straightened, steeled herself. "I am losing my mind," she whispered hoarsely, "I am seeing visions."

It did not occur to her to call for help. Help? Against what! She knew the servants were away, and even if they were not she shrank from disclosing what she believed to be this morbid condition of mind to the ignorant and unsympathetic.

"I will go in," she resolved, "place my hand upon–the shoulder; and it will be over; the illusion will vanish."

In fancy she went through the whole sensation of placing her hand upon a visible, intangible something that would melt away, vanish like smoke before her eyes. An involuntary shudder passed through her frame from head to foot.

As she glided noiselessly into the room in her black garb, Madame Martel, with that light, filmy hair, her wide-open, fearful blue eyes, looked far more like a "spirit" than the substantial figure seated in her armchair before the fire.

She had not time to place her hand upon the shoulder of her ghastly visitant. Before she reached the chair he had turned. She tottered, and springing forward he seized her in his arms.

"Mother! mother! mother! what is it? Are you ill?" He was kissing her hair, her forehead and closed, quivering eyes.

"Wait, Gustave. In a moment, dear son—it will be all right." She was, in fact, rather faint from the shock. He placed her upon the sofa and after bringing her a glass of water seated himself beside her.

"Idiot that I am!" he exclaimed. "I wanted to surprise you and here I've almost thrown you into a swoon." She was looking at him with eyes full of tenderness but for some reason she did not tell him the whole story of her surprise.

How glad she was to see him—her big, manly son of nineteen. And how like his father at that age! The age at which the old ambrotype had been taken; the picture that she had been weeping over and that Gustave was looking at when she first discovered him there.

"Of course you came on the evening train, Gustave?" she asked him quietly.

"Yes, only a while ago. I got to thinking—well, I had enough of Assumption last year. And after all there's no place for a fellow at Christmas like home."

"You knew that I wanted you, Gustave. Confess; you knew it." Madame was hoping for a little disclosure of thought transference—mental telepathy—occultism in short. But he disabused her.

"No," he said. "I'm afraid I was purely selfish, mother. I know that you prefer to be alone at this season," in that tone of subdued respect which was always assumed in approaching the subject of Madame Martel's sorrow. "I came because I couldn't help it; because I couldn't stay away. I wanted to see you, to be with you, mother."

"You know, Gustave, it won't be gay here at home," she said nestling closer to him.

"Oh, well, if we can't be gay, there's nothing to keep us from being happy, mom."

And she was, very, very happy as she rubbed her cheek against his rough coat sleeve and felt the warm, firm pressure of his hand.

Snow

Robert Olen Butler

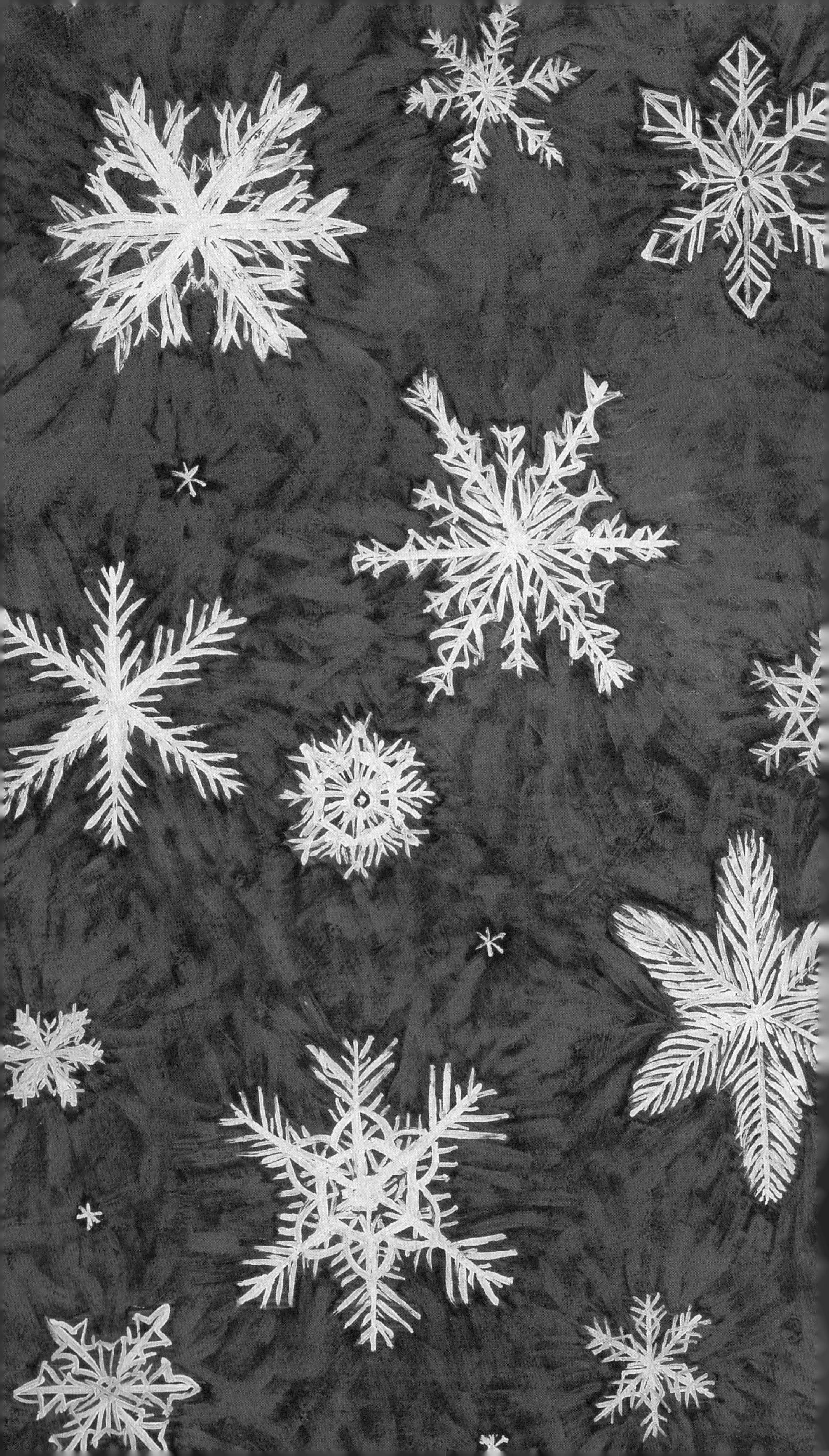

I wonder how long he watched me sleeping. I still wonder that. He sat and he did not wake me to ask about his carry-out order. Did he watch my eyes move as I dreamed? When I finally knew he was there and I turned to look at him, I could not make out his whole face at once. His head was turned a little to the side. His beard was neatly trimmed, but the jaw it covered was long and its curve was like a sampan sail and it held my eyes the way a sail always did when I saw one on the sea. Then I raised my eyes and looked at his nose. I am Vietnamese, you know, and we have a different sense of these proportions. Our noses are small and his was long and it also curved, gently, a reminder of his jaw, which I looked at again. His beard was dark gray, like he'd crawled out of a charcoal kiln. I make these comparisons to things from my country and village, but it is only to clearly say what this face was like. It is not that he reminded me of home. That was the farthest thing from my mind when I first saw Mr. Cohen. And I must have stared at him in those first moments with a strange look because when his face turned full to me and I could finally lift my gaze to his eyes, his eyebrows made a little jump like he was asking me, What is it? What's wrong?

I was at this same table before the big window at the front of the restaurant. The Plantation Hunan does not look like a restaurant, though. No one would give it a name like that unless it really was an old plantation house. It's very large and full of antiques. It's quiet right now. Not even five, and I can hear the big clock–I had never seen one till I came here. No one in Vietnam has a clock as tall as a man. Time isn't as important as that in

Vietnam. But the clock here is very tall and they call it Grandfather, which I like, and Grandfather is ticking very slowly right now, and he wants me to fall asleep again. But I won't.

The plantation house must feel like a refugee. It is full of foreign smells, ginger and Chinese pepper and fried shells for wonton, and there's a motel on one side and a gas station on the other, not like the life the house once knew, though there are very large oak trees surrounding it, trees that must have been here when this was still a plantation. The house sits on a busy street and the Chinese family who owns it changed it from Plantation Seafood into a place that could hire a Vietnamese woman like me to be a waitress. They are very kind, this family, though we know we are different from each other. They are Chinese and I am Vietnamese and they are very kind, but we are both here in Louisiana and they go somewhere with the other Chinese in town–there are four restaurants and two laundries and some people, I think, who work as engineers at the oil refinery. They go off to themselves and they don't seem to even notice where they are.

I was sleeping that day he came in here. It was late afternoon of the day before Christmas. Almost Christmas Eve. I am not a Christian. My mother and I are Buddhist. I live with my mother and she is very sad for me because I am thirty-four years old and I am not married. There are other Vietnamese here in Lake Charles, Louisiana, but we are not a community. We are all too sad, perhaps, or too tired. But maybe not. Maybe that's just me saying that. Maybe the others are real Americans already. My mother has two Vietnamese friends, old women like her, and her two friends look at me with the same sadness in their faces because of what they see as my life. They know that once I might have been married, but the fiancé I had in my town in Vietnam went away in the Army and though he is still alive in Vietnam, the last I heard, he is driving a cab in Hồ Chí Minh City and he is married to someone else. I never really knew him, and I don't feel any loss. It's just that he's the only boy my mother ever speaks of when she gets frightened for me.

I get frightened for me, too, sometimes, but it's not because I have no husband. That Christmas Eve afternoon I woke slowly. The front tables are for cocktails and for waiting for carry-out, so the chairs are large and stuffed so that they are soft. My head was very comfortable against one of the high wings of the chair and I opened my eyes without moving. The rest of me was still sleeping, but my eyes opened and the sky was still blue, though the shreds of cloud were turning pink. It looked like a warm sky. And it was. I felt sweat on my throat and I let my eyes move just a little and the live oak in front of the restaurant was quivering–all its leaves were shaking and you might think that it would look cold doing that, but it was a warm wind, I knew. The air was thick and wet, and cutting through the ginger and pepper smell was the fuzzy smell of mildew.

Perhaps it was from my dream but I remembered my first Christmas Eve in America. I slept and woke just like this, in a Chinese restaurant. I was working there. But it was in a distant place, in St. Louis. And I woke to snow. The first snow I had ever seen. It scared me. Many Vietnamese love to see their first snow, but it frightened me in some very deep way that I could not explain, and even remembering that moment–especially as I woke from sleep at the front of another restaurant–frightened me. So I turned my face sharply from the window in the Plantation Hunan and that's when I saw Mr. Cohen.

I stared at those parts of his face, like I said, and maybe this was a way for me to hide from the snow, maybe the strangeness that he saw in my face had to do with the snow. But when his eyebrows jumped and I did not say anything to explain what was going on inside me, I could see him wondering what to do. I could feel him thinking: Should I ask her what is wrong or should I just ask her for my carry-out? I am not an especially shy person, but I hoped he would choose to ask for the carry-out. I came to myself with a little jolt and I stood up and faced him–he was sitting in one of the stuffed chairs at the next table. "I'm sorry," I said, trying to turn us both from my dreaming. "Do you have an order?"

He hesitated, his eyes holding fast to my face. These were very dark eyes, as dark as the eyes of any Vietnamese, but turned up to me like this, his face seemed so large that I had trouble taking it in. Then he said, "Yes. For Cohen." His voice was deep, like a movie actor who is playing a grandfather, the kind of voice that if he asked what it was that I had been dreaming, I would tell him at once.

But he did not ask anything more. I went off to the kitchen and the order was not ready. I wanted to complain to them. There was no one else in the restaurant, and everyone in the kitchen seemed like they were just hanging around. But I don't make any trouble for anybody. So I just went back out to Mr. Cohen. He rose when he saw me, even though he surely also saw that I had no carry-out with me.

"It's not ready yet," I said. "I'm sorry."

"That's okay," he said, and he smiled at me, his gray beard opening and showing teeth that were very white.

"I wanted to scold them," I said. "You should not have to wait for a long time on Christmas Eve."

"It's okay," he said. "This is not my holiday."

I tilted my head, not understanding. He tilted his own head just like mine, like he wanted to keep looking straight into my eyes. Then he said, "I am Jewish."

I straightened my head again, and I felt a little pleasure at knowing that his straightening his own head was caused by me. I still didn't understand, exactly, and he clearly read that in my face. He said, "A Jew doesn't celebrate Christmas."

"I thought all Americans celebrated Christmas," I said.

"Not all. Not exactly." He did a little shrug with his shoulders, and his eyebrows rose like the shrug, as he tilted his head to the side once more, for just a second. It all seemed to say, What is there to do, it's the way the world is and I know it and it all makes me just a little bit weary. He said, "We all stay home, but we don't all celebrate."

He said no more, but he looked at me and I was surprised to find that I had no words either on my tongue or in my head. It felt a little strange to see this very American man who was not celebrating the holiday. In Vietnam we never miss a holiday and it did not make a difference if we were Buddhist or Cao Ðài or Catholic. I thought of this Mr. Cohen sitting in his room tonight alone while all the other Americans celebrated Christmas Eve. But I had nothing to say and he didn't either and he kept looking at me and I glanced down at my hands twisting at my order book and I didn't even remember taking the book out. So I said, "I'll check on your order again," and I turned and went off to the kitchen and I waited there till the order was done, though I stood over next to the door away from the chatter of the cook and the head waiter and the mother of the owner.

Carrying the white paper bag out to the front, I could not help but look inside to see how much food there was. There was enough for two people. So I did not look into Mr. Cohen's eyes as I gave him the food and rang up the order and took his money. I was counting his change into his palm–his hand, too, was very large–and he said, "You're not Chinese, are you?"

I said, "No. I am Vietnamese," but I did not raise my face to him, and he went away.

Two days later, it was even earlier in the day when Mr. Cohen came in. About four-thirty. The grandfather had just chimed the half hour like a man who is really crazy about one subject and talks of it at any chance he gets. I was sitting in my chair at the front once again and my first thought when I saw Mr. Cohen coming through the door was that he would think I am a lazy girl. I started to jump up, but he saw me and he motioned with his hand for me to stay where I was, a single heavy pat in the air, like he'd just laid this large hand on the shoulder of an invisible child before him. He said, "I'm early again."

"I am not a lazy girl," I said.

"I know you're not," he said and he sat down in the chair across from me.

"How do you know I'm not?" This question just jumped out of me. I can be a cheeky girl sometimes. My mother says that this was one reason I am not married, that this is why she always talks about the boy I was once going to marry in Vietnam, because he was a shy boy, a weak boy, who would take whatever his wife said and not complain. I myself think this is why he is driving a taxi in Hồ Chí Minh City. But as soon as this cheeky thing came out of my mouth to Mr. Cohen, I found that I was afraid. I did not want Mr. Cohen to hate me.

But he was smiling. I could even see his white teeth in this smile. He said, "You're right. I have no proof."

"I am always sitting here when you come in," I said, even as I asked myself, Why are you rubbing on this subject?

I saw still more teeth in his smile, then he said, "And the last time you were even sleeping."

I think at this I must have looked upset, because his smile went away fast. He did not have to help me seem a fool before him. "It's all right," he said. "This is a slow time of day. I have trouble staying awake myself. Even in court."

I looked at him more closely, leaving his face. He seemed very prosperous. He was wearing a suit as gray as his beard and it had thin blue stripes, almost invisible, running through it. "You are a judge?"

"A lawyer," he said.

"You will defend me when the owner fires me for sleeping."

This made Mr. Cohen laugh, but when he stopped, his face was very solemn. He seemed to lean nearer to me, though I was sure he did not move. "You had a bad dream the last time," he said.

How did I know he would finally come to ask about my dream? I had known it from the first time I'd heard his voice. "Yes," I said. "I think I was dreaming about the first Christmas Eve I spent in America. I fell asleep before a window in a restaurant in St. Louis, Missouri. When I woke, there was snow on the ground. It was the first snow I'd ever seen. I went to sleep and there was still only a gray afternoon, a thin little rain, like a mist. I had no idea things could change like that. I woke and everything was covered and I was terrified."

I suddenly sounded to myself like a crazy person. Mr. Cohen

would think I was lazy and crazy both. I stopped speaking and I looked out the window. A jogger went by in the street, a man in shorts and a T-shirt, and his body glistened with sweat. I felt beads of sweat on my own forehead like little insects crouching there and I kept my eyes outside, wishing now that Mr. Cohen would go away.

"Why did it terrify you?" he said.

"I don't know," I said, though this wasn't really true. I'd thought about it now and then, and though I'd never spoken them, I could imagine reasons.

Mr. Cohen said, "Snow frightened me, too, when I was a child. I'd seen it all my life, but it still frightened me."

I turned to him and now he was looking out the window.

"Why did it frighten you?" I asked, expecting no answer.

But he turned from the window and looked at me and smiled just a little bit, like he was saying that since he had asked this question of me, I could ask him, too. He answered, "It's rather a long story. Are you sure you want to hear it?"

"Yes," I said. Of course I did.

"It was far away from here," he said. "My first home and my second one. Poland and then England. My father was a professor in Warsaw. It was early in 1939. I was eight years old and my father knew something was going wrong. All the talk about the corridor to the sea was just the beginning. He had ears. He knew. So he sent me and my mother to England. He had good friends there. I left that February and there was snow everywhere and I had my own instincts, even at eight. I cried in the courtyard of our apartment building. I threw myself into the snow there and I would not move. I cried like he was sending us away from him forever. He and my mother said it was only for some months, but I didn't believe it. And I was right. They had to lift me bodily and carry me to the taxi. But the snow was in my clothes and as we pulled away and I scrambled up to look out the back window at my father, the snow was melting against my skin and I began to shake. It was as much from my fear as from the cold. The snow was telling me he would die. And he did. He waved at me in the street and he grew smaller and we turned a corner and that was the last I saw of him."

Maybe it was foolish of me, but I thought not so much of Mr. Cohen losing his father. I had lost a father, too, and I knew that it was something that a child lives through. In Vietnam we believe that our ancestors are always close to us, and I could tell that about Mr. Cohen, that his father was still close to him. But what I thought about was Mr. Cohen going to another place, another country, and living with his mother. I live with my mother, just like that. Even still.

He said, "So the snow was something I was afraid of. Every time it snowed in England I knew that my father was dead. It took a few years for us to learn this from others, but I knew it whenever it snowed."

"You lived with your mother?" I said.

"Yes. In England until after the war and then we came to America. The others from Poland and Hungary and Russia that we traveled with all came in through New York City and stayed there. My mother loved trains and she'd read a book about New Orleans, and so we stayed on the train and we came to the South. I was glad to be in a place where it almost never snowed."

I was thinking how he was a foreigner, too. Not an American, really. But all the talk about the snow made this little chill behind my thoughts. Maybe I was ready to talk about that. Mr. Cohen had spoken many words to me about his childhood and I didn't want him to think I was a girl who takes things without giving something back. He was looking out the window again, and his lips pinched together so that his mouth disappeared in his beard. He seemed sad to me. So I said, "You know why the snow scared me in St. Louis?"

He turned at once with a little humph sound and a crease on his forehead between his eyes and then a very strong voice saying, "Tell me," and it felt like he was scolding himself inside for not paying attention to me. I am not a vain girl, always thinking that men pay such serious attention to me that they get mad at themselves for ignoring me even for a few moments. This is what it really felt like and it surprised me. If I was a vain girl, it wouldn't have surprised me. He said it again, "Tell me why it scared you."

I said, "I think it's because the snow came so quietly and everything was underneath it, like this white surface was the real earth and everything had died—all the trees and the grass and the streets and the houses—everything had died and was buried. It was all lost. I knew there was snow about me, on the roof, and I was dead, too."

"Your own country was very different," Mr. Cohen said.

It pleased me that he thought just the way I once did. You could tell that he wished there was an easy way to make me feel better, make the dream go away. But I said to him, "This is what I also thought. If I could just go to a warm climate, more like home. So I came down to New Orleans, with my mother, just like you, and then we came over to Lake Charles. And it was something like Vietnam here. The rice fields and the heat and the way the storms come in. But it makes no difference. There's no snow to scare me here, but I still sit alone in this chair in the middle of the afternoon and I sleep and I listen to the grandfather over there ticking."

I stopped talking and I felt like I was making no sense at all, so I said, "I should check on your order."

Mr. Cohen's hand came out over the table. "May I ask your name?"

"I'm Miss Giàu," I said.

"Miss Giau?" he asked, and when he did that, he made a different word, since Vietnamese words change with the way your voice sings them.

I laughed. "My name is Giàu, with the voice falling. It means 'wealthy' in Vietnamese. When you say the word like a question, you say something very different. You say I am Miss Pout."

Mr. Cohen laughed and there was something in the laugh that made me shiver just a little, like a nice little thing, like maybe stepping into the shower when you are covered with dust and feeling the water expose you. But in the back of my mind was his carry-out and there was a bad little feeling there, something I wasn't thinking about, but it made me go off now with heavy feet to the kitchen. I got the bag and it was feeling different as I carried it back to the front of the restaurant. I went behind the counter and I put it down and I wished I'd done this a few moments before, but even with his eyes on me, I looked into the bag. There was one main dish and one portion of soup.

Then Mr. Cohen said, "Is this a giau I see on your face?" And he pronounced the word exactly right, with the curling tone that made it "pout."

I looked up at him and I wanted to smile at how good he said the word, but even wanting to do that made the pout worse. I said, "I was just thinking that your wife must be sick. She is not eating tonight."

He could have laughed at this. But he did not. He laid his hand for a moment on his beard, he smoothed it down. He said, "The second dinner on Christmas Eve was for my son passing through town. My wife died some years ago and I am not married."

I am not a hard-hearted girl because I knew that a child gets over the loss of a father and because I also knew that a man gets over the loss of a wife. I am a good girl, but I did not feel sad for Mr. Cohen. I felt very happy. Because he laid his hand on mine and he asked if he could call me. I said yes, and as it turns out, New Year's Eve seems to be a Jewish holiday. The Vietnamese New Year comes at a different time, but people in Vietnam know to celebrate whatever holiday comes along. So tonight Mr. Cohen and I will go to some restaurant that is not Chinese, and all I have to do now is sit here and listen very carefully to Grandfather as he talks to me about time.

About Grace

Kelly Cherry

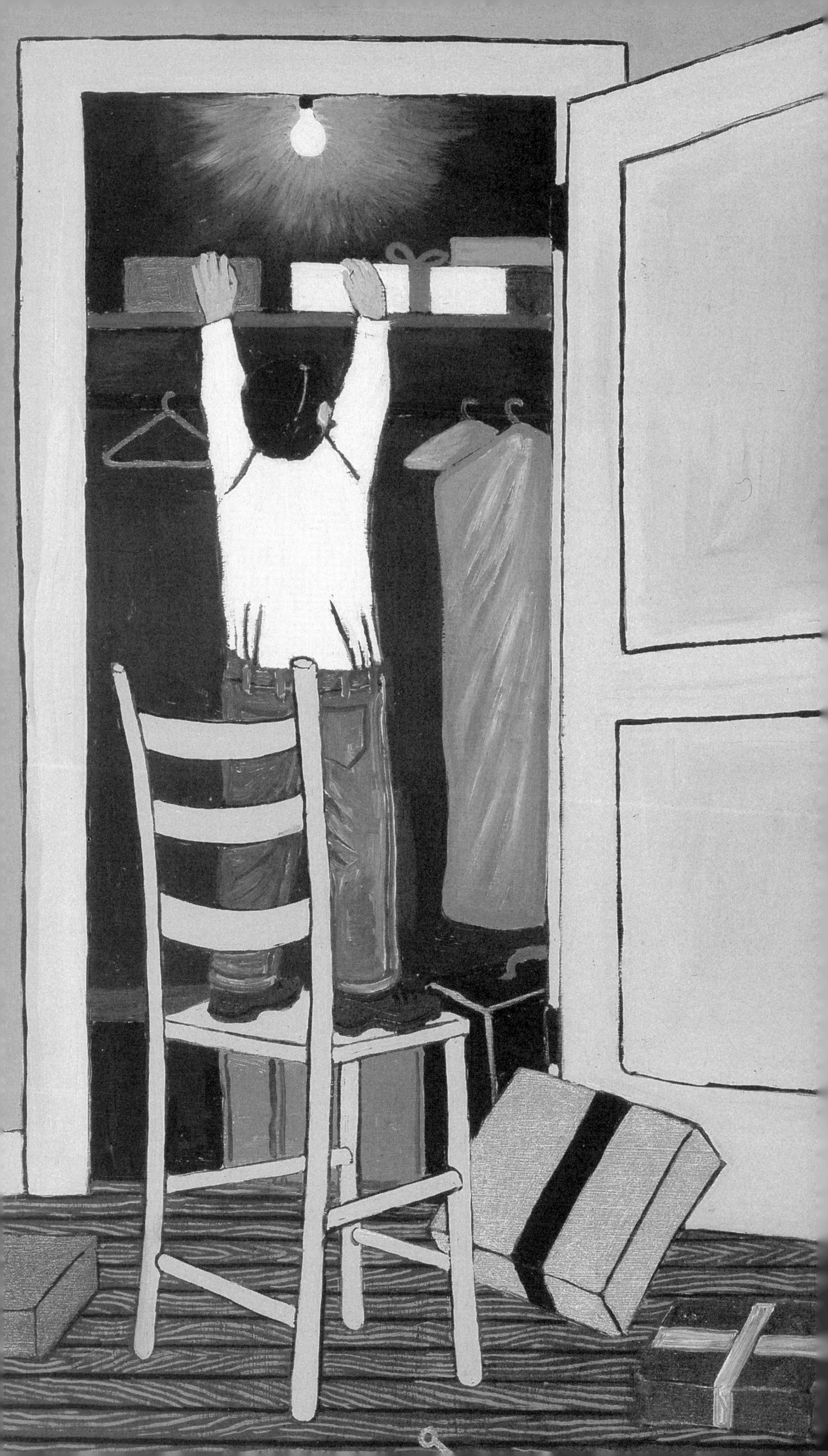

It was Christmas Eve, 1941, and he was very nearly eight years old, a good little boy, rather disconcertingly self-confident but generous and well-intentioned. He was even well-*behaved*, perhaps mostly because his schooling to date had taken place in a convent, whose nuns insisted on strict obedience. They had accepted him even though he was a Protestant. How much he understood of Catholicism remained a question. "Did you have a good day at school?" our mother asked when he returned home, the screen door banging shut behind him. He would have walked home under the hot Louisiana sun that seemed to push down and across the sky like an iron, smoothing out the endless crease of the horizon. "The teacher said a lot of Hail Americas," he said, "and talked about Mike the Dark Angel."

His red hair looked more like an article of clothing than part of his body: a hat or cap or Bible-school beanie. He was clever and planned to be an architect when he grew up, building "moderated" houses.

We were living in Louisiana then; our father taught violin at the University. Our father had been too young for the first war and too old, too married, and too 4-F for the second. Instead, he was a member of the generation that had been catapulted out of college straight into the Great Depression, a war in its own way, a different kind of war, in which men lost not their lives but their self-esteem, although back then people talked about self-respect and not "self-esteem."

The country was enthusiastic about the new war. Despite the demurrers of some, for a great many people the war was a welcome distraction from financial hardship. Soon there was such a surplus of cash as to create a scarcity of consumer goods, and rationing had to be introduced. My brother conducted scrap paper drives, and whenever he earned any money, he was careful to put at least a part of it into defense stamps.

Home from school, he'd throw his books down on the couch in the living room and sit down at the card table in the kitchen and wolf down the bread and butter and sugar sandwich our mother put before him on a milk-green glass plate. He drank a bottle of Coke. This was how some of us ate in those days.

Then our mother would leave him there and return to the living room, where her violin lay waiting on the seat of the ladder-back chair, the music stand like a sentry protecting the sheet music, and ashtrays overflowing their ceramic banks. When I grew up, I would learn to hate those cigarettes, hate what they had done to our parents, but for years they were just an accepted part of life.

For fifty-nine cents our young mother had bought a little machine so she and her husband could roll their own. "With careful planning," she'd written her mother some months earlier, "I managed to spend only $12.50 on groceries for all of July."

She hated to cook, wasn't crazy about eating. She'd gotten married at twenty to a man whose "eyes were a lovely deep shade of brown" and who "played the Brahms Violin Concerto better than anyone I'd ever heard." But now they had two children, and the second, a daughter born one year ago, had actually been planned.

I was that daughter, and I was sitting up in my crib in the living room, peering out behind the bars like a very small, chubby prisoner. Whenever our mother reappeared in the room, I cried "Momma!" and clapped my hands, knowing already that, in our family, applause was always appreciated.

On Christmas Eve afternoon, our parents were practicing for a concert to be given at Grace Presbyterian that night.

Our father went to pick up Clara, who usually sat for us, but came back without her. It seemed she had been indulging in the Christmas cheer.

Our father stood my brother in front of him while he sat on the couch. "We're leaving you in charge tonight," he said. "Clara can't make it, and we think you're old enough to look after your sister anyway."

My brother could hardly believe his ears. What luck! he thought, remembering the presents piled on the top shelf of the hall closet. He was well behaved, it's true, but he was still a boy, and there were no nuns in the house.

After our parents had left, our father in tails and our mother in a long black taffeta gown that had cap sleeves and a net stole draped over the shoulders—as if her shy, white shoulders were butterflies caught in a dress—my brother came to check on me, as they had told him to do.

I was sleeping in my crib, which had been moved back into our parents' room. I've been told I was a pretty baby, pink and ivory. I slept with my round head resting against a toy felt duck. Like any baby's, my skin was so delicate and responsive that when my brother touched my cheek, blood raced to the surface as if to say hello—but I slept on, almost, he must have thought, as if I weren't really there, as if I didn't really exist.

Stealthily, he opened the top drawer of the dresser and fished out the big key to the hall closet.

He wasn't as stealthy as he imagined (he had imagined he was a frogman sabotaging a bridge or establishing a beachhead on a foreign shore, surfacing at our parents' maple bureau). I woke up and clapped my hands. "Bubba!" I cried. My vocabulary was less than extensive.

He snapped on the overhead light and came over to talk to me. "Go back to sleep," he said. "Santa Claus won't come if you don't go to sleep."

I laughed and reached for the key.

He decided to hypnotize me. He swung the key slowly back and forth in front of my big gray eyes (as I've heard them described). "Sleeeeeeeep," he said, in a creaking, Vincent Price voice. "Sleeeeeeeep."

My lashes fluttered, my lids grew heavy and clicked shut like a doll's. He worried that he might have hypnotized me for life: he had forgotten to give me a wake-up cue. Suppose I was in a trance forever, some kind of baby zombie? He wanted to shake me awake but decided he'd wait until after he had looked at the presents in the hall closet.

One by one, he took them down, standing on the ladder-back chair to reach the shelf. When they were all on the floor, he jumped down from the chair and began to unwrap them, being careful to pay attention to just how each was wrapped, how the ribbon was tied. After he'd opened and examined each present, he wrapped it up again.

Here was a Pullman car for his electric train, and here was a regulation-size basketball. A pair of roller skates. A set of three tee-shirts. A crystal radio set. A yo-yo.

A copy of *Treasure Island.* A catcher's mitt. A model airplane kit.

On and on–there were so many toys he began to be afraid he didn't deserve them all. Our parents were poor. He knew this because they often said so, and when our mother and father fought, it was usually about money. Now they had spent all this money on him.

There was a pen-and-pencil set, a new lunch box, a Mickey Mouse watch.

I guess I didn't need a wake-up cue, because while he was still looking at the presents I began to cry loudly and unceasingly. My brother ran back into the bedroom and stood looking at me with concern, his hands plunged into the pockets of his knee-length pants.

In the overhead light, my face was as red as a skinned knee. I was wearing the long, white nightgown that was my wardrobe in most of the family photographs from that first year. I used to bob up and down in it while holding onto the bars of my crib, singing a one-syllable accompaniment to the Huykens Serenade when anyone held up sheet music for me; it didn't matter what the sheet music was for, I always sang the Huykens Serenade. I had started doing this at eight months and it was one of my favorite things to do.

When I didn't stop crying, my brother decided I was hungry. He went out to the kitchen to try to fix some milk for me. He climbed onto the counter to get a can of Carnation Pet Milk down from the cabinet, punched two holes in the can and poured the milk into the bottle. Then he tried to figure out how to heat it up. He ran water into a pan and stood the bottle in it and turned on the gas stove. All this he did correctly. He had seen our mother do this, and he was careful to think through each step as he went. He even remembered to test the milk on the inside of his wrist to make sure it wasn't too hot.

But it put him behind schedule, fixing this bottle for me. He brought it to me, leaned over the crib, placed it in my hands. Air bubbles appeared in the squarish bottle as I swilled the milk. My face grew cool. He stroked my hair back off my forehead.

It was getting late. As soon as I had finished the bottle and fallen asleep again, he raced back out to the living room. He had to get all the presents back up on their shelf.

At last, they were in place—everything was ready for the morning, and no one would ever know that he had peeked into the future.

He stepped down from the chair, shut the door, and turned the key, which broke in the lock.

He was horrified. Half the key was in his hand, and half was in the lock. He wanted to howl but he caught himself just in time, remembering that I was asleep in the next room.

He ran back into the kitchen and again lit the burner under the pan of water. It was still warm from my bottle and didn't take long to boil. He dropped the key-half into the pan and waited for it to melt. He thought that when it was slightly liquid at the end, he could stick it back into the lock and the key would kind of glue itself together. But as he watched, the water boiled away, and the key-half lay at the bottom of the pan unchanged. He turned the stove off and tried to take the key-half out and burned his fingers. Again, he had to remember not to wake me. He hopped around the kitchen, waving his hand in the air, until his fingers stopped stinging. By then the key-half had cooled and he was able to pick it up.

He thought that he had the principle right, if not the technology: the thing to do was to weld the two halves together. Frantically scrabbling through the cabinet that contained all our father's work tools, he uncovered the soldering iron, which he plugged into a socket near the hall closet. He succeeded this time in melting the broken end of the key-half. He felt a rising relief, anticipation of victory. He fitted the key-half into the lock, wriggled it to make sure tip had met tip, and held it there until it had hardened. He turned the made-whole-again key–and the key refused to turn. It wouldn't budge. He had soldered the key to the lock.

With all his might, he twisted the key, whereupon it broke all over again, in exactly the same place.

It was too much for him, my brother who was not yet eight and who should no doubt never have been left alone in the apartment with a baby sister and a closet full of toys anyway. Even so, he didn't scream in frustration–which I am very sure is what he wanted to do. He curled up on the couch, facing the darkened Christmas tree, and cried as softly as possible, still being careful not to wake me.

When our parents came home, they found him asleep on the couch, his red hair poking out wildly in erratic bunches, tear-tracks drying on his sorrow-filled face (which like all Louisiana children's faces was brown as root beer all year long from that almost omnipresent sun). On the hall floor was the soldering iron. My brother, in his sleep, was still clutching one half of the hall closet key.

Our father opened my brother's tight fist and took the key-half away. Then he hoisted his son up in his arms, and my brother drowsily leaned his head against our father's black shoulder, white collar, the collar studs. "I broke the key, Dad," he said, gulping. "Now nobody can have Christmas."

"The baby's fine," our mother said, coming back into the room to report on me. She had taken off her evening gown before changing me and now carried it over her bowing arm. Her slip was the full-length kind women wore then, with darts under the bust that made the cups look important, as if they contained secrets, and the slip's shiny material fitted smoothly across her still-girlish stomach.

My brother looked at her over our father's shoulder–our mother who was so young-looking that when he was a toddler, people on the street used to flatter her by asking him if he was her little brother. He dropped off to sleep again and was only dimly aware of hands taking off his clothes, pulling the top sheet down, tucking him in.

In the morning, he had to force his way back into conscious-ness, not wanting to face the ruinous thing he had done. He dragged himself out of bed, dressed in his middy shirt and shorts, which he thought of as his naval uniform, and trudged toward the living room.

There, under the lighted tree, were the presents, all of the presents that had been in the closet.

Eyes popping, he tore out to the hall. The door to the closet had been removed from its hinges, and now the closet was wide open, and as empty as the tomb of the risen Jesus in the picture in the convent classroom.

"Feel better, son?" Our father had come up behind him, and now rested a hand on his shoulder.

My brother looked up at him and then darted into our parents' room to wake me. He lifted me up over the bars of the crib, and carried me out to the living room and put me down beside the tree, where I was just as happy, in my liberation, to play with the torn wrapping paper and used ribbon as with any of the toys.

Of course, my brother already knew what his presents were, but he pretended not to know. And our parents knew, from the way the presents had been re-wrapped, that he had managed to unwrap them before the key broke, but they were so grateful that there had not been a fire (the stove, the soldering iron) that they pretended to believe in my brother's pretended surprise. And what surprised him most was that he had gotten away with it, that somehow a miracle had happened and the lost Christmas had been rescued even though he had not been a good boy.

As for me, I had hauled myself up to a standing position, holding onto the piano bench, and was joyfully singing my one-syllable rendition of the Serenade, the long white skirt of my starched nightdress flaring out from my feet as if I were dancing. (I wore crocheted booties, a gift from my grandmother.)

Every family has its stories, of course, that serve as parables or summaries. Such stories encapsulate the lessons that life has taught that particular family, and each time they are told, remind the family of what it has learned. This has been one of ours. What my brother learned that morning was something about grace, how it happens in spite of us, how it is a gift. This is why, in my family, even after all this time, we tell this story among ourselves, embroidering a bit here and there, to be sure, or playing with the point of view, but never changing, always cleaving to, the heart of it: to remind ourselves that *good* things can happen even to *bad* people (and certainly to only slightly bad little boys).

Popcorn for Christmas

Debra Gray De Noux

and O'Neil De Noux

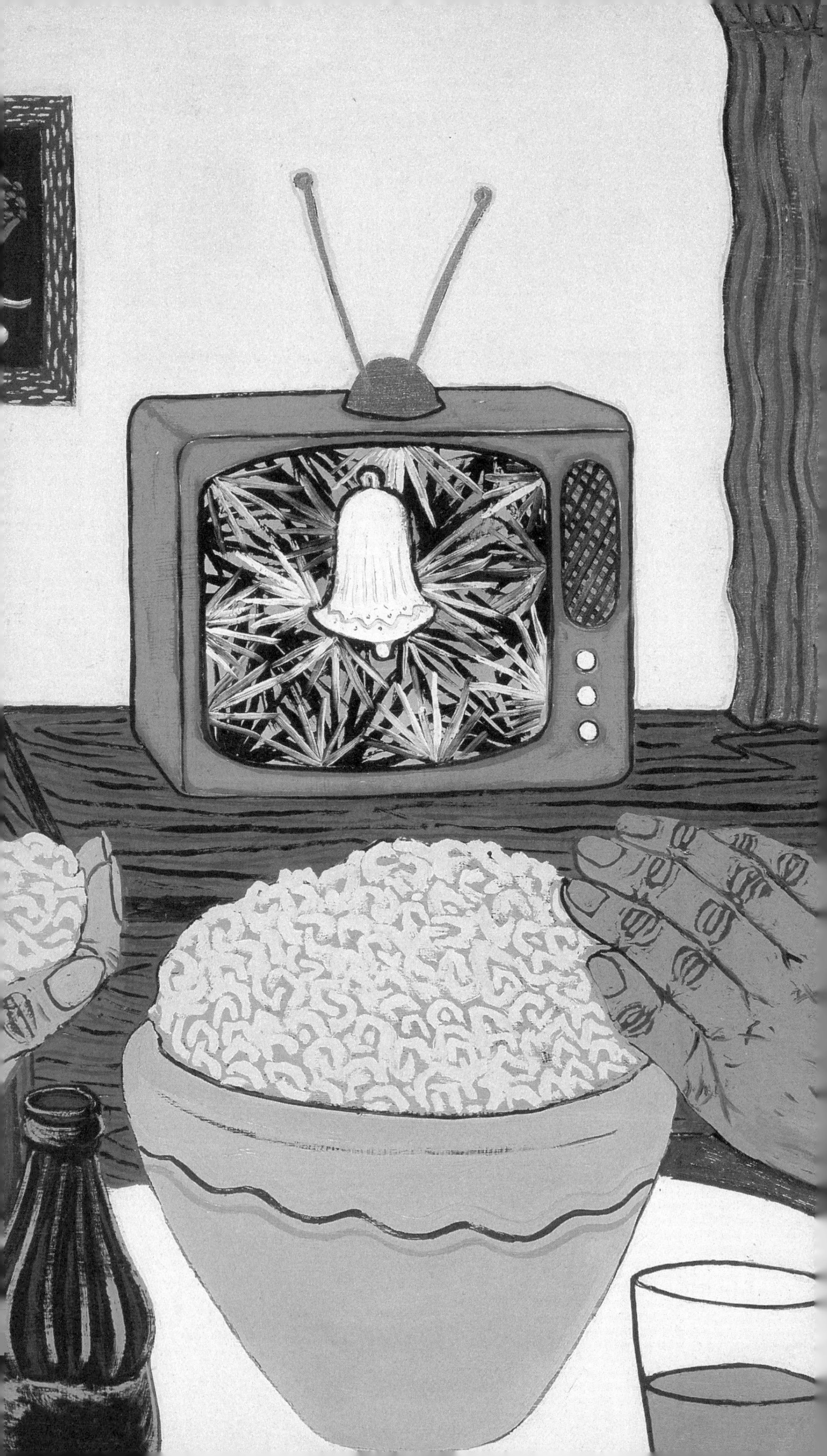

*S*ome sick bastard's throwing a party in the morgue on Christmas Eve. That's what Johnny Russell thought as he passed the Criminal Courts Building after getting off the evening watch at the crime lab at eleven P.M. Still in uniform, Johnny turned off the sidewalk and walked into the coroner's office garage. He could see the door to the morgue was ajar. Someone was singing "The Little Drummer Boy." It sounded like Andy Williams, or maybe Perry Como. Johnny stopped and listened, twirling his PR24 nightstick by the handle, spinning it in circles.

It was dark in the garage of the old building. Built in the thirties, the huge gray concrete-block Criminal Courts Building dominated the corner of Tulane and Broad, in downtown New Orleans. Johnny noticed how chilly it was in the garage. He holstered his nightstick and checked his watch. It was five minutes after eleven. He stretched and thought about getting out of uniform, putting his nine millimeter Beretta away and maybe dropping in on the First District's watch party after all.

Glancing back at the morgue's door, he saw a young woman step out. Illuminated by the bright light from inside, she looked as if she was in a spotlight. Suddenly Johnny was no longer chilly, not even tired anymore. He felt himself inching closer to the woman standing in the light. Wearing a black party dress that barely reached her knees, the woman had short dark brown hair, a slim figure, and nice slender legs, accentuated by her high heels. He could see her face in profile. She had a model's face, smooth and well made-up. He thought she looked beautiful.

Without even noticing him, the woman turned around and went back into the party. Johnny followed. Stepping through the door he paused and tossed his hat on the hat rack next to the door. He was surprised his hat didn't tumble off. Instead, it caught one of the spikes, spun once and stopped.

Before he could move away from the door, a tall blond woman in a Roman toga stepped up and gave him a good looking over. She told him to turn around and nodded approval after he made a complete circle. Pursing her lips, she kissed the air, wheeled and walked back into the party.

There were several people in the hallway, three men and two women, all middle-aged and dressed up for a party. One man, in a bright green suit, stood brooding against the wall. He scowled at Johnny and said, "Evening, Officer," in a gruff voice.

Johnny hesitated a moment. His nostrils registered some strange odors now, ammonia and formaldehyde possibly, along with other rich smells of decay. He was about to grab his hat when he saw the woman in the black dress again. She crossed the hall from the pathologist's office into the autopsy room.

Weird, Johnny thought as he walked down the hall toward the autopsy room. Passing the refrigeration unit on his left, he looked in and saw a blond man in a blue suit kissing a woman in a baby blue dress.

The stereo began a version of "Chestnuts Roasting on an Open Fire" as Johnny moved into the autopsy room. The woman in the toga was sitting on one of the stainless steel autopsy tables. A tall black man was now pressed between her open legs. They were kissing. A gray-haired man was holding hands with a gray-haired woman next to the other autopsy table. The woman in the black dress was leaning against the wall near the far corner, alone, staring straight ahead.

Johnny felt his pulse rise as he looked at her. He could feel a tug at his heart. She was indeed beautiful, striking. She looked a few years younger than Johnny, probably twenty-two or -three. He crossed the room, pausing at the stereo to discover it was Andy Williams after all, before standing back against the wall a few feet from the woman in the black dress. He noticed how small she was, standing next to him. He was six feet even. In her high heels, she was only about five-four. Her hair was a much darker brown than his hair, although her complexion was quite a bit fairer.

The older couple started dancing. Gently caressing each other, they looked romantic gliding along, even in an autopsy room. Johnny noticed the shelves along the walls of the room. They were lined with various glass containers. In the containers were organs and other pieces of human anatomy: eyes, livers, brains, and fingers. Johnny knew the fingers were for printing for identification purposes. Soak them in a certain chemical and they become straight and stiff. Easy to fingerprint.

Weird, Johnny thought to himself again and turned to face the woman in the black dress. She looked at him, and he couldn't speak. The girl's eyes were so dark they looked black. They looked as if there were black holes where no light could escape. Even under the bright light of the autopsy room, he could see no pigmentation in her irises. But it was the look in those eyes that seemed to grab Johnny's throat and freeze his voice. Her eyes were so sad.

Slowly, the woman's expression changed, and she smiled at him. It wasn't a flirty smile, or even a happy one. It was a sad smile. It reminded Johnny of a lost little girl. He smiled back and let out a sigh. For the life of him, he couldn't think of anything intelligent to say. So he gulped and continued smiling at her. *I must look like a moron*, he thought, smiling like a baboon.

Slowly, her smile went away. Her chin dropped momentarily before she raised it, bending her neck back and shaking her hair. A whiff of perfume caught the air now, causing Johnny's heart to stir. Johnny felt his pulse rise even more. He cleared his throat and discovered it was parched.

"Would you like something to drink?" he heard himself ask in a voice that sounded hoarse.

She shook her head no.

He looked around and noticed there were no refreshments.

He looked at the others. No one else had anything to eat or drink either. *Weird party*, he told himself.

"Know what I *would* like?" she asked.

"Huh?"

"I'd like some popcorn," she said. She had a deep voice, sexy, a voice right out of one of those old film noir movies, those gangster movies with Bogie and Cagney and those stiff-backed women with desperate eyes, those dangerous women.

Popcorn, Johnny thought. *She said popcorn.*

"Um," Johnny said, "I'm trying to think of where we can buy some popcorn on Christmas Eve."

The woman turned to face him now, leaning her left shoulder against the wall, crossing her feet as she put her right fist on her hip. "I don't like store-bought popcorn."

He couldn't read the expression on her face, but it wasn't flirty and wasn't as sad. *Damn*, he thought, *she looks so sexy*. He couldn't help looking her up and down, and then felt so obvious about it he looked away.

"Well," he said, "what about movie house popcorn?"

"I like homemade popcorn," she said in that deep, velvet voice. She shook her hair again, slower this time, and asked, "Do you like popcorn?"

"I love it." That was true. Johnny could feel his heart thundering now, along with a stirring between his legs.

"I'm Johnny," he said, extending his right hand.

"Laurie," she said, pulling her hand behind her back as if he would grab it. Arching her right eyebrow, she said, "You wouldn't happen to have some popcorn at home?"

"I sure would."

She blinked and looked down as if she was embarrassed by her own boldness.

"I can pop some up in a minute."

Her eyes were still directed at the floor.

"I don't mean anything by that," Johnny said. "I'll make a deal with you. I'll give you my gun. I won't try anything funny and you won't shoot me, okay?"

Laurie looked up and he could see her eyes were damp. She was biting her lower lip. Cautiously, she reached her right hand out and ran the tips of her fingers across his New Orleans police star-and-crescent badge. Her touch was so light he couldn't even feel it. Laurie nodded once, and pushed herself away from the wall. He liked the way she did that, the smooth movement of her body.

She led the way out, past the old couple still dancing, past the toga lady sitting on the autopsy table with the black man still standing between her legs, past the refrigeration unit with the blondes in blue still kissing, through the hall, past the brooding man in the bright green suit. Johnny followed the movement of her hips. He scooped up his hat on the way out.

True to his word, Johnny withdrew his Beretta before opening his apartment door and tried to hand it to Laurie, who smiled and shook her head. He returned it to his holster and opened the door to his small midcity apartment. It smelled a little musty inside, so Johnny quickly lit a couple of scented candles he kept in the living room. At least the place wasn't too messed up, he told himself as Laurie looked around the living room.

"Kitchen's in here," he said, flipping on the light switch to his tiny kitchen. By the time Laurie slipped in the kitchen doorway, he had his favorite popcorn pot on the stove, the oil already heating up. She leaned against the door frame and watched. Johnny grinned at her, and poured one cup of popcorn kernels into the pot.

He could smell her perfume again, faintly. Stepping away from the gas stove, Johnny unfastened his gun belt and placed it on the small wooden kitchen table. He stepped back to the stove, grabbed two pot holders and shook the pot. When the first kernel popped, he put the lid on the stainless steel pot, leaving it askew to allow the steam to escape, but not enough to allow any of the popcorn to pop out.

Laurie watched intently from the doorway. He noticed how she had moved her left knee forward. She had such nice legs, long slender legs for such a small woman.

Johnny shook the pot continually. When the popping stopped, he moved the pot to another burner and pulled a huge amber-colored glass bowl from the cupboard. He poured the popcorn into the bowl, then thought of maybe two bowls, in case she wanted something on hers.

"You want some popcorn salt?"

"No," she answered, reaching over to grab a few warm kernels. "I like it plain."

"Me too." Johnny was surprised. He was the only person he'd ever known to like it plain.

"Do you like the old maids?" she asked.

"The what?"

"The half-popped seeds."

"I *love* 'em."

"I'll fight you for them," Laurie said, smiling and scooping a handful of popcorn before turning and heading back into the living room.

"When I was a little girl, we always did this on Christmas Eve," she told him in that velvet voice when they were seated in front of the TV. They were facing each other, cross-legged in the center of the living room, the bowl between them. "We always popped popcorn and watched old movies."

Johnny had found *It's a Wonderful Life* on one of the cable channels. They were at the part when James Stewart first met his guardian angel.

"Why don't you do it anymore?" he asked.

"They're all gone now."

"Oh."

Johnny hadn't realized he was hungry until he started in on the popcorn. It was delicious. He enjoyed watching Laurie as she ate. She took generous handfuls of popcorn each time, then ate each kernel one by one. When she took a drink of Coke, she took small sips. He noticed that her hands constantly moved.

She had pushed her dress down between her legs when she

sat cross-legged. She was in her stocking feet, her shoes next to her right knee, her left knee nearly touching his.

"Beat you," she said, a glint in her dark eyes as she plucked out a half-popped kernel and tossed it into her mouth. "I got the first old maid."

Johnny looked into the bowl and searched for an old maid of his own. They made a game of it, each taking turns. After digging through the remainder of the popcorn to grab all of the half-popped seeds, they finished off the rest of the popcorn.

"Want some more?" he asked.

Laurie said no as she rose and moved to the sofa. Johnny finished off his Coke and joined her. Seated at either end of the long sofa, they watched the conclusion of the movie.

Laurie was curled as she sat, almost in a fetal position. Johnny stole glimpses of her face in profile, at her delicate nose and fine lips, at her dark eyes and sculptured chin. She was truly lovely.

"Want some more Coke?"

She shook her head no and scooted down to rest her head on the arm of the sofa. A new movie started. Johnny turned to the TV in time to catch the title shots of *The Ghost and Mrs. Muir*, as it began.

"Oh, wow," he said. "This is a good one."

"I know," she said in a softer voice. "It's a love story." Then very faintly, she added, "A ghost story . . ."

She was asleep before Rex Harrison made his first appearance. Johnny watched Laurie as she slept, watched her chest rise slightly with her steady breathing. Later, when Rex Harrison was making his final scene, the one before the parting shot when he walked off arm-in-arm with Gene Tierney, Johnny noticed how chilly it had become in his apartment.

He pulled two blankets out of his closet, draped one over Laurie and curled up with the other at the far end of the sofa. He focused his eyes on her face, on the lovely lines of her restful face. He noticed there were three earrings in her right ear, all delicate gold hoops.

He wanted to reach over and run his hands along her body, to let his fingers glide along the curves and valleys of her body as she lay there. He wanted to touch her, to feel her skin, to hear her sigh from his touch.

He thought about his family for a minute, of Cajun Christmases on Vermilion Bay, of crawfish pie and etouffee, of feasts and dancing and music to the strains of fiddles, *fais do do* music. He missed those Christmases when he was a little boy and the world was a simple place without shootings and stabbings and people fighting over the damnedest things. He felt his eyes growing tired. He felt his eyelids grow heavy.

He dreamed he was dancing. He dreamed of dancing with Laurie, holding her in his arms. Her eyes were closed as she pressed her face against his neck. When she opened them, he felt her eyelashes brush his throat. He looked down at her eyes, at her dark orbs and her lovely face. In slow motion, ever so slow motion, Laurie closed her eyes, turned her head slightly and parted her lips as she moved her mouth to his.

He dreamed of a kiss, of one kiss. It was a long kiss, a very soft kiss. He dreamed of her lips pressed against his, her warm tongue moving against his. He dreamed of a loving kiss that went on and on, a kiss that spanned time, that spanned lifetimes.

Sunlight streaming through the picture window of Johnny's apartment woke him. Blinking his eyes into focus, he turned to her. But Laurie was no longer on the sofa. He felt something in his heart immediately. He felt frightened. He stumbled off the sofa and looked for her, even though he knew she was gone. Then he climbed out of his uniform, pulled on a gray sweatshirt and jeans and headed for the morgue.

What else could he do? That was the only thing he knew about her. He didn't know her last name, her age, where she lived, what she did.

Some goddam investigator I'd make if I ever get promoted to detective, he told himself. He was so angry at himself he almost got into two wrecks before parking his Toyota in front of the Criminal Courts Building at nine o'clock, Christmas morning.

Autopsies never took holidays. Johnny had been a cop long enough to know they'd be working that morning. He strolled into the morgue and was immediately assaulted by reeking odors, formaldehyde definitely, ammonia, pine oil, and the sweet, stale smell of flesh newly laid open.

A curly-haired pathologist in a gray smock was working over the body of a black man when Johnny walked in. The pathologist looked up through a pair of thick glasses and shrugged. Johnny pulled out his ID folder with his badge attached and said, "I'm looking for someone."

The pathologist went back to his dissecting.

Johnny turned and headed for the coroner's investigators office. The investigators were usually ex-police. Johnny knew a couple by sight. The heavyset black investigator behind the cluttered desk was not one of them. An obese man in a white shirt, the investigator looked up at Johnny with tired eyes and waited for him to speak.

"I'm looking for someone I met here last night." Johnny showed his ID to the man. "There was a party here last night and I met a woman." Johnny felt nervous and found that he was speaking rapidly, more quickly than normal. "She's about five-four, short dark brown hair, very pretty. Her name's Laurie. Jesus, I hope she works around here."

The man squinted his eyes at Johnny and grinned. "Damn cops. You guys are all comedians." The man went back to shuffling his papers. "Fuckin' party on Christmas Eve. Here. Sure!"

Johnny took a step back into the hall and let out a long sigh. He tried to think of what to do next when he caught sight of a morgue assistant rolling a body past on a roller table. It was the woman in the toga.

"Whoa," Johnny said, grabbing the table. "What happened to her?"

The morgue assistant, a huge black man in a blood-splattered lab coat that was once white, looked at Johnny with a face incapable of expression.

"Jesus," Johnny said, turning back to the investigator. "She was at the party last night. What happened to her?"

The investigator climbed out from behind the desk and forced his huge body through the narrow passage between the desk and wall and waddled over. He reached around for the tag attached to the toga woman's right big toe, read it and signaled the assistant to go on. The assistant rolled the table into the autopsy room.

The investigator stepped back to his desk and fished out a piece of paper. He picked it up and said, "Her name was Alice Jones. She collapsed at a party on the twenty-fourth. Pronounced dead at 1:20 A.M. yesterday morning."

Johnny felt the hair rising on the back of his neck. He felt pinpricks down his back all the way to his ass. He felt as if there was no breath in his lungs. He had to lean against the wall.

Yesterday morning. Did he say yesterday morning? Johnny's mind was trying to work its way out of an overload.

"You all right?" the investigator asked, looking at Johnny with narrow, curious eyes.

Just then another assistant started down the hall with another roller table. The brooding man in the light green suit was lying on the roller. Johnny felt as if he had been punched in the stomach. He tried to swallow, but there was no saliva in his mouth. He took in a deep breath and let it out slowly. In a voice that sounded hollow and lost he said, "I'd like to see the rest of the bodies."

"Suit yourself," the investigator answered.

Johnny noticed that the fat man kept a wary eye on him as they moved to the refrigerator units. They found her in the second drawer on the left side of the cooler. Her arms were stiff by her sides, her face waxy and flaccid, her eyelids half open. She was wearing the black party dress and heels. Johnny moved around to get a better look at her face. He counted the three hoops in her right ear and turned away.

It took Johnny a full minute to catch his breath. He felt goose bumps covering his entire body. He felt his face flushed red. He wanted to get out, but his legs wouldn't move.

The investigator began speaking. Johnny noticed the man had more papers in his hands now. "Laurie Blackwell," the investigator read from the papers. "A suicide. Pills. Barbiturates. Pronounced dead last night at 5:45 P.M. She even called the suicide hot line to let 'em know. She also left a note."

Before Johnny could stop the man, the investigator read the note aloud, in a staccato monotone voice. "This is the last Christmas I'll spend alone. I've spent too many holidays alone. This one is especially bad. I can't stop crying. Please forgive me. Please."

Johnny heard the words, not in the bloodless voice of the investigator but in Laurie's sad velvet voice. "This is the last Christmas I'll spend alone. I've spent too many holidays alone. This one is especially bad. I can't stop crying. Please forgive me. Please."

Johnny managed to croak a thank-you to the investigator, and made it to his car without falling on his face. Behind the steering wheel, he closed his eyes and tried to calm himself. His chest ached so much he thought he was going to have a heart attack.

When he finally made it home, he had trouble opening his front door. His hands wouldn't work. It took both hands on the key to get in. Every muscle of his body ached, his heart most of all. He was a good three steps into the flat when he smelled popcorn. He hesitated and then continued forward.

It has to be from last night, he told himself. He flipped on the light switch and saw it. On the floor in front of the TV was the amber bowl full of popcorn.

His knees felt like rubber. Slowly, he moved to the bowl. He knelt next to it and cupped his hands around the bowl. It was warm. He lifted his shaking left hand to the popcorn and reached in. It was warm. He pulled some up to his mouth and placed it on his tongue. No salt.

He sat back heavily, almost falling over. When he felt he could rise, he got up and looked through his apartment. He found the pot on the stove. It was so hot it almost burned his hand. Moving stiffly, Johnny went back into the living room and flipped on the TV. *It's a Wonderful Life* was just ending. He sat cross-legged next to the bowl and reached in for a handful of popcorn. When he put it in his mouth, he realized his cheeks were wet.

The announcer told the audience to stay tuned for another classic. *The Ghost and Mrs. Muir* was next.

Johnny looked into the bowl and found an old maid. He reached for it quickly, popped it in his mouth and whispered, "Beat you."

Little
Miss Sophie

Alice Dunbar-Nelson

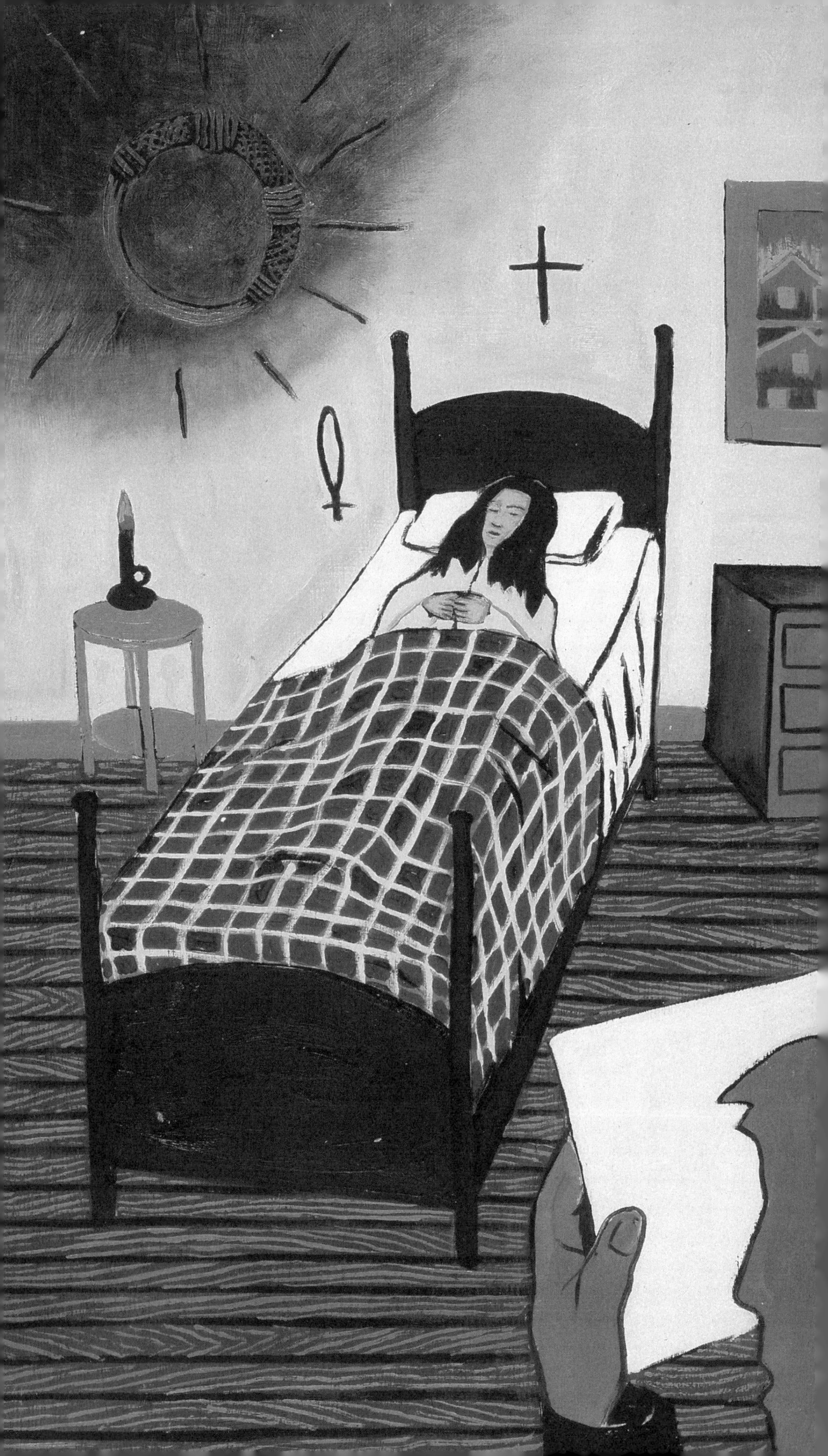

When Miss Sophie knew consciousness again, the long, faint, swelling notes of the organ were dying away in distant echoes through the great arches of the silent church, and she was alone, crouching in a little, forsaken black heap at the altar of the Virgin. The twinkling tapers shone pityingly upon her, the beneficent smile of the white-robed Madonna seemed to whisper comfort. A long gust of chill air swept up the aisles, and Miss Sophie shivered not from cold, but from nervousness.

But darkness was falling, and soon the lights would be lowered, and the great massive doors would be closed; so, gathering her thin little cape about her frail shoulders, Miss Sophie hurried out, and along the brilliant noisy streets home.

It was a wretched, lonely little room, where the cracks let the boisterous wind whistle through, and the smoky, grimy walls looked cheerless and unhomelike. A miserable little room in a miserable little cottage in one of the squalid streets of the Third District that nature and the city fathers seemed to have forgotten.

As bare and comfortless as the room was Miss Sophie's life. She rented these four walls from an unkempt little Creole woman, whose progeny seemed like the promised offspring of Abraham. She scarcely kept the flickering life in her pale little body by the unceasing toil of a pair of bony hands, stitching, stitching, ceaselessly, wearingly, on the bands and pockets of trousers. It was her bread, this monotonous, unending work; and though whole days' and nights' constant labour brought but the most meagre recompense, it was her only hope of life.

She sat before the little charcoal brazier and warmed her

transparent, needle-pricked fingers, thinking meanwhile of the strange events of the day. She had been up town to carry the great, black bundle of coarse pants and vests to the factory and to receive her small pittance, and on the way home stopped in at the Jesuit Church to say her little prayer at the altar of the calm white Virgin. There had been a wondrous burst of music from the great organ as she knelt there, an overpowering perfume of many flowers, the glittering dazzle of many lights, and the dainty frou-frou made by the silken skirts of wedding guests. So Miss Sophie stayed to the wedding; for what feminine heart, be it ever so old and seared, does not delight in one? And why should not a poor little Creole old maid be interested too?

Then the wedding party had filed in solemnly, to the rolling, swelling tones of the organ. Important-looking groomsmen; dainty, fluffy, white-robed maids; stately, satin-robed, illusion-veiled bride, and happy groom. She leaned forward to catch a better glimpse of their faces. "Ah!–"

Those near the Virgin's altar who heard a faint sigh and rustle on the steps glanced curiously as they saw a slight black-robed figure clutch the railing and lean her head against it. Miss Sophie had fainted.

"I must have been hungry," she mused over the charcoal fire in her little room, "I must have been hungry"; and she smiled a wan smile, and busied herself getting her evening meal of coffee and bread and ham.

If one were given to pity, the first thought that would rush to one's lips at sight of Miss Sophie would have been, "Poor little woman!" She had come among the bareness and sordidness of this neighbourhood five years ago, robed in crape, and crying with great sobs that seemed to shake the vitality out of her. Perfectly silent, too, she was about her former life; but for all that, Michel, the quartee grocer at the corner, and Madame Laurent, who kept the rabbé shop opposite, had fixed it all up between them, of her sad history and past glories. Not that they know; but then Michel must invent something when the neighbours came to him as their fountainhead of wisdom.

One morning little Miss Sophie opened wide her dingy windows to catch the early freshness of the autumn wind as it whistled through the yellow-leafed trees. It was one of those calm, blue-misted, balmy, November days that New Orleans can have when all the rest of the country is fur-wrapped. Miss Sophie pulled her machine to the window, where the sweet, damp wind could whisk among her black locks.

Whirr, whirr, went the machine, ticking fast and lightly over the belts of the rough jeans pants. Whirr, whirr, yes, and Miss Sophie was actually humming a tune! She felt strangely light today.

"Ma foi," muttered Michel, strolling across the street to where Madame Laurent sat sewing behind the counter on blue and brown-checked aprons, "but the little ma'amselle sings. Perhaps she recollects."

"Perhaps," muttered the rabbé woman.

But little Miss Sophie felt restless. A strange impulse seemed drawing her up town, and the machine seemed to run slow, slow, before it would stitch all of the endless number of jeans belts. Her fingers trembled with nervous haste as she pinned up the unwieldy black bundle of finished work, and her feet fairly tripped over each other in their eagerness to get to Claiborne Street, where she could board the up-town car. There was a feverish desire to go somewhere, a sense of elation, a foolish happiness that brought a faint echo of colour into her pinched cheeks. She wondered why.

No one noticed her in the car. Passengers on the Claiborne line are too much accustomed to frail little black robed women with big, black bundles; it is one of the city's most pitiful sights. She leaned her head out of the window to catch a glimpse of the oleanders on Bayou Road, when her attention was caught by a conversation in the car.

"Yes, it's too bad for Neale, and lately married too," said the elder man. "I can't see what he is to do."

Neale! She pricked up her ears. That was the name of the groom in the Jesuit Church.

"How did it happen?" languidly inquired the younger. He was a stranger, evidently; a stranger with a high regard for the faultlessness of male attire.

"Well, the firm failed first; he didn't mind that much, he was so sure of his uncle's inheritance repairing his lost fortunes; but suddenly this difficulty of identification springs up, and he is literally on the verge of ruin."

"Won't some of you fellows who've known him all your lives do to identify him?"

"Gracious man, we've tried; but the absurd old will expressly stipulates that he shall be known only by a certain quaint Roman ring, and unless he has it, no identification, no fortune. He has given the ring away, and that settles it."

"Well, you're all chumps. Why doesn't he get the ring from the owner?"

"Easily said; but—it seems that Neale had some little Creole love-affair some years ago, and gave this ring to his dusky-eyed fiancée. You know how Neale is with his love-affairs, went off and forgot the girl in a month. It seems, however, she took it to heart,—so much so that he's ashamed to try to find her or the ring."

Miss Sophie heard no more as she gazed out into the dusty grass. There were tears in her eyes, hot blinding ones that wouldn't drop for pride, but stayed and scalded. She knew the story, with all its embellishment of heartaches. She knew the ring, too. She remembered the day she had kissed and wept and fondled it, until it seemed her heart must burst under its load of grief before she took it to the pawn-broker's that another might be eased before the end came,—that other her father. The little "Creole love affair" of Neale's had not always been poor and old and jaded-looking; but reverses must come, even Neale knew that, so the ring was at the Mont de Piété. Still he must have it, it was his; it would save him from disgrace and suffering and from bringing the white-gowned bride into sorrow. He must have it; but how?

There it was still at the pawnbroker's; no one would have such an odd jewel, and the ticket was home in the bureau drawer. Well, he must have it; she might starve in the attempt. Such a thing as going to him and telling him that he might redeem it was an impossibility. That good, straight-backed, stiff-necked Creole blood would have risen in all its strength and choked her. No; as a present had the quaint Roman circlet been placed upon her finger, as a present should it be returned.

The bumping car rode slowly, and the hot thoughts beat heavily in her poor little head. He must have the ring; but how–the ring–the Roman ring–the white-robed bride starving–she was going mad–ah yes–the church. There it was, right in the busiest, most bustling part of the town, its fresco and bronze and iron quaintly suggestive of medieval times. Within, all was cool and dim and restful, with the faintest whiff of lingering incense rising and pervading the gray arches. Yes, the Virgin would know and have pity; the sweet, white-robed Virgin at the pretty flower-decked altar, or the one away up in the niche, far above the golden dome where the Host was.

Titiche, the busybody of the house, noticed that Miss Sophie's bundle was larger than usual that afternoon. "Ah, poor woman!" sighed Titiche's mother, "she would be rich for Christmas."

The bundle grew larger each day, and Miss Sophie grew smaller. The damp, cold rain and mist closed the white-curtained window, but always there behind the sewing-machine drooped and bobbed the little black-robed figure. Whirr, whirr went the wheels, and the coarse jeans pants piled in great heaps at her side. The Claiborne Street car saw her oftener than before, and the sweet white Virgin in the flowered niche above the gold-domed altar smiled at the little supplicant almost every day.

"Ma foi," said the slatternly landlady to Madame Laurent and Michel one day, "I no see how she live! Eat? Nothin', nothin', almos', and las' night when it was so cold and foggy, eh? I hav' to mek him build fire. She mos' freeze."

Whereupon the rumour spread that Miss Sophie was starving

herself to death to get some luckless relative out of jail for Christmas; a rumour which enveloped her scraggy little figure with a kind of halo to the neighbours when she appeared on the streets.

November had merged into December, and the little pile of coins was yet far from the sum needed. Dear God! How the money did have to go! The rent and the groceries and the coal, though, to be sure, she used a precious bit of that. Would all the work and saving and skimping do good? Maybe, yes, maybe by Christmas.

Christmas Eve on Royal Street is no place for a weakling, for the shouts and carousals of the roisterers will strike fear into the bravest ones. Yet amid the cries and yells, the deafening blow of horns and tin whistles, and the really dangerous fusillade of fireworks, a little figure hurried along, one hand clutching tightly the battered hat that the rude merrymakers had torn off, the other grasping under the thin black cape a worn little pocketbook.

Into the Mont de Piété she ran breathless, eager. The ticket? Here, worn, crumpled. The ring? It was not gone? No, thank Heaven! It was a joy well worth her toil, she thought, to have it again.

Had Titiche not been shooting crackers on the banquette instead of peering into the crack, as was his wont, his big, round black eyes would have grown saucer-wide to see little Miss Sophie kiss and fondle a ring, an ugly clumsy band of gold.

"Ah, dear ring," she murmured, "once you were his, and you shall be his again. You shall be on his finger, and perhaps touch his heart. Dear ring, ma chère petite de ma cour, chérie de ma cour. Je t'aime, je t'aime, oui, oui. You are his; you were mine once too. Tonight, just one night, I'll keep you–then–tomorrow, you shall go where you can save him."

The loud whistles and horns of the little ones rose on the balmy air next morning. No one would doubt it was Christmas Day, even if doors and windows were open wide to let in cool air. Why, there was Christmas even in the very look of the mules on the poky cars; there was Christmas noise in the streets, and

Christmas toys and Christmas odours, savoury ones that made the nose wrinkle approvingly, issuing from the kitchen. Michel and Madame Laurent smiled greetings across the street at each other, and the salutation from a passer-by recalled the many-progenied landlady to her self.

"Miss Sophie, well, po' soul, not ver' much Chris'mas for her. Mais, I'll jus' call him in fo' to spen' the day with me. Eet'll cheer her a bit."

It was so clean and orderly within the poor little room. Not a speck of dust or a litter of any kind on the quaint little old-time high bureau, unless you might except a sheet of paper lying loose with something written on it. Titiche had evidently inherited his prying propensities, for the landlady turned it over and read, –Louis,–Here is the ring. I return it to you. I heard you needed it. I hope it comes not too late.

"The ring, where?" muttered the landlady. There it was, clasped between her fingers on her bosom,–a bosom white and cold, under a cold happy face. Christmas had indeed dawned for Miss Sophie.

Trying to Sing

Sheryl St. Germain

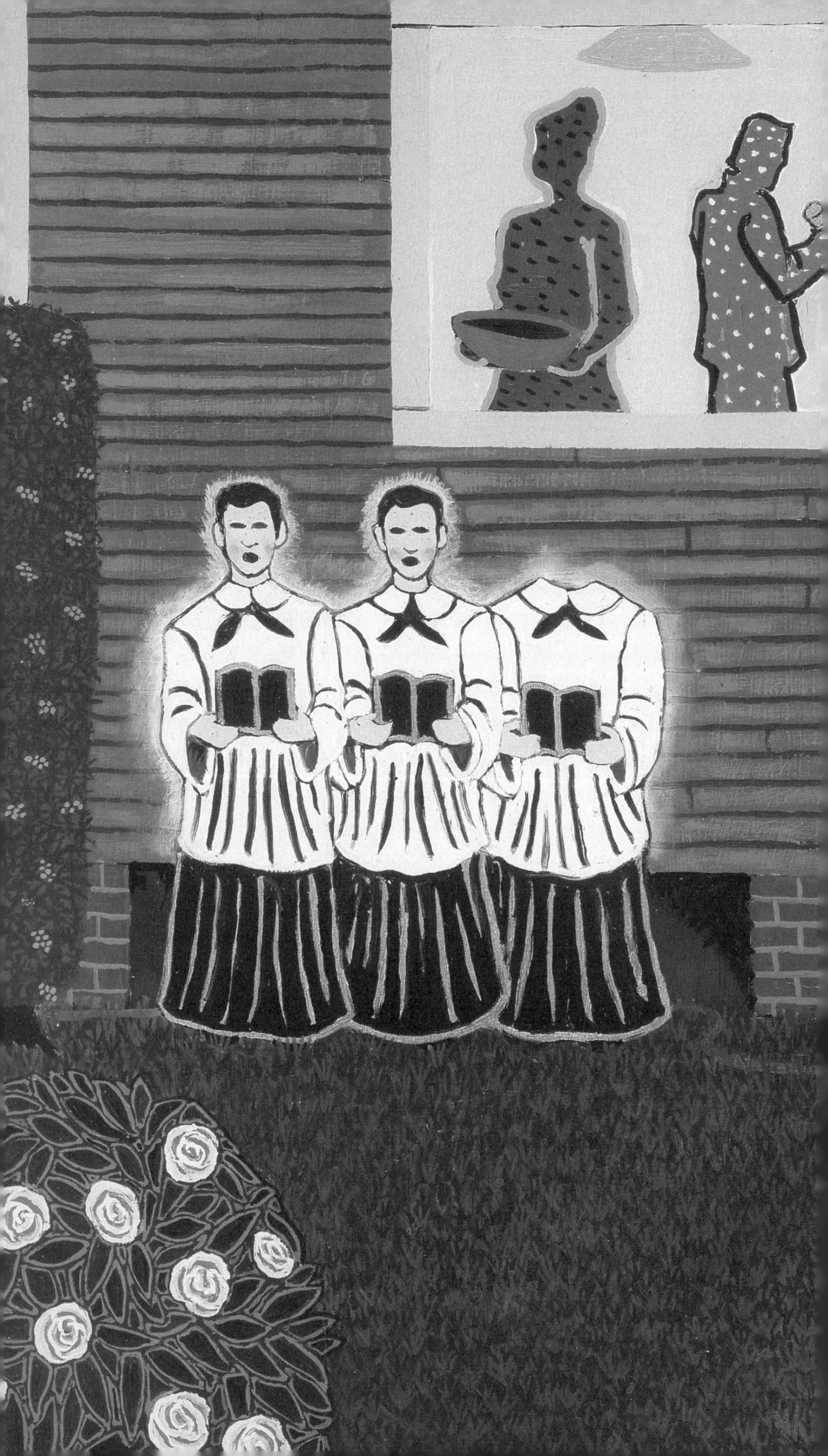

W inter storm warnings in Iowa. It's a couple of weeks before Christmas, and snow has been falling almost without a break for several days. The wind chill makes it feel like forty below outside. I look out of my study at the thick cover of snow that brightens the world as far as I can see. Not only does snow change the color of the land; it also changes the feel of it. With all the corn and soybeans harvested, the Iowa landscape for the last few months has seemed even flatter than usual, more tired and used up. Now, with almost two feet of snow, some of it mounded into soft hills by the wind, the land seems fatter, softer. I'm relieved we're having this heavy snow, even though the weather is so bad the schools are all closed; the snow plows can't keep up with the snow, and it's dangerous to drive even to the neighborhood store. I'm happy because it's as if nature has cleared its throat and stated definitively, *it's winter.* Never was there such clarity about winter in Louisiana. Winter there isn't much different from fall. Air conditioners continue to hum, the grass turns brown, leaves fall off trees, and it almost never snows. We understood snow as we understood God: it was something you were supposed to believe in even though you never saw or touched it.

And like all things you can never have, or are difficult for you to get, we wanted it, especially around this time of year, and especially when we were children. In this I don't think we were alone: most southerners would happily suffer through winter storms if only to have a frosting of brilliant white masking the brown mush that dominates Louisiana winters. In the Midwest, the killing freezes and cover of snow that usually follows provide a new beginning. The slate has been wiped clean, everything is forgiven, and one gets to start all over again. The landscape of the Deep South doesn't allow for that because winters are so mild nothing–not the insects, the rodents, the noxious weeds–ever gets totally wiped out. We can never utterly *begin again.* As if there's too much history, the southern landscape filled with the weight of too much knowledge that can never be scraped away or hidden under ice and snow.

It's dusk, and almost every house in my neighborhood is lit up with Christmas lights. My boyfriend, Peter, who is from England, finds the multicolored lights, giant lighted trees, plastic Santas and reindeers that decorate my neighbors' homes tasteless and garish. On some level I agree. But the decorations and snow also awaken a kind of hope: I can feel knots in my body loosen around the grief and joy I associate with this time of year, one of two seasons–the other was Mardi Gras–when my family seemed happy.

Perhaps my family took Christmas so seriously because we knew Mardi Gras was just around the corner. Hardly were the Christmas trees undressed and tossed into yards when the first King Cake parties would begin. The first week of January marks the beginning of the Mardi Gras season, which is, for us, the season of deception, wit, and irony. Christmas, though it involved pageantry and costuming as well, was the season of earnestness.

Oddly enough the two seasons were more tightly connected historically, and indeed at some time may have been part of the same festival. Christmas has been linked to the Roman feast of Saturnalia, which was a day when everything was opposite: children dressed as kings, slaves as masters, etc. The homes and public places were decorated with some of the items we now associate with Christmas: holly, ivy, evergreen, candles, and torches. Mummers also ran about in the streets. The people chose a Lord of Misrule who presided over the "Feast of the Fools." The playfulness of this celebration is not unlike that of the Mardi Gras season, which not only closely follows Christmas, but also overlaps it. The magi who were said to have followed the star to pay homage to the infant Jesus are the kings honored in the Mardi Gras tradition of the King Cake. January 6, also known as "Little Christmas," or the Feast of the Epiphany, is the day that officially begins the Mardi Gras season. Throughout the Middle Ages that day was also the final day of Christmas, which came to be known as Twelfth Night.

I stare through the window at the house across the street. A lighted, life-size plastic choirboy stands in front of it, his red robes stark against the snow, his mouth open in frozen song. Something about him makes me shiver. He looks very much like one of the three plastic choirboys my father used to set out in front of our house every Christmas: the red flaring robe, that singing O of a mouth, and dark round eyes raised to the heavens. He is the picture of earnestness.

I was seventeen when my father last displayed the plastic choirboys. Nineteen seventy-one: a warmish day in early December, and on our browning front lawn a small mountain of lights and cords. Next to these a life-size plastic Santa lies on its side. The plastic choirboys are set upright but without their heads, which come off so you can put lights inside the bodies. My father replaces the lights inside each of the three bodies, then settles the heads on top of two of them. He looks through the pile of lights and wires, but cannot find the third head. He curses softly, then lights a cigarette and stands smoking and thinking for a few minutes. After he finishes the cigarette, he sets the two boys with heads in the middle of the lawn, and then, almost as an afterthought, puts the third one out too.

That Christmas our house and the mimosa tree and hydrangea bushes in front would be outlined as usual with lots of lights, and would become, as usual, a backdrop for the Santa and the three choirboys, except that this year the middle one would be headless. Maybe my father hoped to find the head somewhere in the attic and never got around to looking for it. Maybe he was being ironic. In any event it had a chilling effect:

the rest of the house decorated in all seriousness and that headless choirboy in the midst of it all like some macabre, cutting
criticism of the whole thing.

This also would be the last year my father would put up
Christmas lights, the last year things would seem relatively quiet
in the family, although it was a kind of uncomfortable quiet. My
father is drinking heavily, but no one has yet begun to call him
alcoholic. My brother François is thirteen, and though he has
always been a difficult child, he hasn't yet been expelled or
arrested, and hasn't yet started doing drugs. Certainly there are
signs of trouble with both my brother and father, but none of us
would have predicted then the paths their lives would ultimately
take. My younger sister Aimée is fifteen and pregnant that
Christmas, though we don't know it yet. She will drop out of
school early the next year to marry and have her child, a boy, my
godchild, who would be killed by a drunk driver a dark New
Year's Eve night years later. The two youngest siblings, Jules and
Marie, are seven and three respectively, their own troubles far
into the future. I have just graduated from high school and will
be leaving home and starting college at Southeastern Louisiana
University in January. I am engaged to be married to my high
school sweetheart, Ricky, who is in his first year at the Naval
Academy in Annapolis.

My maternal grandfather, whom we called Paw-Paw, is very
sick this year. He has stomach cancer, and Christmas Eve 1971
will be the last time I will see him alive. But I am infected with
the hopefulness of the season, naive in all ways about death, and
believe he will recover.

I am happy. Except for my grandfather's illness, everything
seems possible, as untarnished and bright as Louisiana in
December can manage. That Christmas Eve I work until 7 P.M. at
Woolco, the department store in Kenner where I have a part-time
job. It is just cool enough to wear a jacket, although it will warm
up later in the evening. Ricky, who is home on Christmas break
from Annapolis, picks me up from work. He has agreed, with
much prodding on my part, to wear his dress uniform that night

to my family's annual Christmas Eve party. I know Paw-Paw, who had been in the navy, will be there. My father had also been in the navy as a young man, and I tell Ricky they will both be proud to see my fiancé in his white midshipman's uniform.

Ricky and I will break up the next month, and he will resign from the Naval Academy, which he hates, before the end of the year, but no matter. We believe, at least for this night, that we'll be together forever.

That week my family's small house has been transformed as Mother went into her annual cleaning frenzy, sweeping and dusting where no sweeping or dusting had occurred all year, and clearing off cluttered countertops whose surfaces we hadn't seen since the previous Christmas. She had even gotten on her hands and knees and scrubbed the floors. She had to use a butter knife to get at the flat hardened gum—like hard dark nipples—that turned up wherever she scrubbed. The house, which the week before had been cluttered and overstuffed, suddenly revealed itself to be clean, with space somehow cleared for a tree and crèche.

I never fully understood where all the clutter went, although I knew a lot of it went into my parents' bedroom, which became something of a junk room during the holiday season. The house had the feeling, in the days leading up to Christmas, of having sucked in its breath for a few days; you knew that soon the breath would be let out and the fat stomach of the house would make itself known again.

Christmas music filled the house the entire month of December, mostly because of my mother, who loved this time of year and had a large collection of seasonal music. The record player was stacked with LPs waiting to be dropped and played: Robert Goulet, Mario Lanza, Frank Sinatra, Johnny Mathis, and Bing Crosby, as well as Handel's *Messiah* and Eydie Gorme y Los Panchos and their *Blanca Navidad* album, which my mother played over and over, though all the lyrics were in Spanish and none of us spoke a word.

Our finest piece of furniture was the spinet piano my parents struggled for years to purchase. The children all eventually took piano lessons, and most everyone else in the family could play by ear. François, who actually had a good ear for music, had a horrendous experience with the man the rest of us took lessons from for eight years, Mr. Harry, our next door neighbor, who was not particularly gifted as a teacher. I was dutiful and dull; I practiced and did everything he asked of me, so we got along fine. But François challenged him every step of the way, and refused to practice. He couldn't be bothered with counting measures or with correct fingering, and saw no need to learn how to sight-read when he could pick any melody out by ear. His weekly lesson soon became a shouting session, and eventually my mother stepped in, mercifully, and cancelled the lessons.

Every Christmas Eve those of us who were currently taking piano lessons with Mr. Harry would take part in an informal piano recital where we played a piece we'd been practicing for several months. In 1971 I would play the largo from Chopin's *Fantasie Impromptu* and Aimée would play something from Debussy. Marie and Jules were still too young for lessons, and François had already stopped taking lessons. He still played piano, but only picked things out by ear that he liked. Rarely would he play in front of anyone.

My father and Maw-Maw also played by ear and would play some popular songs and Christmas carols as well. Eventually we'd all sing carols around the piano, and sometimes we'd go caroling in the neighborhood later. I was always the instigator of these trips because I loved to sing. During all four years of high school I belonged to both the high school chorus and our church choir, though my voice was not a strong one and I couldn't, as a soprano, always hold the melody if I were placed right next to someone singing alto or second soprano.

Still, if anyone had asked me what I wanted to be when I grew up, I would've said a *singer*. I remember many summer evenings swinging in our backyard, singing my heart out as I swung, mostly popular songs from the radio and musicals I'd watched with my mother. I had the idea that maybe someone would pass by, someone would recognize what a good voice I had, raw, yes, but also pure and strong. When I sang as a child it felt like a string vibrating through my body, from mouth and tongue to the tips of my toes, a string to which all other sounds were tuned. I lost the exuberant faith of that swinging child after I became an adult and with it the ability to feel the physical excitement she felt when she sang.

This Christmas my mother was a little more subdued than usual, because she understood, certainly more clearly than any of the children, that her father was dying. She had a complicated relationship with Paw-Paw, a loud, gruff man she loved, but who had not, she thought, treated her mother right. He was German, square-jawed and blue-eyed, and she had inherited both his jaw and his eyes. He loved to cook, and he loved poetry–as did she. He also loved to argue with his wife's mother, who was French, about why the Germans were better than the French. My mother thought he was intelligent, and liked to tell the story of how, when he was in high school, he had pointed out to one of his teachers that their mathematics textbook had a mistake in it. My great-grandfather pulled him out of school when he was fifteen though, to help with the family business, and he never returned to graduate. He and his father eventually parted ways, and Paw-Paw spent most of his life working as a painter for a hospital in New Orleans, a job that offered no benefits, a job for which he was clearly overqualified, and a job that left him bitter and in the bars most nights. My grandparents remained poor all of their lives and were never able to buy a house of their own. They rented half of a shotgun house–a house where the rooms were arranged one after the other such that if you shot a gun through the first room the bullet would pass through all the rooms. They lived there, in an old neighborhood in east New Orleans, for almost half a century.

They made the ten-mile trip from New Orleans to Kenner every other Sunday, though, in their ancient car, to visit. Paw-Paw always brought a nickel box of Crackerjacks for each of the kids, and gave us full-bodied hugs and spirited kisses. I don't remember ever feeling his face against mine for a kiss when it wasn't covered with white stubble. He loved to eat and drink beer, as his ample belly betrayed.

My mother would not tell me until years later the details of Paw-Paw's betrayals of Maw-Maw. All I know this Christmas is how glad I will be to see him again, as I haven't seen him for several months. He has been too ill to travel for the last three months, and I take it as a good sign that they are able to make the trip from New Orleans to Kenner for the party. Even though I'm older now, graduating from high school, I still look forward to watching him hand out Crackerjacks. I still crave the crisp, rich peanuts and sticky caramel popcorn, the sweetness that would catch itself in my teeth for hours.

In some ways Paw-Paw reminded me of Scrooge. Flinty, inscrutable, but somewhere in him a generosity ready enough to show itself to children, but needing the right coaxing around adults. I had been thinking of him the night before when we gathered, mother, father, and the five children, around the hi-fi to listen to Basil Rathbone as Scrooge in *A Christmas Carol*. My mother turned all the lights in the house off and lit some candles. We each had a mug of eggnog with freshly grated nutmeg sprinkled on top. My father lay in his easy chair, my mother sat on the sofa with Marie in her lap and Jules sitting close next to her. Aimée, François, and I lay on the newly cleaned floor. I listened to the voices and sounds and music and stared at the small red light that indicated the record player was on, the light that looked like my grandfather's nose when he'd been drinking. The melancholy clanging of Marley's chains sounded deep in my body, a metaphoric ringing the literal movie versions could never manage. I wondered what chains Paw-Paw might be dragging around. I wondered if whatever it was that made my mother sad about him could be changed. Maybe, I thought, he could be redeemed, pulled back from his sickness, which was surely a punishment for something he'd done in his life.

Before I could read, my mother would read *A Christmas Carol* to me, and later she gave me illustrated editions of the story and took me to see its film versions whenever they came out. Christ-mas after Christmas, this tale entered me, and with it the belief that characters change—for better or ill. If I could not effect trans-formation in my own life or those of my family members, I would continue to believe that stories might change and inspire us for a time.

By the time Ricky and I arrive at my family's house this Christmas Eve, he in his white Naval Academy dress uniform and I waving around a small diamond engagement ring, most everyone else has already arrived. In the living room are my aunt Alta and my uncle Emile as well as my paternal grandpar-ents, who are deaf-mutes. The only people who can communi-cate with them efficiently are my father and Aunt Alta. Though my grandparents can't speak, it doesn't mean they don't like to have a good time. They both love to eat, and they both like to drink a lot on occasion. My grandmother can perceive some low sounds and claps along to music if there is a deep bass line whose vibrations she can feel. Sometimes she makes a low moaning that sounds like singing. She is clapping and trying to sing when we walk in. She looks happy, slightly drunk, pleased with her one syllable "Ahhh." Albin, my grandfather, is sitting next to her, bending over to dip a potato chip into the garlic dip, for which he has an unholy love. We all love my mother's dip, made with lots of garlic, sour cream, and cream cheese, dyed green or red. The house will smell of garlic for days after Christ-mas day. Tomorrow morning it will be in all of our breaths, like a secret we have all shared.

Frank Sinatra, singing "Jingle Bells," wafts from the hi-fi in the back of the house. All along one side of the living room is my mother's crèche, set out on a long table covered with fake snow and pine branches from the Christmas tree. The lights are dimmed, and the Christmas tree, against the back wall, wel-comes us with blinking lights of red and blue and green and gold.

The house smells warm and full, a complex polyphony of scents—pine and whiskey, tomato sauce and coconut.

Underneath, like a chorus of full, deep bass notes, the everyday odor of the house–the smell of books and the smell of my mother's perfume, my father's cigarettes. The tree has a pile of presents underneath it. Sometime during the night these presents will all get opened, and then, much later, after we are in bed, my mother, with the help of my father, will put the presents from Santa under the tree. My mother has a Christmas Club account where she saves five dollars a week to have money to buy presents, and my father also usually takes on an extra job at this time of year to help pay for presents. No matter how poor we are, there are always lots of presents under the tree Christmas morning.

My father, dressed in a paisley silk shirt, jumps up when Ricky and I arrive, and walks over to give me a hug. He smells of garlic and scotch, Old Spice and smoke. He makes a joke about Ricky's uniform and asks what he wants to drink.

"I'll have a Hammer if y'all have it this year," Ricky says.

"How about you, Sherry, what do you want, sweetie?" Even though I'm not old enough to legally drink, all the children are allowed to drink on Christmas Eve.

"I'll have a Hammer too, Daddy, thanks."

A "Hammer" is a potent drink my mother always concocts gallons of for Christmas Eve. It's a sort of heavy-duty piña colada made with all the white liquors, pineapple juice, and coconut cream. Usually the younger crowd, who hadn't yet developed a sophisticated taste for liquor, favored this mix. My father serves us our Hammers in large plastic cups, and Ricky and I wander to the back of the living room to look at the tree.

My favorite ornaments on the tree are the plastic clear ones that look like round houses but have small blades inside. When you place them over the lights the heat from the light rises and makes the blades turn, causing the tree to seem alive, casting small, quick shadows about so that it looks as if large insects, or small birds, or fairies are darting about, although all you can see is the movement of their shadows before they disappear.

You can hardly see any of the ornaments on the tree this year, though, because of the icicles, which cover it from top to bottom. Mother always says it's the icicles that make the tree. She would caution, when we helped decorate, that we should add one icicle at a time, and not throw them on in clumps. She would show us, yet again, how to carefully drape them. Eventually we would tire of this, though, especially my brothers, who would wind up throwing them on in clumps with great glee. She'd redo our handiwork after we went to bed. Mother saved icicles from year to year, painstakingly removing each one from the tree and laying it flat in the icicle box—hundreds and hundreds of them. Often they were crinkled and creased from several years of use. Long after this Christmas the memory of those recycled icicles would be a painful reminder of how poor we were. When I become an adult I will never be able to bring myself to buy tinsel, though it costs less than a dollar a box.

"I'm hungry." Ricky nudges me, and we turn from the tree and walk toward the kitchen where people are sitting around the kitchen table, and where the serious food is located. My mother always makes the same dishes for Christmas, and this is comforting in the same way the familiar narratives of the season are. Ricky grabs a couple of crustless ham sandwiches from a platter on a small table near the door and wolfs them down. I helped my mother make the meatballs that are now simmering in a spicy tomato sauce on an electric skillet. I walk over to the meatballs and jab one with a toothpick. It always took a long time to get the meatballs just the way Mother wanted them. She had the magical ability to roll them just right, all the same size. Mine were always coming out too big or too small, or somehow lopsided, and I'd have to start over. The meatballs are slightly sweet with barbecue sauce, and spicy with Tabasco sauce. The sweet and the hot are a lovely combination in my mouth, a combination that always reminds me of my family at this time of year.

My mother is standing up against the counter holding a glass of wine, and Maw-Maw is sitting at the kitchen table, drinking a glass of beer. A beautiful, dark-haired woman with high cheekbones and olive complexion, she does not look like a typical grandmother. Raising four children with a difficult husband during the depression has not visibly taken its toll on her, at least not in her physical countenance.

"Hello, dawlin," she says, "how ya doin?" and gives me a beery kiss. Maw-Maw has lived deep in the heart of New Orleans all her life and has a thick New Orleans accent, as does most everyone in my family, although Maw-Maw's and Paw-Paw's accents are the heaviest. To an untrained ear this accent, primarily associated with downtown New Orleans, sounds a bit like a New York City or Hoboken, New Jersey, accent, except that northerners don't, of course, use the expression *y'all*, which always gives a New Orleanian away, and which we sometimes use not only as a pronoun but as a possessive: "y'all got y'all books?"

I would come to love this accent in my middle age, and would come to think of its slow sloppiness that connects every syllable to every other syllable as being like the water that dominates the landscape, slow and sloppy and muddy and lovely. But it embarrassed me as a young adult, and I eventually tried to lose it. I thought I *had* lost it after I moved to Texas in my twenties. But even after twelve years in another state I'd still fall back into it whenever I visited home, or even on the phone, whenever my mother called, forgetting I was a college graduate, forgetting I was an English major, saying things like *wheah ya at sweethawt,* or *dat doan mean nuttn, ya awta seen da way she pawks dat caw,* the sounds I was fed like milk as a child, the "aw" sound predominating as if it was just too much work to pronounce the "r." I tried hard to get rid of it, to make my voice sound as if I had nothing to do with the black smell of the lake, nothing to do with my mother's cooking, nothing to do with my father's breath, my brother's track marks.

That Christmas Eve, though, I have never been outside of Louisiana, and I can't really hear the accent; it is just the way we all talk, and as linguistically comfortable as an old nightshirt. My mother is the only one in the family at this point who can choose to speak without a pronounced accent if she wants to, though my father would always say she was "putting on airs" when she spoke in unaccented, grammatically correct sentences. Today, when I return home, I cannot imagine speaking to any of my brothers and sisters in unaccented grammatically correct sentences. If, because of so many years of being an English teacher and living away from Louisiana, I happen to fall into standard English when speaking to my family, the air becomes immediately and almost unbearably tense; it feels as if I have switched to an almost foreign language, a language in which it will be impossible to say anything meaningful.

Jules and Marie are playing on the floor with toys they'd received earlier in the evening from some relative or another. Mr. Harry and his wife, Lucille, are also in the kitchen. Mr. Harry gives us lessons for free in exchange for my mother letting him play the piano whenever he wants. She always gives him an extraspecial gift for Christmas to repay him for the lessons.

I say hello to everyone, then attack the artichoke balls, which are my favorite, and which I also helped make the day before. We'd mashed up artichoke hearts in a big bowl, added lemon juice, olive oil and lots of garlic, Italian breadcrumbs and Parmesan cheese, then rolled the mixture into small balls. The balls are soft and squishy in your mouth, and when you bite into them you're likely to bite into bits of garlic. The artichoke balls contributed significantly to the family's collective garlic breath that would infect the church that night when we sang at Midnight Mass, and which would not begin to dissipate until the day after Christmas.

Maw-Maw pops an artichoke ball into her mouth too, and between chews notes how fine Ricky's uniform is and how beautiful my engagement ring is.

"Where's Paw-Paw?" I ask.

Maw-Maw swallows, sips her beer, and looks at my mother. My mother, in turn, looks at her hands. "He's in the back bedroom." She means my parents' bedroom.

"Oh, is he okay?"

"Well, he's tired, and can't really get up, but I'll tell him you're here and y'all can go back and say hello." My mother carefully steps over my sister and brother and the trucks and dolls on the kitchen floor and makes her way down the hall to her bedroom.

Mr. Harry has started a conversation with Ricky. He is speaking much louder than he usually does, which means he too has had a lot to drink. I sip the sweet Hammer drink, which reminds me we made some sweet things yesterday too. I search the counters for the stuffed dates. We used pitted dates and stuffed them with marshmallows and topped them with half a pecan, then rolled the whole thing in granulated sugar.

I pop one into my mouth, the rich date flavor and pecan and sugar filling my mouth, all sticky and even more complicated than the Crackerjacks. Robert Goulet sings *Fall on your knees, oh hear the angel voices,* and Mother enters the kitchen again, the scent of her perfume, Chanel #5, enveloping me, so sweet I wish I could taste it. My mother looks pretty, her blond hair curled and pulled back off her face with an ornate barrette, but her face is flushed.

"He knows you're here. You can go see him. Don't stay too long, though." She bends to pick up Marie, who has started crying. I look at Ricky. "Ready?" I say.

"Ready."

I fluff my hair, grab Ricky's hand, and lead him into the hall, underneath the entrance to the attic and past my own bedroom to my parents' bedroom. Only the lamp on the night table is lit. The room is filled with the detritus that has been removed from the rest of the house to make more space for the party. The gifts from Santa are also stuffed into this room, in the closet and underneath the bed. Christmas boxes and ribbon and paper are piled on the floor, as this is also the room where gifts got wrapped. This is the room, in fact, where many important things happened. It is the room where my youngest brother and sister were conceived, but it is also the room where my mother sat Aimée and me on her bed and explained about menstruation. It is the room where, many years ago, my mother sat me down on the bed and explained, that no, Sheryl, there actually isn't really a Santa Claus, not a man, anyway, but a spirit, a spirit you could still believe in. It is also the room to which my parents retreated when they talked about the possibility of divorcing. It is the room where my mother would lie in bed for hours at a time and read books into the small hours of the morning, my father not home yet. And now it is the room where I will speak to my grandfather for the last time.

A pathway leads from the entrance between my mother's bureau, cluttered with jewelry and makeup, to the bed where Paw-Paw lies, breathing heavily. Three months I have known about the cancer, but nothing could have prepared me for this, for the way the body looks when it has given up, skin crying out in retreat, eyes flagged in surrender, belly gone flat and valleyed. I fall silent for a moment.

The music from the front room pauses, as if on cue, as another LP drops down. Ricky shifts nervously next to me, then Bing Crosby's voice singing "White Christmas" begins to fill the house. Paw-Paw likes this song, and would always talk about how one Christmas, mark his words, it would snow.

I have never been around any kind of dying before. I've only read about it in books. But it's not his conspicuous dying that causes me to recoil; it's not knowing how to kiss the face shaved so clean, and it's the strangeness of his sober lips, robbed of the yeasty breath I recognize as his. Boyfriend planted like a hedge at my side, I finally open my mouth, chatter about our engagement, and hold my hand out to show him the ring. His eyes are bright blue pools of agony. Sunken into the bed, he looks at the ring, then at Ricky. He gathers himself up, voice sudden, and speaks, looking right at Ricky: *You take good care of her, son.* Ricky doesn't respond, but smiles weakly and squeezes my hand. Then, becoming something like the man I thought I knew, so that it seems as if belly rolls over belt again, whiskers grow again, Paw-Paw pulls himself up and charges: *Promise me, boy.* He falls back onto the bed.

Ricky gulps out the promise like a belch.

These days when I think of my grandfather I like to think of him extracting that promise, becoming himself one last time. I hold on to the idea of it like some treasure or inheritance. Ricky and I left that dark room and went into another, drinking our way from room to room until it was sufficiently late and we were drunk enough to attend Midnight Mass with my mother and father, brothers and sisters. This was the only time of the year my father went to church, and the only time we all stood together and sang hymns to celebrate Christ's birth.

Afterwards, Ricky kisses me in the car, and holds me for a time, staring at the lights on the house, and at the lighted Santa and choirboys in front of it.

"What happened to the head of that one choirboy?" he asks, twisting the ring on my finger.

"Someone must have stolen it," I say. I press his hand and close my eyes.

When I walk into the house half an hour later there's no music on the hi-fi but I can hear someone playing "Silver Bells" softly on the piano. I tiptoe into the living room. François, who clearly thinks he is alone, is sitting at the piano, pecking the notes out, staring at the keys as if they hold some secret to his life. My mother is standing in the darkened hallway, listening, though I'm sure he doesn't know she is there. When the lights from the tree flash on, I can see that her lips are pressed together. Tears, reflected in the light like tiny glass ornaments, fill her eyes.

We are sometimes given moments—I do not know if we are blessed or cursed with these moments—when we can see the future with stark clarity. I do not mean epiphanies, for those are often the result of much thinking and unconscious work. I mean something more like a gift. You are given the gift of sight for a moment. I think my mother, early this Christmas morning, was experiencing such a gift. She could see something of her son's future from that hallway, something clear, something irrevocable, something I could not see. I tiptoe past them both and go to bed, falling asleep almost immediately.

The snow continues to fall outside in large, wet, fluffy flakes, the kind we used to draw as kids, the kind that feel like cold, sloppy kisses when they land on your cheek. I am forty-six now, and have lived in the Midwest for seven years. During that time, for several Christmases, I have gotten what I so wanted as a child: snow. My sister Aimée also has snow. She lives in Nebraska now, where they see even more snowfall than we do in Iowa. We both miss Louisiana, but we've both made lives away from it, both in places with killing freezes and winter storm warnings, and it seems unlikely either of us will return to Louisiana to live, though we both visit frequently. My youngest brother and sister, who are both now married with children of their own, still live in Louisiana, and often speak wistfully, when I call, of hoping for snow.

This year my mother dubbed off a tape of the Basil Rathbone *A Christmas Carol* for me. The record had become scratched and warped with so many years of playing, and the tape had recorded all the hisses and pops of the old album. I put it on the cassette player and watch the snow outside my window as I listen. I think I can hear the small seasonal joy of our family through the pops and hisses, can almost see the ghosts of all those who are no longer here. It's not Marley I hear when the chains sound, but my brother, my father, my grandfather. And when the carols come in at the end of the tape, after Scrooge's transformation, it's all of us together again, singing at Midnight Mass, all of us alive, our imperfect, passionate, drunk voices ringing in the snowless night.

The
Holy Assumption
of Mr. Tinsel

Patty Friedmann

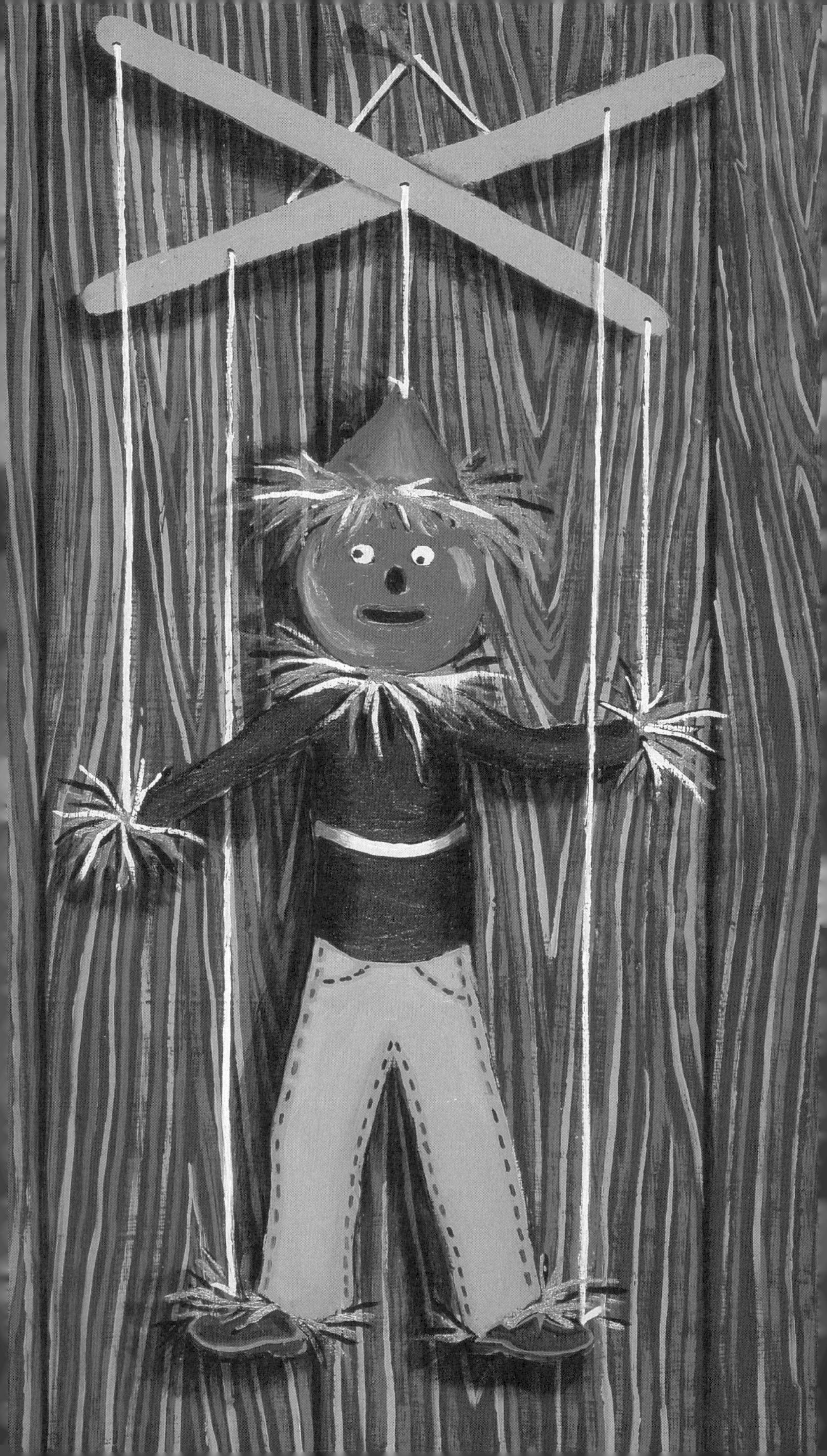

People often passed as Walter let himself in through the street door, but no one ever turned to look. It seemed to him that having keys to a door on Bourbon Street counted for something, but even down at his end everyone was looking for women and men in feathers and spangles, and he never attracted any curiosity, any particular envy.

He didn't like having to go through the narrow corridor to the stairs, and he'd have liked some admiration for doing so every day. He'd once figured that the passage was half a block long, and so high, two stories up to the ceiling, that if there was a light fixture at all, it hadn't had a bulb in it for as long as he could remember. A queer little slit of a transom was set over the door at the street, thick and semiopaque with the grease and dust thrown off by bad behavior. By late fall no light filtered through, and now, with the winter solstice only a few weeks away, all Walter could do was leave the street door open, open maybe to prying eyes of tourists and desperate project boys, while he checked to see that all was the same as ever, and then he'd slam the door, count ninety-seven paces, careful to keep on a straight line so that his white shirt, still clean, would sweep no slick wet walls, take no mildew. Too, he'd given himself quite a nick in the shoulder once, bumping into the row of electric meters which he now knew were on the wall eighteen paces in. Ninety-six steps, and then his hand would find the banister in the dark.

For the past few weeks, Walter had been having a strange experience every time he was walking down the corridor. He tried not to let the thoughts work their way into his mind, but still the image of Riley popped into his head, there in the dark.

Riley hadn't lived there in twenty-one years, but lately something about being in the hallway made him think about the man who'd lived in the apartment that shared a landing with his before Dorcas moved in.

Riley was fat. And Riley lived with his father, who was fat, too. The two of them never left their apartment at the same time, and rarely left it at all, but a few times Walter had found himself coming in or going out at the same time as Riley. He could hear Riley puffing slowly through the corridor, too large to move straight forward, sidling along; when Riley reached the electric meters he had to line himself up perpendicular to the outside door, grunting from little scrapes and bruises. When they came to light, Riley smiled at Walter, and Walter felt he was a friend of sorts.

Riley's father died one morning. Through a crack in his apartment door, Walter could see the police arrive. They went in for what seemed like a very short time, reeled out as if they'd seen or smelled something overpowering, one heading back down the steps, flashlight in hand, the other calling after him, "Hey, look out for stalactites." "Stalagmites," the first one called back. "How you gonna tell which way's up in a place like this?" said the one still upstairs, and Walter heard a deep hoot of derision come from the corridor below.

It took the ambulance attendants almost two hours to arrive, and Riley stood in his doorway all that time, with Walter watching politely. The attendants had a terrible time getting Riley's father out to the street, their stretcher bearing a great mound, covered in taut rubber. "This sonofabitch gonna need twenny pallbearers," one said, grunting the way a person does when something won't go around a corner, no matter what. Riley walked slowly behind them, a slow-motion processional; his eyes were red-rimmed now, darting a little, expecting something. Riley left the door to his apartment wide open. Walter wanted very much to see how they managed to get through the downstairs passageway, but he couldn't think of a discreet way to follow them down the old wooden steps to listen. When Riley didn't return in about four weeks, Walter slipped into his apartment and took the vinyl reclining lounger. He was glad he did it, because a couple of days later the landlord put all of Riley's stuff out on the sidewalk.

Dorcas moved in shortly after that, and she'd lived there ever since. She was a night nurse with about seventeen cats, and Walter could never figure out how she always looked so crisp when she lived with all those cats. She baked him a cake once, courteously leaving it outside his doorway while he was at work, and he'd brought it to the store the next day. He put it on the lunchroom table at noon, cutting a big swath out of it to show he wasn't afraid of cat hairs, but no one else took any all the time he was in the lunchroom. He figured that one of the bus girls took it home, because it was gone when he came in for lunch the next day.

Walter was basically happy with the experiences he'd had with his neighbors, and he thought his place was supreme. He felt that over the years he had made his one-room apartment into a real bachelor pad. He had a refrigerator, a bed with wooden headboard and footboard, a dresser, and a black-and-white console television that his aunt Pearl had left him, and of course the recliner. The bed stood next to the wall, making it a little hard for him to make up each morning, but he felt it was worth the trouble. He'd won a painting at the store's Fourth of July picnic eight years ago, and the painting was as long as the bed, so it looked perfect hanging on that wall. It was quite a piece of art, a locomotive coming from the valley up the steep rise of a mountainside, as perfect as a photograph.

Walter's refrigerator always had a few beers in it, along with a paper sack in which a half-eaten doughnut had sat for about eight months. At first he'd planned to eat the rest of the doughnut, then he'd considered throwing it away, and with the lapse of time he'd eventually become unable even to peer into the sack, which was neatly folded closed at the top.

Walter liked the image of himself when he was home. He'd take a beer out of the refrigerator, turn on channel six, the only channel poor Aunt Pearl's TV could pick up any more, and plop himself down in his recliner. He was sure he looked exactly like those guys he saw on TV who sat in front of their own sets, throwing back beers, jumping up and down excitedly while a crowd roared on the tube, and trying to ignore their nagging wives who were always harping about some kind of dish detergent. Walter was an all-American man. Once or twice it occurred to him that it was too bad that Aunt Pearl and Riley's father had had to die before he got the television and the recliner. He might have invited Riley over to watch a football game.

He was lucky that, if his TV could only pick up one channel, it would be channel six. Walter had his own television show; at least, five weeks out of the year he did. He was the creator of Mr. Tinsel, whom he tended and succored and curried forty-seven weeks out of the year. Every weeknight from mid-November to Christmas Eve, Mr. Tinsel was on TV at five forty-five. For the past couple of years, Walter had been bothered that Mr. Tinsel was followed by the Muppets. He didn't know why exactly, but the Muppets made him feel bad. The toy department was full of books and stuffed dolls and games with Muppet pictures on them, and the only Mr. Tinsel for kids was an inflatable balloon toy that Newman's brought out every Christmas for a dollar sixty-nine. The colors on it weren't even close to correct. He once asked George, who was a producer at channel six, why the Muppets followed his show. "You come on first; that way the kids keep watching," George said. Walter liked George after that, but he still didn't particularly care for the Muppets.

He'd taped today's episode only yesterday morning, and it was fresh enough in his mind to keep him chuckling with anticipatory laughter. That Mr. Tinsel was a feisty one; it was hard to remember sometimes that he was a marionette. Walter had fashioned the original Mr. Tinsel out of lamp globes and chandelier bulbs–some as delicate as eggshells and all painted with iridescent paint–and Christmas tree tinsel twenty years ago. Mr. Tinsel was supposed to look as if he were made of Christmas ornaments, and the general manager of Newman's department store had been delighted with the idea of using the fragile puppet to promote Christmas toy sales. Over the years, Mr. Tinsel became a media celebrity and in the process eventually had had every globe shattered and replaced. Walter had put him through several metamorphoses, and these days he was made of kapok sheathed in shiny Mylar. These days, too, Walter didn't have to do live television, and so he could go home and watch the taped broadcast of the program in the comfort of his own recliner.

In today's episode, Mr. Tinsel was trying to educate his thickheaded moose friend, Choklit, about barber poles and magnetic poles. Their painted-on eyes swayed in and out of focus as marionette eyes do, though Walter had tried to aim them as much as possible toward a red-and-white barber pole standing like a monolith on the puppet stage. Mr. Tinsel and Choklit were caught up in an absolutely uproarious conversation. "I think I've, uh, found the, uh, North Pole here, Mr. Tinsel. Uh, looks like a, uh, candy cane. Except, you know, uh, there's no hook." Simple people said "uh" a lot. Choklit's cloven hand made a smooth arc in the air, and Walter shimmered with the pleasure that comes of pure talent.

Walter knew that in all their homes, all over the city, little Santa-believing kids were squealing, "No, silly, that's not the North Pole!" And so that's exactly what Mr. Tinsel said, "No, silly, that's not the North Pole!" in a voice that was the same one Walter used in his everyday life. Mr. Tinsel was good-hearted, and he always stood out as the leader among all the characters. Walter saw him as a wellspring of information, though it wasn't easy to gauge how much the children were learning from his shows. Walter had never talked to children, though he eavesdropped on them whenever he was near them in the store.

Each plot also had to give Walter a lead to talk about toys that Santa would bring and about how the kids who were friends of Mr. Tinsel's should come down to see Santa and all his toys at Newman's. Mr. Tinsel was good for Newman's department store.

In fact, Mr. Tinsel was so good for the store that tomorrow a three-story-tall model of the puppet would be mounted on the facade of the building, which had dominated Canal Street since

1903. Newman's did that every year, so kids whose mamas took them down to Canal Street would pester until they got to go to Newman's. The mamas used to be refined white ladies who parked at Solari's; now more of them were black girls who came on the bus with their babies, but every child on earth was horribly spoiled, as far as Walter could tell from the fussing. Newman's had a suburban store now, too, but Walter never had seen it, and he couldn't see that it mattered much. Walter couldn't wait for tomorrow, when a hollow plaster-cast Mr. Tinsel would have his holy assumption over Canal Street.

His thoughts were broken by the deep-falsetto voice of Kermit the Frog, and Walter knew he was finished with television for the evening. He tipped the recliner slightly forward, until his toe could reach the on-off button on the TV. Once the old set had swallowed the picture into the center of itself, Walter swiveled around until he could reach the refrigerator. He prided himself on being able to control his whole world from a sitting position, and he pulled a second beer from the meat compartment right under the little freezer of his refrigerator. He liked his beers icy cold.

Walter liked to think that he was a valued employee of Newman's because he wasn't a ten-to-six person; he lived his job. During his days he wrote scripts and refurbished his puppets and, at Christmas season, he taped a show each weekday. But, really, he'd given up his nights to his job, too, because he was a creative person, and his mind had to be working all the time. Tonight, he decided, he would have to start working up plots in which Mr. Tinsel could be more hero-like; kids were crazy about that kind of thing, if he could judge by what he saw on the shelves of the toy department. He wouldn't have weapons, of course, the way so many of the good warriors did; he would have a cape and a reassuring voice, and that would be enough. Mr. Tinsel deserved a chance to show how he could save lives and have girls falling in love with him; that was logical for a fellow who knew all the answers to all the questions. Perhaps he'd begin by creating Mrs. Tinsel—wait, no, that might make Mr. Tinsel look as if he were nothing more than part of some ornamental species. Walter wanted him to be one of a kind. Well, Walter thought, tipping back the cold beer in the dry-heated room, I have to figure out how to introduce someone for Mr. Tinsel to rescue. She should have about as much savvy as those girls the store hired every year straight out of high school to work in the hosiery department, he planned. As light and delicate as air. With no kapok. And a great deal of gratitude. Walter was well on his way to next year's series when he fell asleep at seven-thirty.

Usually he could manage to be on his way to work by first light, because he always fell asleep so early. This particular morning, though, he was already perched on a counter stool at Chez Donut while the sky was still matte black. Walter wasn't tamping down his excitement at all, clacking thick china cup against saucer with the idea that a thirty-six-foot Mr. Tinsel was going to defy all the laws of gravity that ruled Canal Street.

Even after he had drunk two cups of hot chocolate, the doughnut seemed too dry to swallow, and when the clock behind the cash register reached seven o'clock, Walter decided he'd had enough to do with breakfast. Ever the one to profit from experience, he left the bitten-out doughnut on the plate.

Chez Donut was on Iberville Street, the first street that ran parallel to Canal inside the French Quarter; it was one-way toward the river, lined with the rude, flat backsides of stores. Walter couldn't actually see the facade of Newman's until he rounded the corner onto Canal. When he turned, the little streaks of light in the sky were enough now for him to see a splendid sight: there lay Mr. Tinsel, a good part of a city block in length, filling two lanes of the downtown side of a street that soon would be busy with buses, secretaries, shoppers, and hundreds of lost automobiles, their drivers speeding with annoyance. No one ever drove on Canal Street on purpose. Mr. Tinsel was protected only by a cadre of orange traffic cones, straight and military watchmen around his Gulliver-body. Walter figured that the warehousemen must have brought him out late last night. Going by what had been done in years past, Walter knew workmen would begin hoisting Mr. Tinsel up onto the front of the building around nine-thirty, when rush hour was pretty well past and the store still wasn't open for business. It made a lot of sense to Walter.

Walter strolled happily around to the back entrance and let himself into the store with his own key. Only he and the security guard were there this early in the morning, but he treasured padding through the gray silence at an hour when everyone else from the store was still home asleep. One morning he'd worn his church shoes to work, just to be different, and the sound of the hard leather on the polished floors had felt like such a violation of the rules that he'd never worn anything but Hush Puppies slip-ons after that.

Mr. Tinsel and the whole cast of supporting characters were waiting for him in the studio. Walter was never grudging about sharing the spotlight with any of them. As he walked in and flooded the room with fluorescent light, his expression changed, from pure reverence for the dark to beatific pleasure over their sweet patience. "Good morning, guys," he said, and probably his voice could be heard all over the second floor. "Catch that game on TV last night?" Walter's off-stage imaginings about Mr. Tinsel were quite different from the ones he could actually put into scripts. He couldn't have Mr. Tinsel and his friends sitting in front of the television set betting on a football game. "So who d'you think's going to make the play-offs?"

Choklit had been particularly irrepressible lately. Walter moved closer to him, perfectly naturally, and Choklit said, "How about them Mets?" Walter moved along, passing each puppet on the shelf, going through a medley of knowing chuckles. When he reached Mr. Tinsel, Mr. Tinsel said in a kind, tolerant voice, "Oh, they play baseball, you must have your mind on baseball."

"I was just kidding," Choklit said from the corner of Walter's mouth.

Walter gave him a hearty laugh, then clapped his hands once, loudly, wanting the mood to lift. "What a caution!" he said. "Now, look, guys, today's a big day, you know." Locker room time; he could almost smell the ammonia. "Your leader will be enshrined on the front of our building." He said "enshrined" as if he had just learned the word. "Now this occasion's gotten me to do a lot of thinking. You're going to see some changes around here! What you fellows need are some women." They were all fully androgynous to an outsider, but Walter had never questioned that the puppets were all men of their species. He marched up and down like a general, knees unbending, strides long. The marionettes sat up neat and straight, their strings hung taut from the shelf above. Walter liked to leave them that way at night, as if they were a team before a game, waiting for him to come in the next morning and give them a talk.

"Okay!" Walter said, and gave another rousing clap, though he wasn't looking into the paint-eyes anymore. He began fingering a chunk of Styrofoam that he'd left on his work table. By Christmas next year Mr. Tinsel would have himself an ingénue.

Nine-thirty passed, ten o'clock arrived, customers began drifting up to the second floor, with the nervous hum of people who are considering spending money, and yet no one had come to tell Walter that it was time to come down to the street to see the sculpture raised onto the store's front. Walter decided at ten-thirty to go out onto Canal Street to check things out, see if he could help. Mr. Tinsel was still where he'd been at daybreak, supine in the middle of the street, guarded by traffic cones. Walter didn't want to approach anyone to find out what was going on, but he moved as close as he could to a couple of workmen who looked particularly cranky.

"Goddamn," one said. "I like to get killed by that fucking rock. Wouldn't you figure they could of known earlier that this dumb tinker toy can't hang on no building without pulling the whole damn thing down?"

"I hate doing shit that's stupid," said another. "Don't tell me it's not fucking stupid, leaving this big bastard smack in the middle of the street until they fix the building. Old as that building is, we going to be walking over this thing come Easter." He waved his hand over Mr. Tinsel in disgust.

Walter couldn't move. He was more frightened by the men than hurt by their insults, and he didn't take a step away from where he stood until the workmen drifted away, bored and embarrassed. Slowly Walter began a tour around the body. He was looking for cracks, chinks, but Mr. Tinsel seemed perfect, unmoved. Feeling relief that probably Mr. Tinsel hadn't actually been raised onto the building yet, but rather that something had happened when they were attaching the supports, he stepped back just the tiniest bit. A car with Texas plates came tearing past, horn blaring, coming so close that road dust wiped onto Walter's white shirt. "Asshole!" the driver said from his open window. "Close call," Walter said to no one in particular.

Satisfied that everything was under control, that in fact people at his level had no need to be out on the street, Walter headed for the lunchroom.

All store employees except the general manager ate in the single lunchroom, unless, of course, they had the money and the nerve to go out somewhere else and get a meal down in thirty minutes. Walter loved the lunchroom, with its smells of bay leaf and hot peas and women's cologne, and he always took his only meal of the day there.

There were three rows of long tables pushed end to end. Walter always sat down by himself, but he always had someone sitting close by, if not right next to him. He especially liked it when salesgirls clustered near him, chattering about empty, heavenly things. "I swear, my whole paycheck goes on clothes before I even get it. I got to steer clear of Lingerie; you can blow a hundred dollars on stuff nobody sees. Well, almost nobody." Giggles and knowing sniffs. "You look good in yellow, you know it? Me, I wear yellow, I look like I got a disease." They never realized he was there, eating mutely and staring straight at the food on his tray while he listened to them. He marveled to himself that humans could exchange the kinds of information these girls did.

Times came each day, five minutes before the hour or twenty-five minutes after the hour, when almost everyone but Walter filed out of the lunchroom to do some last minute toileting.

Because Walter put in such long hours, no one kept him to a thirty-minute lunch break, and everyone up to the general manager respected that.

Between lunch shifts, the lunchroom was almost quiet, and Walter could hear the piped-in music. He really didn't mind it, because Newman's kept the radio on a pop station, and Walter listened to it to keep up on what was happening in the world. The Craig Marshall show always overlapped with some part of Walter's lunch break, and the sonorous voice, which moved at an unbelievably fast clip, came right out at Walter from the speaker on the wall by the kitchen door.

"Okay! It's a sad time for the rug rats today," Craig said. "What the hell a rug rat is?" one bus girl said to another. "You kids, fool. What else you think squirm around on the rug?"

"In my house, plenty," the first one said, and both laughed.

Walter strained to hear over them. "We've had a confirmed report that the holiday hero of all the short people is dead as a doornail. Yes, Mr. Tinsel–" Craig boomed the name the way the voice-over on TV might say Superman or Mighty Mouse after a great buildup. "Mr. Tinsel has gone to his reward, all over the downtown side of Canal Street." He chuckled a little, and Walter was beginning to be confused. "Hey, we've actually been getting calls from moms saying the kids are positively grief stricken over the passing of their good friend. We'll have more details when Kerry does the news at twenty past and twenty of the hour."

Craig ran the first few measures of a tinny recording of "The Stars and Stripes Forever," and before he'd even cut it off for a full-gut laugh, Walter was out of the lunchroom. He left his dirty dishes on his tray on the table for the first time in all the years he'd worked for Newman's. Walter prided himself on always bringing his tray back to the kitchen.

He didn't stop running until he reached the radio station five blocks from Newman's. It was a tiny cinder block building, a minor landmark only for having been the first radio station in the city. Walter had no trouble walking in, or even finding Craig's studio. Through the glass he could see Craig's mobile mouth moving in quick patter. Craig couldn't see him and dropped a few words when, without warning, Walter pushed his way through the studio door.

"Hey, what you doing?" Craig said, still on the air. It was the same voice Walter had heard in the lunchroom. But Craig didn't look as slick and trim as his male-model voice. He had cowlicks in his hair and acne pits on his cheeks, and he was so fat that he filled his swivel chair, with a thick strip of thigh hanging over the side.

"I'd like to speak on the radio," Walter said shyly. Radio listeners at home and in their cars couldn't hear him, but Walter didn't know that.

A thick-necked engineer, as big as Craig, had picked up on the interruption in the show and had come running to back Craig up. When he saw Walter, whose belt was on the fifth hole, he stopped short, as if Walter were a cockroach he could take his time with. "Okay, buddy, come along. You want to be on the radio, okay. You get yourself an FCC license, how about it?"

The engineer was edging Walter inch by inch toward the door, and Walter saw his chance to speak rapidly disappearing. Blindly he began struggling and scratching his way out of the man's gentle grip, then grabbed the microphone from in front of Craig.

"Hello, boys and girls," he said. His heart was light. His voice was his regular voice, the one he also reserved for Mr. Tinsel. "I was busy working down at Newman's, and I heard the most awful thing on the radio. Somebody thought I was dead. No sirree, they must have gotten the wrong fellow. See, I had to lie down on Canal Street until the building got strong enough for me. I'm a big guy, you know. I . . ."

Craig and the engineer, as thick and gamy as two slabs of meat, had their wits back now, and they managed to pull Walter in one direction and the microphone in another. As the engineer began trying to drag him from the studio, and while Craig tried to move himself back in under him, Walter strained back. Stretching his neck as far as he could and still be able to talk,

Walter kept up his speech. "No, kids, I'm not even sick or hurt." A sob fought its way out of him against his will. "I am not dead!" he said before the engineer dragged him away.

Won't You Lead Us in "Jingle Bells"?

Harnett T. Kane

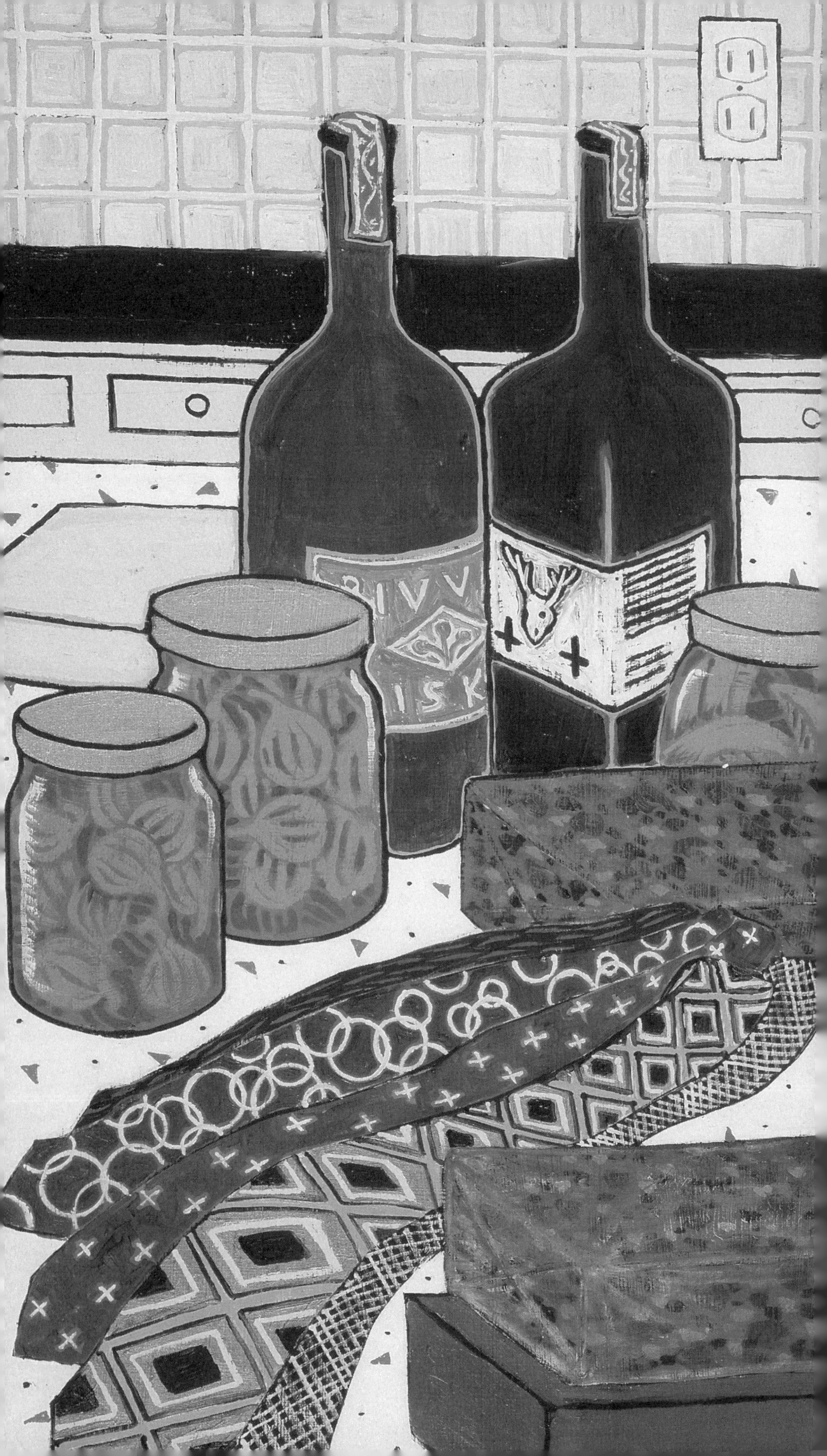

Christmas comes but once a year, and for a writer a Christmas volume probably arrives only once in a lifetime. In late '58 I did mine, *The Southern Christmas Book*, the result of a study of history, customs, and folkways. The trip that followed was different from any other, in an atmosphere ranging from easy-humored to jovial to down right teary.

During its course I found myself draped in a red hood as an honorary St. Louis Christmas Caroler. (I had to give the hood back, but at any future Christmas season I am privileged to join several hundred thousand others and roam the city streets, lifting my voice in a defective baritone.) At other times I met Santa Clauses with two guns and Texas boots, and barely escaped being a Kriss Kringle myself. I became an overnight judge of holiday delicacies ranging from German-style North Carolina cookies to fruit cake and eggnog. And I was called upon to pass judgment among dozens of holiday toddies, gaining ten pounds and fifteen hangovers in the process.

Not least of the tributes were Christmas songs dedicated to the book, to me, and one, oddly, to my house on Ferret Street. ("The Home Where This Book Was Composed," according to the poetic words; my family has never gotten over that one.) From Tennessee there arrived a neatly wrapped box, "to show you the effect which that volume had on me." When I ripped open the package, out fell a piece of badly scorched bread; the lady had been so interested, she said, that she let it burn as she read. My sister Florence commented: "It's a good thing that you didn't help wreck a chicken fricassee."

The joyous season started early for me, on October 19,

publication day. My first gift came on that day from a girl I know in the Sunny South of Portland, Oregon. It was a Christmas tie, and not bad for one of that variety. She informed me it was a holiday gift and publication gift combined; she had no intention of sending two presents.

From then on, in recognition of the book's publication, I acquired twelve more ties from readers, five stickpins, six pairs of cuff links, two bottles of bourbon, and several five-pound boxes of candy; light fruit cakes, dark fruit cakes, hampers of homemade preserves, cordials, a variety of cakes of all shapes and content, and a reinforced box of old-time beaten biscuits. (A hundred strokes until they begin to blister, or they are not really beaten.)

With each such gift my two nieces showed a growing affection and admiration. "Aren't you going to write another Christmas book?" Kathy asked me a few months ago. "And one with ice cream in it?" inquired Judy, who favors that type of fattener.

When the David McKay Company first announced the book, my mail from men's and women's clubs jumped quickly, and within a few weeks the autographing trip was outlined and speeches settled along the route. Now if anything sounds non-controversial, it might be a *Southern Christmas Book.* But on one of my first stops, I found that a schism had developed in the ladies' organization.

Only a day or two before, a number of members born in other places had held a rump session and delivered an ultimatum: If that fellow talked on Christmas in the South, there would have to be someone else to tell about the Northern kind. In a word, equal time . . . Since it was so late, however, the rump ladies had been unable to locate much material on their subject, and they made a request: Would I mind writing out the remarks for their Northern representative to make?

Hastily I explained that, without advance preparation, I would not have time to write out even an outline for the other talk. This sent the rump element into a fury; it called my attitude "Southern pettiness" and boycotted the meeting. At last report the split continues.

But I could only comply when, on another morning, Madame Chairman introduced me and announced: "Before he talks, so that we will all get into the proper spirit, I am going to ask Mr. Kane to favor us by leading us in the singing of 'Jingle Bells.'" As the girls applauded in a spontaneous rush of enthusiasm, the chairman added: "There will be no accompaniment, as Mrs. Jones, our pianist, has a daughter down with the mumps."

This new intelligence created an even greater stir, and remarks and questions sprang up from the floor: "Oh, please tell her how sorry we are." "You know you have to watch mumps." One matron called out solicitously: "You've never had mumps, have you, Mr. Kane?" A moment later, red-faced, I began the piano-less singing, and many months later I sometimes still wake from a harassing nightmare in which I have again been leading the ladies in "Jingle Bells" or even "Rudolph the Red-Nosed You-Know-What."

On the trip I enjoyed many a program at which choral groups did two or three numbers, then sat down. I came, however, to flinch when that pleasant custom developed into something else. Members of the choral organization after agreeing to give the ladies a pair of offerings, were occasionally caught up by the merry, merry mood, and also the sound of their own voices, and sang ten, eleven, or more numbers. One chorus went on and on for forty minutes, leaving me ten for my talk. Another was still vocalizing away by the time I had to leave.

Again a leader of the singers, set off by a round of sherry, signaled the girls to keep steadily on until they ran out of numbers. At once she started the repertoire all over again, despite the frantic efforts of Madame Chairman. When Madame eventually intervened, the conductor-lady led the chorus in a fury. "We've been insulted," she shrieked. "Next year, do your own singing!"

In the next town an imaginative chairman arranged a surprise. Just before I began she broke the news. A chorus was going to do a "soft accompaniment" to my address, "a lovely tinkle of fairy singing." At my question she blushed and assured me: "Not at all; it's just a ladies' chorus." The ladies would be in the next room with the folding doors closed, would start with "Silent Night" and carry on through "Little Star of Bethlehem." And oh, yes, she added, the girls had to go on to another appearance, and would I mind cutting my talk in half? "Just keep your ears open, and when they reach 'Little Star,' end in a minute or two. The timing, if you do your part right, should make things right interesting."

It was all right interesting. Nobody heard a word of mine. The girls, swept away, commenced by singing as loudly as usual; then to make sure that no single distant tinkle would be lost on the audience, they opened the folding doors and finished in a shout.

Once again, when I arrived at a meeting place, Madame Chairman greeted me excitedly. "Oh, Mr. Kane, our Santa Claus has developed a bad chest cold. But we have his costume." As I gazed at her in wonder, I asked myself: She couldn't mean what I thought, could she? She could. Growing coy, she dimpled:

"I saw pictures of you and realized right away that you would fit the part, without too much–well, changing of the suit." She finished with a beam: "Won't you be our Kriss Kringle?"

"But–but I'm due on a plane right afterward, and I think they'd wonder about it." I had done a lot of things on or in connection with plane flights, but I had no intention of boarding one with a white beard and red cap.

"Couldn't you change in the taxi?"

When I declined a second time, Madame accepted, though her face had a suggestion of hurt. Later she told a friend that I had behaved stuffily. "Success has made the man arrogant."

In the meantime I had brought Christmas ahead of time to many places. The clubs put up Santa Clauses, ranging from six inches to six feet in height, with trees, snow, holly, and ornaments to match. In several Texas towns pistol-packing Kringles wore the usual Christmas costumes with high leather boots and five- or ten-gallon hats.

At Nashville my reservation read: Noel Hotel. It turned out that there was actually a place by that name, though I still think Phil Worden of the Cokesbury store sent me there with tongue in cheek.

By this time I realized that practically everybody in the South is an eggnog authority. Each man and woman has his own special recipe, the only good and right one; the rest are nauseous brews. Half the people I met assured me: "There's one way to serve eggnog–cold." The other half were no less definite: "There's one way to serve eggnog and only one–warm." Some declared that milk in the mixture was desecration; it must be "cream and only cream." Others insisted that it had to be milk and nothing else. The Southern moderates favored a middle of the road, common-sense approach–a little of each.

One man quoting George Washington's recipe from my book, made our evening party glow with a truly potent nog, which included brandy, rye, sherry, *and* Jamaica rum. This was a case in which I almost literally drank my own words; I have only a vague recollection of the way the evening ended.

And steadily, for more than thirty days, I ate my way across America. In nearly every town I visited, club officials arranged a "real Christmas dinner"–turkey with cranberry sauce, dressing, potatoes, and the rest, with slight variations: mincemeat pie in some cities, pumpkin in others. This was all very well at the start, but nearly thirty turkey meals in a row are a lot of turkey, and repeatedly the cooks used sage, not lightly, in the dressing. I yield to no man in my fondness for sage, but after the first twelve times it began to pall. For months I have not been able to swallow it again.

Ruth Delmar Sullivan, the comedy radio-TV personality of Corpus Christi, riled her listeners on New Year's Day when, after my visit there, she read passages from the book. Among holiday traditions she quoted: "On New Year's morning never let a woman enter your house first, or your luck will sour." And if the woman be a widow, "may the Lord have mercy on your soul."

Before the program ended, the switchboard at KSIX lighted up. "If you'll excuse the expression," says Ruth, "like a Christmas tree." Women demanded to speak to her, called for her home telephone number, insisted that the station manager put them in touch with her. The ladies, it appeared, had just been paying calls at the houses of friends; or they were matrons who had others as guests. What, they asked, was Ruth trying to do–subvert Texas womanhood?

"It's just an old folk belief, an ancient saying," Ruth told them.

"Well, don't you believe it, and don't you say it." But she was happy; the ladies had let the station know how many listeners she had.

And a shining hour of the trip came toward the end, when a well-upholstered, well-furred lady rushed in. "Ah, Mr. Kane, I hear your book has a lot of fine Christmas food in it, with recipes. I entertain a great deal, and it sounds like just the thing I need."

I showed her the chapter, and she looked about her. "Isn't there a chair?" Getting one, draping her minks around her, she whipped out a large pad and started to copy intently. For an hour and a quarter she ignored everything that went on, transferring directions to her pages, covering sheet after sheet. Then, closing the book, she handed it back to me.

"Thank you so very much! This will make my holidays a whole lot nicer." Her eyes had only peace on earth, good will to all men.

"Merry Christmas," I told her weakly. At that she flashed a warming smile; "And a Happy New Year to you, sir!"

FROM

Requiem for a Year

Genaro Kỳ Lý Smith

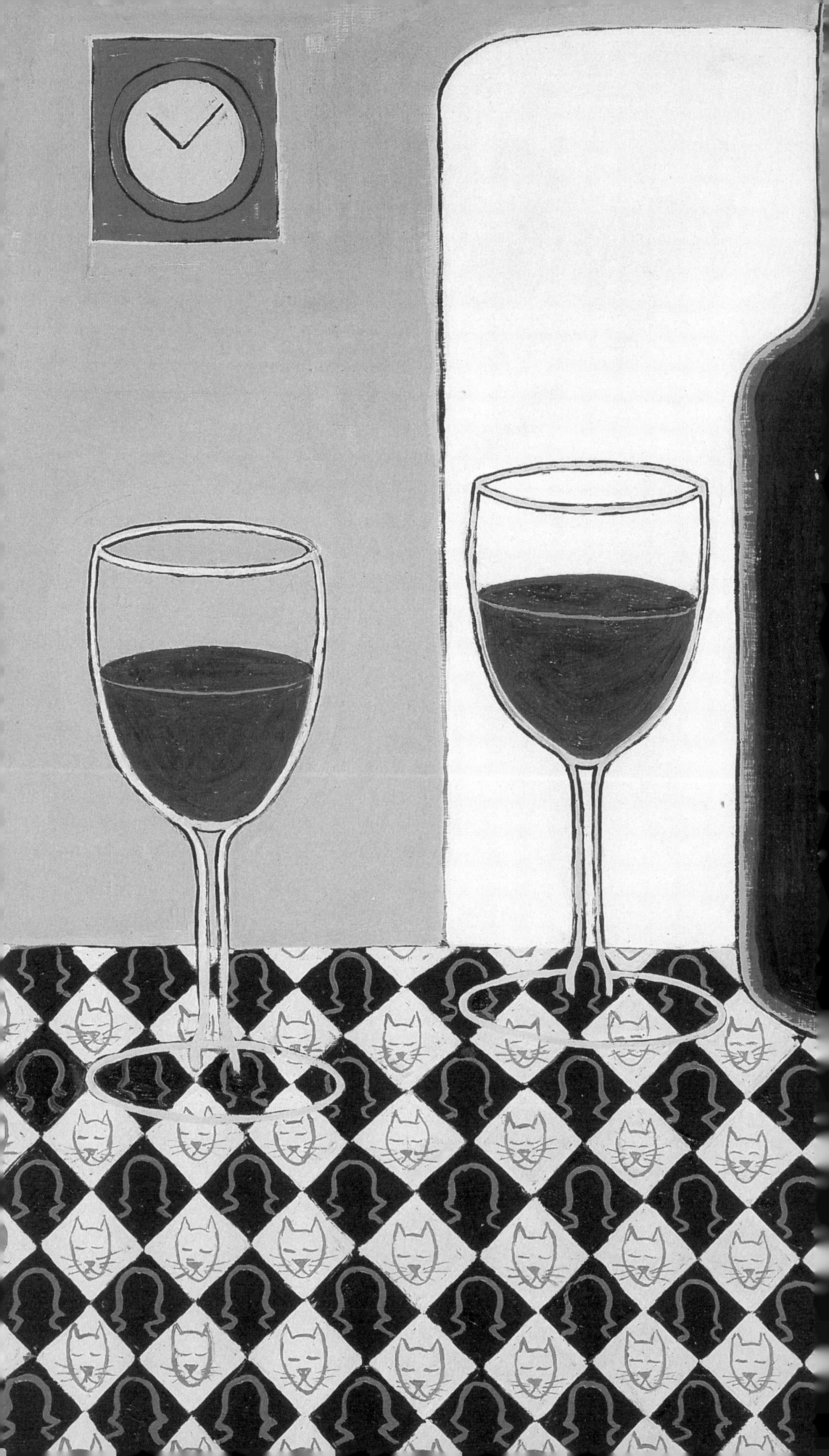

For Christmas Ann and I drive down to Lake Charles to be with her mother and sisters. We have Kiddie, Kiddie with us because when I came back from Portland, she was skinnier. Her head remained the same size, but her body was just grotesquely thin. I could see her ribs through her fur, and her hind legs were bony like chicken wings you buy at a super-market. It was like her muscles, tendons, the organs, and cells had atrophied—fed off her insides due to a lack of food. Her back paws were green from the urine she sat in, and even after wash-ing them with soap and warm water, the whiteness of her fur there remained dirty. It was futile washing her paws because she urinated on herself all day and night. And she never moved from atop her litter box. She just sat there, slept there, and urine would stream down the sides of the box and collect in puddles on the floor.

That night I spoon-fed her, and she was only able to eat two spoonfuls. I let her alone, and to take my mind off Ann and her need to move, I watched a couple of movies. I was lying there on the sofa when I heard a loud thud, one that carried throughout the house. I went into the bathroom and Kiddie, Kiddie was on the floor on her side, curled into a "c." She had fallen in between the litter box and sink cupboard, her head underneath, and I stared at her stomach to see if she was breathing. When she took in air, I slid the box aside to get to her. I brought her out into the open space and set her down. Her eyes remained open; she stared, and when I began petting her, they moved to gaze at me out of the corners. Besides her breathing and the eyes, she remained still. She breathed noisily through her nose, and I didn't know if what she was going through was a seizure or heart attack. I kept petting her, and in doing so I felt her heart, and it was the same as when Ann and I came home from Lake Charles the first time. It beat rapidly, and I thought her heart would just swell up, burst through her bones, tear through her skin and fur and onto the bathroom floor, and beat in the open until it lost momentum and quit. But like before, her heart rate slowed, and she lifted her head for a moment, then sat up on her own.

She is in the back seat now, in her pet carrier with a towel beneath her. An hour into the four-hour drive, Ann cracked open the windows to air out the urine smell. She sighs and plays with her short hair, and we rely on music to fill the silence between us. Ever since Portland, I don't know how to speak to her anymore. I figure keeping quiet and not being in the same room with her was the best thing. Even when we slept, I would just lie on my side of the bed. I wanted to spoon her from behind, fit my knees behind the crook of her knees, drape my arm over her waist, curl my hand into hers, breathe into the back of her neck, and feel her breathing pressed against my chest. And she made no efforts to engage in intimate sleep. It is like sleeping with someone for the first time, and you're uncertain as to what that person likes, whether that person wanted to be touched in slumber or simply left alone.

As soon as we get to her mother's house, I place Kiddie, Kiddie in the garage, get her bowl and fill it with water and dried food, let her out of the cage, and set the towel out to air. Ms. Lynch had a litter box from when she had a cat. She kept everything, like her husband's belongings, like the dried-out flowers Barbara placed on the workbench when they died.

Ms. Lynch comes out to the garage; no doubt Ann mentioned it the moment she walked in.

"She doesn't look well." Ms. Lynch's mouth remains open as she stands over me.

"No. She has anemia. That's why she only weighs three and a half pounds."

"Oh dear," she murmurs.

When I arrived home that Sunday from Portland, I could not take her in because the vet's office was closed. But the next morning I took her in for X-rays and blood tests, and Dr. Davis gave me three different types of medicine: Winstrol V tablets, Doxycycline, and Val/Colife syrup, which looks and smells more like iodine. He said they should help stimulate her appetite so she would eat. All that week, I woke up at 5:30 in the morning to administer all the medicine, and I did it again before going to bed at night. I'd place her between my legs, force her mouth open to give her the syrup first, and then the two pills. The capsule was the hardest; it looked too big for her to swallow. She was so weak during the first couple of days that after she ate, she would sit there. Even worse were the times she'd get down from her litter box, walk down the hallway to eat in the kitchen, and halfway there she'd stop. Kiddie, Kiddie would look up at me, and I'd urge her on, but her hind legs would tremble, and she'd slowly fall over on her side. I didn't understand it. It was like all the energy she had only brought her so far, and then left her. It was like God, if there was one, said, "The moment you are born, you have a maximum of one hundred years to live, barring diseases, sickness, natural geological disasters, car accidents, and homicides. Good luck to you." It was like the brain suddenly went blank, erasing all history of movement.

"Do you plan on leaving her in the garage?" Ms. Lynch asks.

"I'm afraid so. She urinates on herself. She doesn't know she does it, she just does whether on my lap, the windowsills, carpets, everywhere."

I stand up and we both just look down at her.

"It's good to see you," I say and kiss her on the cheek.

"Come on. I have dinner ready. Barbara is here, too. Jillian will be here tomorrow afternoon."

"Good. Everyone is here."

Ms. Lynch flicks a switch and the garage door slowly swings shut. She leaves the light on for now, leaves it for Kiddie, Kiddie so she can see. She closes the door behind us, and Kiddie, Kiddie rests atop her carrier, next to Mr. Lynch's workbench filled with dead flowers.

Barbara does most of the talking. She is in from Wyoming where she and her husband live, and she is glad to be out of the cold, away from snow which has fallen since October. She and her husband are going to expand on their two-story house, add a couple of rooms, and every day they'd stare at blueprints and argue over changes, over windows and closet space and door styles, door sills, hinges, and knobs–brass or crystal–over light fixtures, ceiling fans, baseboards–concave or plain, carpet or hardwood–*hardwood*–vents, blinds, shutters, or curtains; and they discussed the bathroom: linoleum tile or ceramic or hardwood–*hardwood*–glassed-in spa-styled bathtub or claw foot, brass showerhead or cheap plastic passing for crystal, silver or brass rosary chain for the plug, polyester or linen shower curtain, see-through, solid, or patterned, a free-standing sink or a cabinet sink, marble or porcelain, a single operated faucet or double-knobbed, and if knobs, *white*?

Barbara, thoughtful Barbara, always said she preferred the one over the other but she made sure to hold him at night or at least put her head on his chest and fall asleep to the sound of his heart.

"The ground is still frozen solid," she says as she wiggles the tines through a portion of her meatloaf, "so we have to wait until late May when it thaws for them to dig."

"That's really strange," I say.

"What is?" Barbara asks, the fork full of meatloaf poised before her open mouth.

"Just the idea of waiting for the ground to thaw. I never thought of that, thought that the ground can be frozen."

"I know," she slips the fork in her mouth and chews. "Living here in the South, you're surprised by all the things out there. I mean, there's not a humid day in Wyoming, and when I stepped off the twin-engine plane here in Lake Charles, it was like," she holds out her hands, mouth open to form a simile, "like literally walking into a wall and having it just collapse on you."

We chuckle and continue eating.

"How much is all this going to cost?" Ann asks.

"Umm," she looks up at the ceiling fan. "We're still getting bids. One company wants twenty-five thousand, but there is another who will go as low as twenty-one, five."

"Well, whatever it is, add twenty percent to it."

"Huh?" they all look at me.

"Yes, add twenty percent to what they offer because you over-look the little things."

"The little things?" Barbara leans in my direction.

"Yeah, like each nail and screw and bolt. What they gave you was just an estimate. I mean, they may screw up on something as small as a door hinge for instance and they'll have to replace the door sill, or just use putty, but either way it costs. It's those little things like that. I mean I'm sure you've heard this?"

Barbara nods her head and says, "I remember something about that on *Oprah*, or some show."

"Yes, and you remember what they said about couples adding onto the house." I smile and wag my fork at her. "The divorce rate is high among them, so *be* careful, Barbara."

"Really?" Ms. Lynch sits back, and Ann stares at me, eyes wide and unblinking, a wad of food resting in her closed mouth.

"Statistics," I say, mixing a couple of peas into my mashed potato. "Couples have a higher risk, believe it or not, when they build onto their houses." I shove a fork full of peas and potatoes in my mouth.

"Why?" asks Barbara.

"Well, you know. The house is pretty much in disarray. It's chaotic. You have these men who come and walk in and out of your home, in and out of your lives practically, six days a week, and regardless of how many weeks and months it takes, they're still strangers. So you feel violated, you don't have the privacy you once had, and basically, you take it out on each other. You're at each other's throats because there are changes and constant changes. Not only to the house but you rearrange your schedule pretty much. You sleep in different rooms, sometimes in separate rooms. It's the changes they can't handle," I wag my fork again, "and the changes get to them. What starts out as an agreed-upon model will wind up as something different all together, and you worry about more money you will definitely have to dole out."

The women look at me, and I meet each one's gaze and open mouth. Ann closes her mouth, presses her lips tight together, and stabs her meatloaf with the fork, the tines ringing against ceramic.

"I . . . heard this on *Oprah*." I shrug.

Barbara and Ms. Lynch nod their heads slowly, their eyes closed to near slits, their foreheads creased. We continue eating in silence.

Barbara chews and stares at her mother's plate before shaking her head and saying, "I don't remember that part on *Oprah*."

Ann is out with her friends having drinks at Pappy's, and no doubt she is telling them about her moving to Portland, and she is enjoying that moment when their mouths open in surprise, the long drawn out "ooohs" of envy. I could go out with my friends, but I spend the evening with Ms. Lynch, watching *Pleasantville*, and she seems a little depressed after visiting her husband's grave this afternoon. Of the family members, Ms. Lynch spent the longest time at the grave. She carried on a conversation, smiling and nodding her head at times. Barbara told him about the lotus she brought, how it symbolized perfection, purity, creation, the past, present, and future, and how the gift of a lotus flower also expressed the great admiration of the donor for the recipient. And Jillian, the youngest, read a poem she wrote. True to her nature, Ann spent the least amount of time, and though I was two rows back, I tried to read her lips, but all I caught was, "Can you forgive me?" She even leaned forward and pressed her palm flat against the tombstone and let her head drop for a moment.

What did I say? I said I wished he were here to clean his guns in front of me. To grip my shoulder, squeeze the muscle in his large hand and ask, "What are your intentions with my daughter?"

After the movie ends, Ms. Lynch stops the tape and rewinds it, and we sit in the blue hue of the living room. She sighs, and I remain quiet.

"So," she says, "are you planning to move to Portland as well?"

"You know about that?"

"Well, are you?"

"Yes, but not immediately. I plan on staying a third year. It looks better on a résumé."

Ms. Lynch turns to stare at the blue screen. We sit there and I am literally twiddling my thumbs. I pat my hands together, rub them against my thighs and say, "Well, I better check on Kiddie before heading to bed."

Ms. Lynch nods her head.

Kiddie, Kiddie is on top of her pet taxi, eyes wide open when I turn on the lights, and it seems she has been up all this time, staring into the darkness, afraid of closing her eyes. There is a foul smell, and on the garage floor, next to the litter box is a puddle of congealed diarrhea. She had made an effort to use the litter box, for the edge is dirtied.

"Jesus," I sigh and look around the garage for something to wipe up the mess.

Just as I turn to leave the garage to try and find something in the kitchen, Ms. Lynch is standing at the doorway.

"How is she?"

"Uh," I say. "Uh, she . . . she went to the bathroom on the garage floor."

"Oh," she says and looks past me, though I know she cannot see the litter box from where she's standing.

Before I can even enter the house, Ms. Lynch returns with a plastic bag from Kroger's and a roll of paper towels. I reach out to take the items from her, but she walks past me. She gets down on one knee, unfurls several pieces, rips them at the perforated seams, folds them in half, and wipes up the mess. Kiddie, Kiddie trains her eyes on Ms. Lynch's hands.

"You don't have to do that," I come up behind her.

"It's okay," she says. "I'm used to this."

She stuffs the soiled paper towels into the plastic bag, takes the pooper-scooper, and sprinkles some litter over the spot. I take Kiddie, Kiddie from off the litter box, set her between my thighs, and grab her medicines from the compartment. I lay them out, and I tighten my legs around her when she starts squirming.

"You have to give her all those at once?" Ms. Lynch asks.

"Yeah. All three of them twice daily."

I uncap the two bottles, place half a pill in the tube, one whole capsule, slip the plunger through the top end, and with my free hand I wedge my fingers between the sides of her mouth to pry it open, but she wags her head.

"Do you need help?"

"No. I've been doing this all week. The first couple of days she was so weak she couldn't resist, but now," I say, swallowing. "Now she's fighting. I guess that's a good sign."

Ms. Lynch nods. I manage to pry her mouth open, and I shove the tube in and press the plunger, emptying the two pills. Kiddie, Kiddie gags and sticks her tongue out, and the capsule falls to the garage floor. My shoulders slouch. I pick up the capsule, slip it into the tube, set the plunger in place and begin again.

"Do you want me to help?" she asks.

"No," I say, "I've been doing this for a week," my voice cracks, and I lean over Kiddie, Kiddie, for I feel it catch in my throat. No matter how hard I concentrate on prying her mouth open, it unhitches and travels up my throat and forces my mouth open, and I let out a harsh breath. Tears stream down my cheeks. I sit up briefly to wipe my eyes and nose with the back of my forearm and I lean forward again to slip my fingers into her mouth.

"I can do this," I say, the words warbled like liquid.

As soon as I get her mouth open, I stick the tube in and press the plunger, but the capsule rests on her tongue and falls to the floor. Ms. Lynch snatches up both the pill and the tube and plunger, and in one swift motion, she inserts the tube deep into Kiddie, Kiddie's mouth and pushes down on the plunger. And just like that, without my even seeing her throat move to swallow, Kiddie, Kiddie gets up and walks to her litter box, stares at the top, and hops onto her spot.

Ms. Lynch and I sit there on the floor watching Kiddie, Kiddie curl her paws within her chest. I sniffle and Ms. Lynch tears off a paper towel and hands it to me.

"She has to get better," I wipe my nose. Silence, and then, "Thank you."

She nods before saying, "I used to do this: injections, nitro-glycerin rubs, pills. I understand what you're going through."

"She's going to die."

"You don't know that."

I shake my head. "She's going to die."

We stare at each other, look away, and watch Kiddie, Kiddie. I take up the third medicine, the Val/Colife syrup, extract 3 cc's of it into the disposable syringe. I lean forward, grab the loose skin behind her neck and stuff the syringe inside her mouth and drain all of it at once. She licks her lips and nose, her breast stained by the few drops of medicine she didn't swallow.

"Sometimes, she can be difficult." I replace the cap on the bottle of syrup.

"Cats don't like medicine. What pet does?" she smiles. "Come inside and have a drink." Ms. Lynch stands up. "Just have a drink and talk."

We go into the kitchen, and as I take a seat, Ms. Lynch takes down two wine glasses from the cupboard and fills them with red wine. Talk, she said, but we just sit there sipping our wine. I want to tell her about that evening, tell someone who would understand what it was like to hear that sound and find Kiddie, Kiddie still on the bathroom floor.

Although I am an atheist, I prayed while I stroked Kiddie, Kiddie to calm her heartbeat. I told her *please, please just until tomorrow morning, that's all. Tomorrow morning I'll take you in for treatment, just stay alive for another day, a couple more hours.* I sat there on the bathroom floor and watched her for at least an hour: Kiddie, Kiddie, still and wide-eyed.

I watched her waiting for another attack of some sort to occur, and in that hour, I told myself, if it happened again, let it take her this time, and if it didn't finish her, I would. In that hour I thought of possible ways to do it. Drowning would only leave deep scratches on my arms and hands. Tying her legs and placing her in a plastic bag would be harsh, especially seeing her writhe and try to bite through the plastic.

Not to dwell on it any longer, I went outside with a glass of red wine and my pack of cigarettes, and I sat at the edge of the porch steps. The moths fluttered down from the trees after I turned on the porch light, and it occurred to me it had been a while since I caught moths for Kiddie, Kiddie. They came in all colors and sizes, lined, plain, and spotted wings dusty and soot-like. There were a couple with small bulbous bodies but their wings were so large they literally looked like stingrays. Their wings spread out, then narrowed to a thin tail. I felt something brush against my arm, and it was Kiddie, Kiddie, who had made her way out to the porch. She sat there staring at the moths flying about and above her, but she kept still, her paws tucked underneath her chest.

I stared at the driveway, the bricks lining it, and I thought, *That is what I'll do.* I sat there and turned to Kiddie, Kiddie, making certain to breathe without making a sound, for I felt she would know somehow. I crushed the cigarette beneath my boot and set the glass down. Ann was still in Portland. I told myself, *Why wait until tomorrow?* She would probably have another attack and I couldn't do anything for her.

I stood up from the porch steps, went to the driveway, and picked up one of the red bricks. I brought it back with me and stood at the bottom step staring at Kiddie, Kiddie. She looked at it the way she looked at all the moths flying around her. When they came close to her ears, she merely twitched or shook her head, but her paws remained beneath her chest. I felt the coolness of the brick in my hands, how solid it was, the sharp edges pressing into my fingers, the smoothness of the surface. I stood there, and my hand began to tremble, my fingers loosened, and I gripped it tighter, but the tighter I held it, the heavier it became. I imagined bringing it down on her head, and I wondered would it crack in pieces or at least in half if I did it right. My forearm ached, and the feeling traveled up my arm until my shoulder tightened. The muscles on the right side of my body strained to hold something as small as a red brick. I let it drop.

In that moment it took to decide, the moths had settled against the wall, close to the light. There must have been thirty of them. I faced the collage of moths, and I plucked the biggest one. I cocked my hand back and I threw it against the wall. There was a dull thud before it floated to the wooden porch. That smack, that sound of something light but plump hitting the wall sent the other moths fluttering about the bulb. It was like they knew they were in danger, like they heard the sound and recognized it as one of their own. But as they settled, I grabbed another one, and threw it against the wall. Like the first one, it whirled on its way down. I kept at it, plucking moths between two fingers, even snatching those in nervous flight, and I kept going until there remained a few small ones. The wings of the dazed and bruised moths flickered like a dying lightbulb. Kiddie, Kiddie, with her wide green eyes, just stared at them, stared at the moths twitching in tight circles, stared at things that will eventually die.

Ms. Lynch and I continue to sit there at the table, and it's not like imagining her husband cleaning his guns, but still I feel threatened by her silence. The way Ms. Lynch pinches the stem of the wine glass between her thumb and forefinger and slides them up and down says she knows more about Portland than I do, knows I am failing just as I failed giving Kiddie, Kiddie her medicine.

"You picked a hard one," she finally says.

"I kind of didn't have a choice. She came up to me and I couldn't resist her. It was out in the parking lot. When I saw her little tail–"

"I meant Ann."

"Oh. I thought . . ." I laugh and shake my head and stare into the glass. I bite on my upper lip and look up at Ms. Lynch who is smiling. "Ann can be difficult at times. And now this Portland thing."

"Do you want to move there?"

"It would be nice. I never saw the Pacific Northwest," I shrug, "so, yeah, why not?"

"Do *you* want to move to Portland?"

"No." I shake my head. "My place is here."

"But why not? You just said you wanted to see the Pacific Northwest."

I take a deep breath and let it out.

"It feels like," I stop. Ms. Lynch sits forward, her head tilted to one side, her mouth barely working as though to help me complete the sentence. "It feels like running away."

Christmas Gifts

Ruth McEnery Stuart

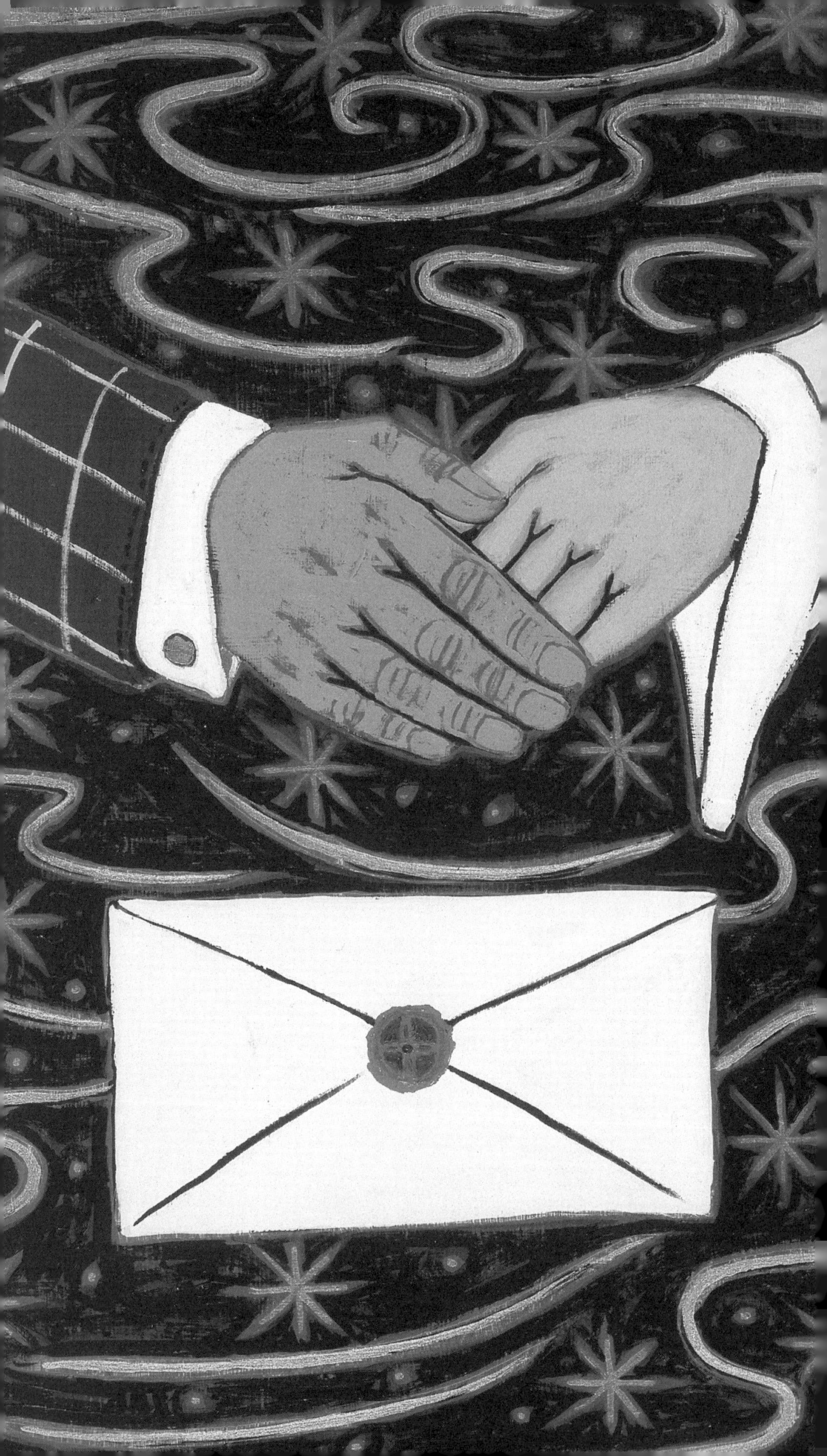

Christmas on Sucrier plantation, and the gardens are on fire with red flames of salvia, roses, geraniums, verbenas, rockets of Indian shot, brilliant blazes of coreopsis, marigold, and nasturtium, glowing coals of vivid portulaca.

Louisiana acknowledges a social obligation to respond to a Christmas freeze; but when a guest tarries, what is one to do?

She manufactures her ice, it is true. Why not produce an artificial winter? Simply because she does not care for it. If she did—? Such things are easily arranged.

Still, when he comes, a guest, she would not forget her manners and say him nay, any sooner than she would shrug her shoulders at a New England cousin or answer his questions in French.

She does the well-bred act to the death, summons her finest, fairest, most brilliant and tender of flower and leaf to await his coming: so today all her royal summer family are out in full court dress, ready to prostrate themselves at his feet.

This may be rash, but it is polite.

Her grandfather was both; and so the "Creole State," in touch with her antipodal brother in ancestor-worship, is satisfied.

But winter, the howling swell, forgetful of provincial engagements, does not come. Still, the edge of his promise is the breeze today, and the flaring banana leaves of tender green look cold and half afraid along the garden wall.

The Yule log smolders lazily and comfortably in the big fireplace, but windows and doors are open, and rocking-chairs and hammocks swing on the broad galleries of the great house.

It is a rich Christmas of the olden times.

Breakfast and the interchange of presents are over.

Cautious approaches of wheels through the outer gates during the night, in the wee short hours when youth sleeps most heavily, have resulted in mysterious appearances: a new piano in the parlor; a carriage, a veritable ante-bellum chariot, and a pair of bays, in the stable; guns, silver-mounted trappings, saddles, books, pictures, jewels, and dainty confections, within and piled about the stockings that hung around the broad dining-room chimney.

For there were sons and daughters on Sucrier plantation.

An easy-going, healthy, hearty, and happy man, of loose purse-strings and lax business habits, old Colonel Slack had grown wealthy simply because he lived on the shore where the tide always came in—the same shore where since '61 the waters move ever to the sea, and those who waited where he stood are stranded.

His highest ambitions in life were realized. His children, the elect by inheritance to luxurious ease, were growing up about him, tall, straight, and handsome, and happily free from disorganizing ambitions, loving the fleece-lined home-nest.

The marriage of an eldest daughter, Louise, to a wealthy next-door planter, five miles away, had seemed but to add a bit of broidery to the borders of his garment.

His pretty, dainty wife, in lieu of wrinkles, had taken on avoirdupois and white hair, and instead of shriveling like a four-o'clock had bloomed into a regal evening-glory.

So distinctly conscious of all these blessings was the old colonel that his atmosphere seemed always charged with the electric quality which was happiness; but on occasions like today, when the depths of his tendernesses were stirred within him by the ecstasy of giving and of receiving thanks and smiles and thanks again from "my loyal slaves"—ah, this was the electric flash! It was joy! It was delight and exuberance of spirit! It was youth returned! It was Christmas!

In his heart were peace and good-will all the year round, and on Christmas—hallelujahs.

He had often been heard to say that if he ever professed religion it would be on Christmas; and, by the way, so it was, but not this Christmas.

A tender-souled, good old man was he, yet thoughtless, withal, as a growing boy.

Down in the quarters, this morning, the negroes gaudily arrayed in their Sunday best, were congregated in squads about the benches in front of their cabins, awaiting the ringing of the plantation bell which should summon them to "the house" to receive their Christmas packages.

In the grove of China-trees around which the cabins were ranged a crowd of young men and maidens flirted and chaffed one another on the probable gifts awaiting them.

One picked snatches of tunes on a banjo, another drew a bow across an old fiddle, but the greater number were giddily spending themselves in plantation repartee, a clever answer always provoking a loud, unanimous laugh, usually followed by a reckless duet by the two "musicianers."

Sometimes, when the jokes were too utterly delicious, the young "buck" would ecstatically hug the China-trees or tumble down upon the grass and bellow aloud.

"What yer reck'n old marster gwine give you, Unc' Torm?" said one, addressing an old man who had just joined the group and sat sunning his shiny bald head.

"'Spec' he gwine give Unc' Torm some hair-ile, ur a co'se comb," suggested a pert youth.

"Look like he better give you a wagon-tongue ur a bell-tongue, one, 'case yo' tongue ain't long 'nough," replied Uncle Tom quietly, and so the joke was turned.

"I trus' he gwine give Bow-laigged Joe a new pair o' breeches!"

"Ef he do, I hope dey'll be cut out wid a circular saw!" came a quick response, which brought a scream of laughter.

"Wonder what Lucindy an' Dave gwine git?"

Luncinda and Dave were bride and groom of a month.

In a minute two big fellows were screaming and holding their sides over a whispered suggestion, when the word "cradle" escaped and set girls and all to giggling.

"Pity somebody wouldn't drap some o' you smart boys on a *corn-cradle* an' chop you up," protested the bride, with a toss of her head.

"De whole passel ob 'em wouldn't make nothin' but rotten-stone, ef dee was *grine* up," suggested Uncle Tom, with an intolerant smile.

"Den you mought use us fur tooth-powder," responded the wit again, and the bald-headed old man, confessing himself vanquished, good-naturedly bared his toothless gums to join in the laughter at his own expense.

A sudden clang of the bell brought all to their feet presently, and, strutting, laughing, prancing, they proceeded up to the house, the musicians tuning up afresh *en route*, for in the regular order of exercises arranged for the day they were to play an important part.

The recipients were to be ranged in the yard in line, about fifty feet from the steps of the back veranda where the master should stand, and, as their names should be called, to dance forward, receive their gifts, curtsey, and dance back to their places.

At the calling of the names music would begin.

The pair who by vote should be declared the most graceful should receive from the master's hand a gift of five dollars each, with the understanding that it should supply the eggnog for the evening's festivities, where the winners should preside as king and queen.

An interested audience of the master's family, seated on the veranda back of him, was a further stimulant to best effort.

The packages, all marked with names, were piled on two tables, those for men on one and the women's on the other, and the couples resulting from a random selection from each caused no little merriment.

All had agreed to the conditions, and when Lame Phoebe was called out with Jake Daniels, a famous dancer, they were greeted with shouts of applause.

Phoebe, enthused by her reception, and in no wise embarrassed by a short leg, made a virtue of necessity, advancing and retreating in a series of graceful bows, manipulating her sinewy body so dexterously that the inclination towards the left foot was more than concealed, and for the first time in his life Jake Daniels came in second best, as, amid deafening applause, Lame Phoebe bowed and wheeled herself back among the people.

Then came Joe Scott, an ebony swell, with Fat Sarey, a portly dame of something like three hundred avoirdupois—a difficult combination again.

That Sarey had not danced for twenty years was not through reluctance of the flesh more than of the spirit, for she was "a chile o' de kingdom," both by her own profession and universal consent.

Laughing good-naturedly, with shaking sides she stepped forward, bowed first to her master and then to her partner, and, raising her right hand, began, in a wavering soft voice, keeping time to the vibrating melody by easy undulations of her pliable body, to sing:

"Dey's a star in de eas' on a Chris'mus morn.
Rise up, shepherd, an' foller!
Hit'll lead ter de place whar de Savior's born.
Rise up, shepherd, an' foller!
Ef yer take good heed ter de angels' words,
You'll forgit yo' flocks an' forgit yo' herds,
An' rise up, shepherd, an' foller!
Leave yo' sheep an'
Leave yo' lamb an'
Leave yo' ewe an'
Leave yo' ram an'
Rise up, shepherd, an' foller!"

Joe took his cue from the first note, and, accommodating his movements to hers, elaborating them profusely with graceful gestures, he fell in with a rich, high tenor, making a melody so tender and true that the audience were hushed in reverential silence.

The first verse finished, Sarey turned slowly, and by an uplifted finger invited all hands to join in the chorus.

Rich and loud, in all four parts, came the effective refrain:

"Foller, foller, foller, foller,
Rise up, shepherd, rise an' foller,
Foller de Star o' Bethlehem!"

Still taking the initiative, Sarey now bent easily and deeply forward in a most effusive parlor salutation as she received her gift; while Joe, as ever quick of intuition, also dispensed with the traditional dipping courtesy, while he surrendered himself to a profound bow which involved the entire length of his willowy person.

Turning now, without losing for a moment the rhythmic movement, they proceeded to sing a second verse:

"Oh, dat star's still shinin' dis Chris'mus day.
Rise, O sinner, an' foller!
Wid an eye o' faith you c'n see its ray.
Rise, O sinner, an' foller!
Hit'll light yo' way thoo de fiel's o' fros',
While it leads thoo de stable ter de shinin' cross.
Rise, O sinner, an' foller!
Leave yo' father,
Leave yo' mother,
Leave yo' sister,
Leave yo' brother,
An' rise, O sinner, an' foller!"

A slightly accelerated movement had now brought the performers back to their places, when the welkin rang with a full all-round chorus:

"Foller, foller, foller, foller,
Rise, O sinner, rise an' foller,
Foller de Star o' Bethlehem!"

A few fervid high-noted "Amens!" pathetically suggestive of pious senility, were succeeded now by a silence more eloquent than applause.

Other dancers by youthful antics soon restored hilarity, however, and for quite an hour the festivities kept up with unabated interest.

Finally a last parcel was held up—only one—and when the master called, "Judy Collins!" adding, "Judy, you'll have to dance by yourself, my girl!" the excitement was so great that for several minutes nothing could be done.

Judy Collins, by a strange coincidence, was the only "old maid" on the plantation, and, as she was a dashing, handsome woman, she had given the mitten at one time or another to nearly every man present.

That she should have to dance alone was too much for their self-control.

The women, convulsed with laughter, held on to one another, while the men shrieked aloud.

Judy was the only self-possessed person present.

Before any one realized her intention, she had seized a new broom from the kitchen porch near by, and stepped out into the arena with it in her hand.

Judy was grace itself. Tall, willowy, and lithe, stately as a pine, supple as a mountain-trout, she glided forward with her broom.

Holding it now at arm's length, now balancing it on end and now on its wisps, tilting it at hazardous angles, but always catching it ere it fell, poising it on her finger-tips, her chin, her forehead, the back of her neck, keeping perfect time the while with the music, she advanced to receive her parcel, which, with a quick movement, she deftly attached to the broom-handle, and, throwing it over her shoulder, danced back to her place.

The performance entire had proven a brilliant success, and Judy's dance a fitting climax.

Needless to say, Judy insisted on keeping the broom.

The awarding of the prizes by acclamation to Joe Scott and Fat Sarey was the work of a moment, prettily illustrating the religious susceptibility of the voters.

Then followed a "few remarks" from the speaker of the occasion, and a short and playful response from the master, when the crowd dispersed, opening their bundles *en route* as they returned merrily to their cabins.

The parcels had been affectionately prepared. Besides the dresses, wraps, and shoes given to all, there were attractive trinkets, bottles of cologne, ribbons, gilt ear-rings or pins for the young women, cravats, white collars, shirt-studs, for the beaux, and for the old such luxuries as tobacco, walking-canes, spectacles, and the like, with small coins for pocket-money.

This year, in addition to the extra and expected "gift," each young woman received, to her delight, a flaring hoop-skirt; and such a lot of balloons as were flying about the plantation that morning it would be hard to find again.

Happy and care-free as little children were they, and as easily pleased.

Having retired for the moment necessary for their inflation and adornment, the younger element, balloons and beaux, soon returned to their popular holiday resort under the China-trees.

Though the branches were bare, the benches beneath them commanded a perennial fair-weather patronage; for where a bench and a tree are, there will young men and maidens be gathered together.

Lame Mose was there, with his new cushioned crutch, and Phil Thomas the preacher, looking ultra-clerical and important in a polished beaver; while Lucinda and Dave, triumphant in the cumulative dignity of new bride-and-groomship, hoop-skirt and standing collar, actually strutted about arm in arm in broad daylight, to the intense amusement of the young folk, who nudged one another and giggled as they passed.

Such was the merry spirit of the group when Si, a young mulatto household servant, suddenly appeared upon the scene.

"'Cindy," said he, "marster say come up ter de house–dat is, ef you an' Dave kin part company fur 'bout ten minutes."

"I don' keer nothin' 'bout no black ogly-lookin' som'h'n-'nother like Dave, nohow!" exclaimed Lucinda flirtatiously, as she playfully grasped Si's arm and proceeded with him to the house, leaving Dave laughing with the rest of her antics.

The truth was that, confidently expecting the descent of some further gift upon her brideship, Lucinda was delighted at the summons, and her face beamed with expectancy as she presented herself before her master.

"Lucindy," said he, as she entered, "I want you to mount Lady Gay and ride down to Beechwood this morning, to take some Christmas things to Louise and her chicks."

Lucinda's smile broadened in a delighted grin.

A visit to Beechwood today would be sure to elicit a present from her young mistress, "Miss Louise," besides affording an opportunity to compare presents and indulge in a little harmless gossip with the Beechwood negroes.

Lady Gay stood, ready saddled, waiting at the door. After a little delay in adjusting the assertive springs of her hoop-skirt to the pommel of the saddle, Lucinda started off in a gallop.

When she entered the broad hall at Beechwood, the family, children and all, recognizing her as an ambassador of Santa Claus, gathered eagerly about her, and as boxes and parcels were opened in her presence her eyes fairly shone with pleasure. Nor was she disappointed in her hope of a gift herself.

"I allus did love you de mos' o' all o' ole Miss's chillen, Miss Lou," she exclaimed presently, opening and closing with infantile delight a gay feather-edged fan which Louise gave her.

"I does nachelly love red. Red seem like hit's got mo' color in it 'n any color."

"Dis heah's a reg'lar courtin' fan," she added to herself, as she followed the children out into the nursery to inspect their new toys, fanning, posing, and flirting as she went. "Umph! ef I'd 'a' des had dis fan las' summer I'd 'a' had Dave all but crazy."

After enjoying it for an hour or more, she finally wrapped it carefully in her handkerchief and put it for safe keeping in her pocket. In doing so, her hand came in contact with a letter which she had forgotten to deliver.

"Law, Miss Lou!" she exclaimed, hurrying back, "I mos' done clair forgittin' ter gi' you yo' letter wha' ole marster tol' me ter han' you de fur' thing."

"I wondered that father and mother had sent no message," replied Louise, opening the note. Her face softened into a smile, however, as she proceeded to read it.

"Why, you wretch, Lucindy!" she exclaimed, laughing, "you've kept me out of my two best Christmas gifts for an hour. I always wanted to own Lady Gay, and father writes that you are a fine, capable girl."

Lucinda cast a quick, frightened look at Louise and caught her breath.

"And I am so glad to know that you are pleased. Why didn't you tell me that you were a Christmas gift when you came?"

There was no longer any doubt. Lucinda could not have answered to save her life. The happy-hearted child of a moment ago was transformed into a desperate, grief-stricken woman.

"Why, Lucindy!" Louise was really grieved to discern the tragic look in the girl's face. "I am disappointed. I thought you loved me. I thought you would be delighted to belong to me–to be my maid–and not to work in the field any more–and to have a nice cabin in my yard–and a sewing machine–and to learn to embroider–and to dress my hair–and to–"

The growing darkness in Lucinda's face warned Louise that this conciliatory policy was futile, and yet, feeling only kindly towards her, she continued.

"Tell me, Lucindy, why are you distressed. Don't you really wish to belong to me? Why did you say that you loved me the best?"

Words were useless. Louise was almost frightened as she looked again into the girl's face. Her eyes shone like a caged lion's, and her bosom rose and fell tumultuously.

After many fruitless efforts to elicit a response, Louise called her husband, and together they tried by kind assurances to pacify her; but it was in vain. She stood before them a mute impersonation of despair and rage.

"You'd better go out into the kitchen a while, Lucindy," said Louise finally, "and when I send for you I shall expect you to have composed yourself." Looking neither to right nor left, Lucinda strode out of the hall, across the gallery, down the steps, through the yard to the kitchen, gazed at by the assembled crowd of children both black and white.

"'Cindy ain't but des on'y a little while ago married," said Tildy, a black girl who stood in the group as she passed out.

"Married, is she?" exclaimed Louise, eagerly grasping at a solution of the difficulty. "That explains. But why didn't she tell me? There must be some explanation. This is so unlike father. We are to dine at Sucrier this afternoon. Go, Tildy, and tell Lucindy that we will see what can be done."

"Fo' laws-o'-mussy sakes, Miss Lou, please, ma'am, don't sen' me ter 'Cindy now. 'Cindy look like she gwine hurt somebody."

If she could have seen Lucinda at this moment, she might indeed have feared to approach her. When she had entered the kitchen a little negro who had followed at her heels had announced to the cook and her retinue,

"'Cindy mad caze ole marster done sont 'er fur a Chris'mus gif' ter Miss Lou." Whereupon there were varied exclamations:

"Umph!"

"You is a sorry-lookin' Chris'mus gif', sho!"

"I don't blame 'er!"

"What you frettin' 'bout, chile? You in heab'n here!"

"De gal's married," whispered someone in stage fashion, finally.

"Married!" shrieked old Silvy Ann from her corner where she sat peeling potatoes. "Married! Eh, Lord! Time you ole as I is, you won't fret 'bout no sech. Turn 'im out ter grass, honey, an' start out fur a grass-widder. I got five I done turned out in de pasture now, an' ef dey sell me out ag'in, Ole Abe'll be a-grazin' wid de res'."

"Life is too short ter fret, honey! But ef yer *boun'* ter fret, fret 'bout *some'h'n'!* Don't fret 'bout one o' deze heah long-laigged, good-fur-nothin' sca'crows name' Mister Man! Who you married ter, gal?"

"She married ter cross-eyed Dave," some one answered.

"Cross-eyed! De Lord! Let 'im go fur what he'll fetch, honey! De woods roun' heah is full o' straight-eyed ones, let 'lone game-eyes!" And the vulgar old creature encored her own wit with an outburst of cracked laughter.

"Ain't you 'shame o' yo'se'f, Aunt Silvy Ann! 'Cindy ain't like you; she *married–wid a preacher.*"

"Yas, an' *un*married '*dout no preacher!* What's de good o' lockin' de do' on de inside wid a key, ef you c'n open it f'om de outside 'dout no key? I done kep' clair o' locks an' keys all my life, an' nobody's feelin's was hurt."

While old Silvy Ann was running on in this fashion, Texas, the cook, had begun to address Lucinda:

"Don't grieve yo' heart, baby. My ole man stay mo' fur 'n ole marster's f'om heah–'way down ter de cross-roads t'other side de bayou. How fur do daddy stay, chillen?" she added, as she broke red pepper into her turkey-stuffing.

"Leb'n mile," answered four voices from as many little black pickaninnies who tumbled over one another on the floor.

"You heah dat! *Leb'n mile,* an' ev'y blessed night he come home ter Texas! Yas, ma'am, an' 'is lone star keep a lookout fur 'im too–a candle in de winder an' a tin pan o' 'membrance on de hyearth."

Seeing that her words produced no effect, Texas changed her tactics.

Approaching Lucinda, she regarded her with admiration: "Dat's a quality collar you got on, 'Cindy. An', law bless my soul, ef de gal ain't got on hoops! You gwine lead de style on dis planta–"

Texas never finished her sentence.

Trembling with fury, Lucinda snatched the collar from her neck and tore it into bits; then, making a dive at her skirts, she ripped them into shreds in her frantic efforts to destroy the hoop-skirt. Dragging the gilt pendants from her ears, tearing the flesh as she did so, she threw them upon the floor, and, stamping upon them, ground them to atoms.

Her new brogans attracting her next, she kicked them from her feet and hurled them, one after another, into the open fire. No vestige of a gift from the hand that had betrayed her would she spare.

While all this was occurring in the kitchen, a reverse side of the tragedy was enacting in the house.

A few moments after Lucinda's departure, while Louise and her husband were yet discussing the situation, another messenger came from Sucrier, this time a man, and again a gift, the "note" which he promptly delivered proving to be a deed of conveyance of "two adult negroes, by name of Lucinda and David." Then followed descriptions of each, which it was unnecessary to read.

The bearer seemed in fine spirits.

"Ole marster des sont me wid de note, missy," said he, courtesying respectfully, "an' ef yer please, ma'am, I'll go right back ef dey ain't no answer. We havin' a big time up our way ter-day."

"Why, don't you know what this is, Dave?"

"Yes, 'm, co'se I knows. Hit's—hit's a letter. Law, Miss Lou, yer reck'n I don' know a letter when I see it?"

"Yes, but this letter says that you are not to go back. Father has sent you as a Christmas gift to us."

"Wh-wh-h-how you say dat, missy?"

"Please don't look so frightened, Dave. From the way you all are acting today, I begin to be afraid of myself. Don't you want to belong to me?"

"Y-y-yas, 'm, but yer see, missy, I—I—I's married."

The hat in his hand was trembling as he spoke.

"And where is your wife?" Could it be possible that he did not know?

"She-sh-she—" This boy was actually crying. "She stay wid me. B-b-but marster des sont 'er on a arrant dis mornin'. Gord knows whar he sont 'er. I 'lowed maybe he sont 'er heah, tell 'e sont me."

The situation, which was plain now, had grown so interesting that Louise could not resist the temptation to bring the unconscious actors in the little drama together, that she might witness the happy catastrophe.

She whispered to Tildy to call Lucinda.

That Lucinda should have been summoned just at the crisis of her passion was most inopportune.

Tildy stood at a distance as she timidly delivered the message. Indeed, all the occupants of the kitchen had moved off apace and stood aghast and silent.

As soon as Lucinda heard the command, however, without even looking down at herself, with head still high in air and her fury unabated, she followed Tildy into the presence of her mistress.

Louise was frightened when she looked upon her; indeed it was some moments before she could command herself enough to speak.

The girl's appearance was indeed tragic.

In tearing the ribbon from her hair she had loosened the ends of the short braids, which stood in all directions. Her ears were dripping with blood, and her torn sleeve revealed her black arm, scratched with her nails, also bleeding.

Below her tattered skirt trailed long, detached springs, the dilapidated remains of the glorious structure of the morning.

Her tearless eyes gave no sign of weakening, and the veins about her neck and temples, pulsating with passion, were swollen and knotted like ropes.

She seemed to have grown taller, and the black circles beneath her eyes and about her swelling lips imparted by contrast an ashen hue grimly akin to pallor to the rest of her face.

As her mistress contemplated her, she was moved to pity.

"Lucindy"–she spoke with marked gentleness–"I showed you all our Christmas gifts this morning; but after you went out we received another, and I've sent for you to show you this, too."

She hesitated, but not even by a quivering muscle did Lucinda give a sign of hearing.

"Look over there towards the library door, Lucindy, and see the nice carriage-driver father sent me."

Ah! now she looked.

For a moment only young husband and wife regarded each other, and then, oblivious to all eyes, the two Christmas gifts rushed into each other's arms.

The fountains of her wrath were broken up now, and Lucinda's tears came like rain. Crying and sobbing aloud, she threw her long arms around little Dave, and dragging him out into the floor, began to dance.

Dave, more sensitive than she, abashed after the first surprise, became conscious and ashamed.

"Stop, 'Cindy! I 'clare, gal, stop! Stop, I say!" he cried, trying in vain to wrest himself from her grasp.

"You, 'Cindy! You makes me 'shame! Law, gal! Miss Lou, come here to 'Cindy!"

But the half-savage creature, mad with joy, gave no heed to his resistance as she whirled him round and round up and down the hall.

"Hallelujah! Glory! Amen! Glory be ter God, fur givin' me back dis heah little black, cross-eyed, bandy-legged nigger! Glory, I say!"

The scene was not without pathos. And yet—how small a thing will sometimes turn the tide of emotion! By how trifling a by-play does a tragedy become comedy!

In her first whirl, the trailing steels of Lucinda's broken hoop-skirt flew over the head of the cat, who sat in the door, entrapping her securely.

Round and round went poor puss, terror-stricken and wildly glaring, utterly unable to extricate herself, until finally a reversed movement freeing her, she sprang with a desperate plunge and an ear-splitting "Miaou!" by a single bound out of the back door.

This served to bring Lucinda to a consciousness of her

surroundings. Screaming with laughter, she threw herself down and rolled on the floor. In rising, her eyes fell for the first time, with a sense of perception, upon herself.

Suddenly conscience-stricken, she threw herself again before her mistress.

"Fo' God sake, whup me, Miss Lou!" she began; "whup me, ur put me in de stocks, one! I ain't no mo' fitt'n fur a Chris'mus gif' 'n one o' deze heah tiger-cats in de show-tent. Des look heah how I done ripped up all my purties, an' bus' my ears open, an' broke up all my hoop-granjer, all on 'count o' dat little black, cross-eyed nigger! I tell yer de trufe, missy, I ain't no bad-hearted nigger! You des try me! I'll hoe fur yer, I'll plough fur yer, I'll split rails fur ye, I'll be yo' hair-dresser, I'll run de sew'-machine fur yer, I'll walk on my head fur yer, ef yer des leave me dat one little black scrooched-up some'h'n-'nother stan'in' over yonner 'g'inst de do', grinnin' like a chessy-cat. He ain't much, but, sech as 'e is an' what dey is of 'im, fo' God sake, spare 'im ter me! Somehow, de place whar he done settled in my heart is des nachelly my *wil'-cat spot!*"

Sitting in her rags at her mistress's feet, in this fashion she approached the formal apology which she felt that her conduct demanded.

Somehow the conventional formula, "I ax yo' pardon," seemed inadequate to the present requirement.

She hardly knew how to proceed.

After hesitating a moment in some embarrassment, she began again, in a lower tone:

"Miss Lou, dis heah's Chris'mus, ain't it?"

"Yes; you know it is."

"An' hit's de day de Lord cas' oft all 'is glory an' come down ter de yearth, des a po' little baby a-layin' in a stable 'longside o' de cows an' calves, ain't it?"

"Yes."

"An' hit's de day de angels come a-singin' peace an' good-will, ain't it?"

"Yes."

"Miss Lou–"

"Well?"

"On de 'count o' all dat, honey, won't yer please, ma'am, pass over my wil'-cat doin's dis time, mistus?"

She waited a moment, and, not understanding how a rising lump in her throat kept her mistress silent, continued to plead:

"Fo' Gord sake, mistus, I done said all de scripchur' I knows. What mo' kin I say?"

"What–what–what–what–what's all this?"

It was old Colonel Slack, standing in the front hall door.

At the sound of his voice, the three grandchildren ran to meet him, Louise following.

"You dear old father!" she exclaimed, kissing him. "You've grown impatient and come after us!"

"Certainly I have. What sort of spending the day do you call this? It's two o'clock now. But what's all this?" he repeated, approaching Lucinda, who had risen to her feet.

Dave had gradually backed nearly out of the door.

"Why, Lucindy, my girl! you look as if you'd had a tiff with a panther."

"Tell de trufe, marster, I done been down an' had a han'-ter-han' wrestle wid Satan ter-day, an' he all but whupped me out."

"How did you happen to send these poor children to us separately, father?" said Louise. "They have been almost broken-hearted, each thinking the other was to stay at Sucrier."

"Well, well, well! I am the clumsiest old blunderer! It's from Scylla to Charybdis every time. I didn't want my people to suspect they were going, just because it's Christmas, you know, and saying good-bye will cast a sort of shadow over things. Dave and Lucindy are immensely popular among the darkies. I knew they'd be glad to come; it's promotion, you see. Never thought of a misunderstanding. And so you poor children thought I wanted to divorce you, did you? I'd tear mine off too. Rig her up again somehow, daughter, and let her go up to the dance tonight."

Opening his pocket-book, he took out two crisp five-dollar bills.

Handing one of them to Lucinda, he said:

"Here, girl, take this, and–don't you tell 'em I said so, but I thought you beat the whole crowd dancing this morning, any-how. And Dave, you little cross-eyed rascal you, step up here and get your money. Here's five dollars to pay for spoiling your Christmas. Now, off with you!"

As they passed out, Lucinda seized Dave's arm, and when last seen as they crossed the yard she was dragging the little fellow from side to side, dancing in her rags and flirting high in air the red fan, which by some chance had escaped destruction in her pocket.

Magnificent in a discarded ball-dress of her new mistress, Lucinda was the center of attraction at the Sucrier festival that evening, and when questioned in regard to her toilet of the morning, she answered, with a playful toss of the head:

"What y'all talkin' 'bout, niggers! I wushes I ter on'erstan' dat I's a house-gal now! Yer reck'n I gwine wear common orna-ments, same as you fiel'han's?"

FROM

Twelve Years a Slave

Solomon Northrup

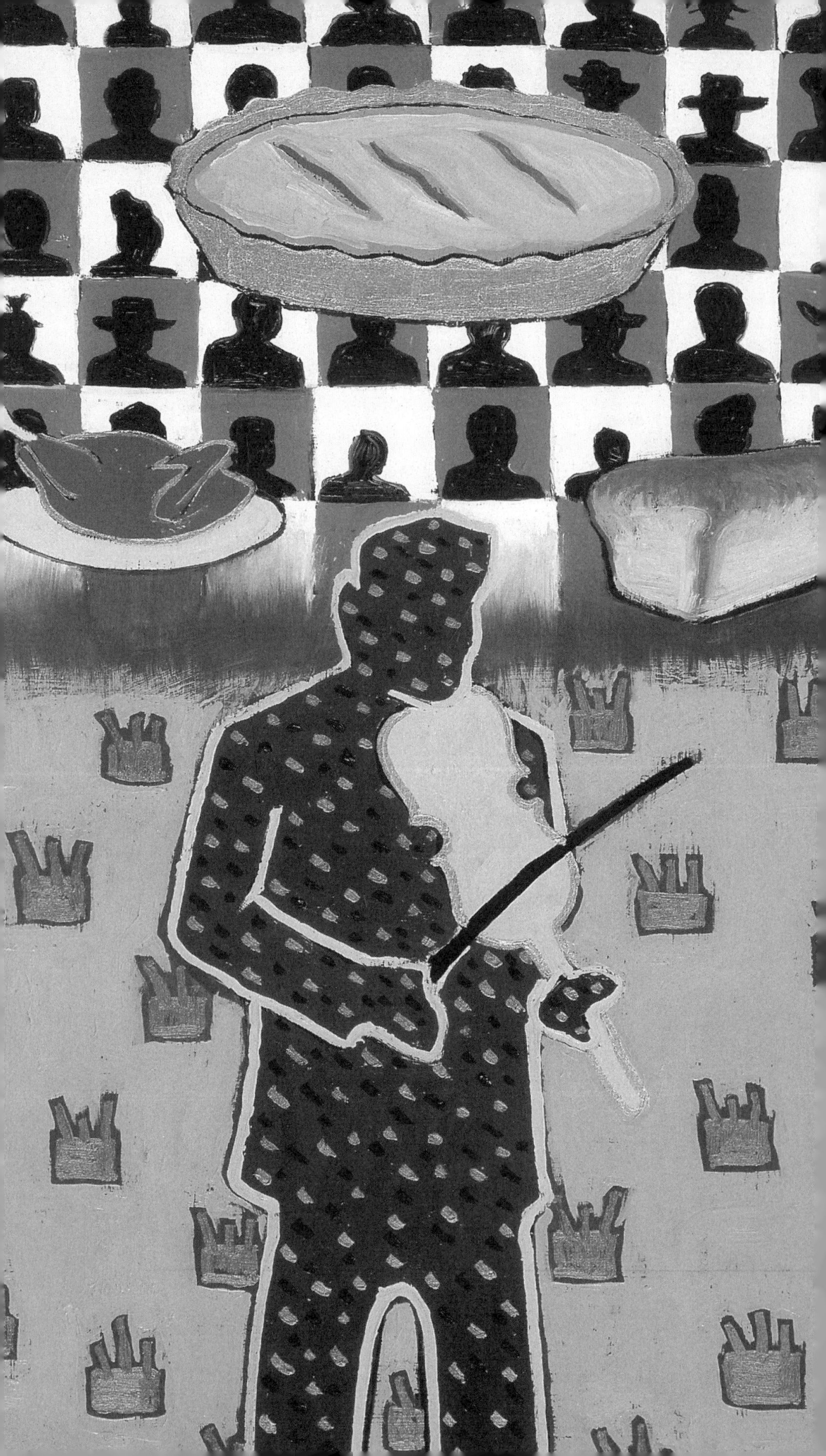

The only respite from constant labor the slave has through the whole year is during the Christmas holidays. Epps allowed us three–others allow four, five and six days, according to the measure of their generosity. It is the only time to which they look forward with any interest or pleasure. They are glad when night comes, not only because it brings them a few hours repose, but because it brings them one day nearer Christmas. It is hailed with equal delight by the old and the young; even Uncle Abram ceases to glorify Andrew Jackson, and Patsey forgets her many sorrows amid the general hilarity of the holidays. It is the time of feasting, and frolicking, and fiddling–the carnival season with the children of bondage. They are the only days when they are allowed a little restricted liberty, and heartily indeed do they enjoy it.

It is the custom for one planter to give a "Christmas supper," inviting the slaves from neighboring plantations to join his own on the occasion; for instance, one year it is given by Epps, the next by Marshall, the next by Hawkins, and so on. Usually from three to five hundred are assembled, coming together on foot, in carts, on horseback, on mules, riding double and triple, sometimes a boy and girl, at others a girl and two boys, and at others again a boy, a girl and an old woman. Uncle Abram astride a mule, with Aunt Phoebe and Patsey behind him, trotting towards a Christmas supper, would be no uncommon sight on Bayou Boeuf.

Then, too, "of all days i' the year," they array themselves in their best attire. The cotton coat has been washed clean, the stump of a tallow candle has been applied to the shoes, and if so fortunate as to possess a rimless or a crownless hat, it is placed jauntily on the head. They are welcomed with equal cordiality, however, if they come bare-headed and bare-footed to the feast. As a general thing, the women wear handkerchiefs tied about their heads, but if chance has thrown in their way a fiery red ribbon, or a cast-off bonnet of their mistress' grandmother, it is sure to be worn on such occasions. Red—the deep blood red—is decidedly the favorite color among the enslaved damsels of my acquaintance. If a red ribbon does not encircle the neck, you will be certain to find all the hair of their woolly heads tied up with red strings of one sort or another.

The table is spread in the open air, and loaded with varieties of meat and piles of vegetables. Bacon and corn meal at such times are dispensed with. Sometimes the cooking is performed in the kitchen on the plantation, at others in the shade of wide branching trees. In the latter case, a ditch is dug in the ground, and wood laid in and burned until it is filled with glowing coals, over which chickens, ducks, turkeys, pigs, and not unfrequently the entire body of a wild ox, are roasted. They are furnished also with flour, of which biscuits are made, and often with peach and other preserves, with tarts, and every manner and description of pies, except the mince, that being an article of pastry as yet unknown among them. Only the slave who has lived all the years on his scanty allowance of meal and bacon can appreciate such suppers. White people in great numbers assemble to witness the gastronomical enjoyments.

They seat themselves at the rustic table—the males on one side, the females on the other. The two between whom there may have been an exchange of tenderness, invariably manage to sit opposite; for the omnipresent Cupid disdains not to hurl his arrows into the simple hearts of slaves. Unalloyed and exulting happiness lights up the dark faces of them all. The ivory teeth, contrasting with their black complexions, exhibit two long, white streaks the whole extent of the table. All round the bountiful board a multitude of eyes roll in ecstasy. Giggling and laughter and the clattering of cutlery and crockery succeed. Cuffee's elbow hunches his neighbor's side, impelled by an involuntary impulse of delight; Nelly shakes her finger at Sambo and laughs, she knows not why, and so the fun and merriment flows on.

When the viands have disappeared, and the hungry maws of the children of toil are satisfied, then, next in the order of amusement, is the Christmas dance. My business on these gala days always was to play on the violin. The African race is a music-loving one, proverbially; and many there were among my fellow-bondsmen whose organs of tune were strikingly developed, and who could thumb the banjo with dexterity; but at the expense of appearing egotistical, I must, nevertheless, declare that I was considered the Ole Bull of Bayou Boeuf. My master often received letters, sometimes from a distance of ten miles, requesting him to send me to play at a ball or festival of the whites. He received his compensation, and usually I also returned with many picayunes jingling in my pockets–the extra contributions of those to whose delight I had administered. In this manner I became more acquainted than I otherwise would, up and down the bayou. The young men and maidens of Holmesville always knew there was to be a jollification somewhere, whenever Platt Epps was seen passing through the town with his fiddle in his hand. "Where are you going now, Platt?" and "What is coming off tonight, Platt?" would be interrogatories issuing from every door and window, and many a time when there was no special hurry, yielding to pressing importunities, Platt would draw his bow, and sitting astride his mule, perhaps, discourse musically to a crowd of delighted children, gathered around him in the street.

Alas! had it not been for my beloved violin, I scarcely can conceive how I could have endured the long years of bondage. It introduced me to great houses–relieved me of many days' labor in the field–supplied me with conveniences for my cabin–with pipes and tobacco, and extra pairs of shoes, and oftentimes led me away from the presence of a hard master, to witness scenes of jollity and mirth. It was my companion–the friend of my bosom triumphing loudly when I was joyful, and uttering its soft, melodious consolations when I was sad. Often, at midnight, when sleep had fled affrighted from the cabin, and my soul was disturbed and troubled with the contemplation of my fate, it would sing me a song of peace. On holy Sabbath days, when an hour or two of leisure was allowed, it would accompany me to some quiet place on the bayou bank, and, lifting up its voice, discourse kindly and pleasantly indeed. It heralded my name round the country–made me friends, who, otherwise would not have noticed me–gave me an honored seat at the yearly feasts, and secured the loudest and heartiest welcome of them all at the Christmas dance. The Christmas dance! Oh, ye pleasure-seeking sons and daughters of idleness, who move with measured step, listless and snail-like, through the slow-winding cotillion, if ye wish to look upon the celerity, if not the "poetry of motion"– upon genuine happiness, rampant and unrestrained–go down to Louisiana, and see the slaves dancing in the starlight of a Christmas night.

On that particular Christmas I have now in my mind, a description whereof will serve as a description of the day generally. Miss Lively and Mr. Sam, the first belonging to Stewart, the latter to Roberts, started the ball. It was well known that Sam cherished an ardent passion for Lively, as also did one of Marshall's and another of Carey's boys; for Lively was lively indeed, and a heart-breaking coquette withal. It was a victory for Sam Roberts, when, rising from the repast, she gave him her hand for the first "figure" in preference to either of his rivals. They were somewhat crest-fallen, and, shaking their heads angrily, rather intimated they would like to pitch into Mr. Sam and hurt him badly. But not an emotion of wrath ruffled the placid bosom of Samuel as his legs flew like drum-sticks down the outside and up the middle, by the side of his bewitching partner. The whole company cheered them vociferously, and, excited with the applause, they continued "tearing down" after all the others had become exhausted and halted a moment to recover breath. But Sam's superhuman exertions overcame him finally, leaving Lively alone, yet whirling like a top. Thereupon one of Sam's rivals, Pete Marshall, dashed in, and, with might and main, leaped and shuffled and threw himself into every conceivable shape, as if determined to show Miss Lively and all the world that Sam Roberts was of no account.

Pete's affection, however, was greater than his discretion. Such violent exercise took the breath out of him directly, and he dropped like an empty bag. Then was the time for Harry Carey to try his hand; but Lively also soon out-winded him, amidst hurrahs and shouts, fully sustaining her well-earned reputation of being the "fastest gal" on the bayou.

One "set" off, another takes its place, he or she remaining longest on the floor receiving the most uproarious commendation, and so the dancing continues until broad daylight. It does not cease with the sound of the fiddle, but in that case they set up a music peculiar to themselves. This is called "patting," accompanied with one of those unmeaning songs, composed rather for its adaptation to a certain tune or measure, than for the purpose of expressing any distinct idea. The patting is performed by striking the hands on the knees, then striking the hands together, then striking the right shoulder with one hand, the left with the other—all the while keeping time with the feet, and singing, perhaps, this song:

"*Harper's creek and roarin' ribber,*
Thar, my dear, we'll live forebber;
Den we'll go to de Ingin nation,
All I walls in dis creation,
Is pretty little wife and big plantation.
Chorus. Up dat oak and down dat ribber,
Two overseers and one little nigger"

Or, if these words are not adapted to the tune called for, it may be that "Old Hog Eye" is—a rather solemn and startling specimen of versification, not, however, to be appreciated unless heard in the South. It runneth as follows:

"Who's been here since I've been gone?
Pretty little gal wid a josey on.

Hog Eye!
Old Hog Eye,
And Hosey too!

Never see de like since I was born,
Here come a little gal wid a josey on.
Hog Eye!
Old Hog Eye!
And Hosey too!"

Or, may be the following, perhaps, equally nonsensical, but full of melody, nevertheless, as it flows from the negro's mouth:

"Ebo Dick and Jurdan's Jo,
Them two niggers stole my yo'.

Chorus. Hop Jim along,
Walk Jim along,
Talk Jim along," &c.

Old black Dan, as black as tar,
He dam glad he was not dar.

Hop Jim along," &c.

During the remaining holidays succeeding Christmas, they are provided with passes, and permitted to go where they please within a limited distance, or they may remain and labor on the plantation, in which case they are paid for it. It is very rarely, however, that the latter alternative is accepted. They may be seen at these times hurrying in all directions, as happy looking mortals as can be found on the face of the earth. They are different beings from what they are in the field; the temporary relaxation, the brief deliverance from fear, and from the lash, producing an entire metamorphosis in their appearance and demeanor. In visiting, riding, renewing old friendships, or, perchance, reviving some old attachment, or pursuing whatever pleasure may suggest itself; the time is occupied. Such is "southern life as it is" three days in the year, as I found it–the other three hundred and sixty-two being days of weariness, and fear, and suffering, and unremitting labor.

Like a Bowl Full of Jelly

Laura J. Dulaney

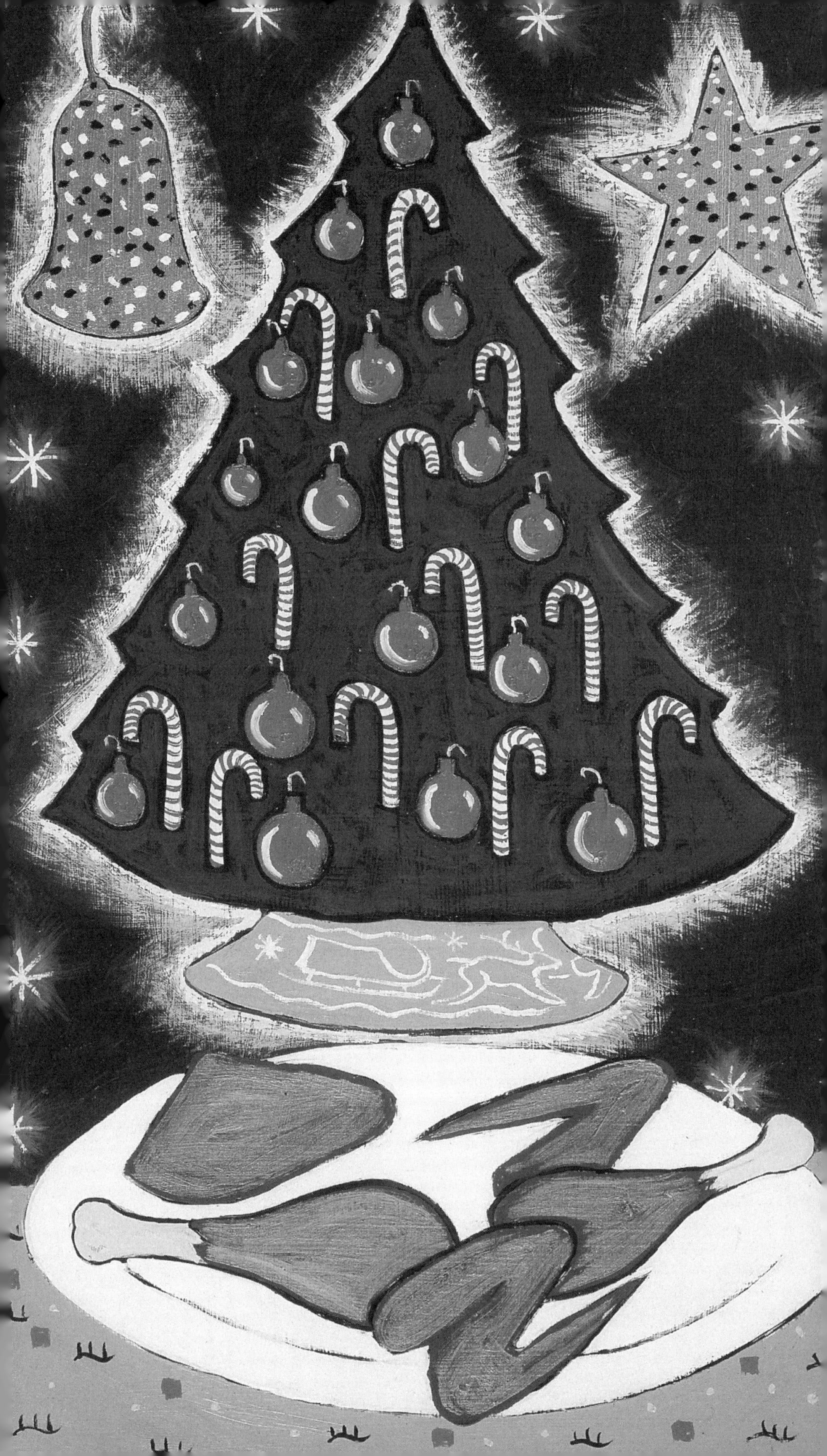

Santa gazed at the plate in wonder. A rice cake? A stinking, dried-up rice cake? Who left rice cakes for Santa Claus? Was this some kind of joke? Clearly whoever did this had no intention of receiving presents this year. Santa's eyes narrowed. This was too bizarre. The Barretts always left him homemade pecan pralines and a tall glass of milk. He pondered. Then his eyebrows shot up and an expectant energy coursed through his body. Of course! This was a joke! A real reward must await him in the kitchen, and the rice cake was a setup to see if he would find it.

Black boots shuffling in rhythm to his humming, Santa blew through the swinging door into the kitchen. His stomach rumbled in anticipation as he perused the contents of the refrigerator. Leftover fried chicken! Now this was a proper offering for a man of his stature. He snatched the platter from the shelf. And what to drink? He spied a lone Dixie beer and grabbed that too, pulling the cap off with his teeth and spitting it in the general direction of the trashcan. It clattered on the linoleum as he retreated to the living room and sank into the La-Z-Boy. Santa launched into the platter of chicken, gurgles of delight bursting through the muffled smacking sounds. As he ate, he considered leaving an extra present or two to show his approval. True, he could have done without the game of "find the prize," but he wasn't complaining. The chicken was tasty, the beer refreshing, and it was good to sit and put his feet up for a few minutes.

Santa was into his third drumstick when he heard the sound of soft crying coming from behind the sofa. Damn. Crying was never a good thing when you were Santa Claus. Santa sighed and heaved his weight forward, bringing the chair to an upright position. Momentarily remembering his wife's admonitions, he finished chewing before speaking, thinking how sad it was that everyone wasn't sleeping so that he could rest and eat in peace and quiet.

"Hello?" he called. The sound of sniffling responded. "Who's there? Mandy or Tommy?"

"M-M-Mandy," came the hesitant voice from behind the sofa.

"Well, Mandy, why don't you come on out and talk to me, tell me what's the matter?" A frightened-looking girl of nine slowly peered around the corner of the couch. Her eyes were red, her nightgown spotted from her tears. She sniffed as she stared at the enormous man in the recliner.

Santa put on his best friend-of-the-children smile and spoke gently. "Now, Mandy, tell Santa what the problem is. Are you afraid I didn't bring you the presents that you asked for?" He added a soft "hohoho" for good effect.

"No sir." Mandy stayed behind the safety of the couch, but her tears had stopped and she sniffled less. She stared with fascination at the platter of chicken in Santa's lap.

"You're not? Hmm. Well, you're gonna have to tell me what's bothering you then." Santa noticed her focused gaze and held forth the platter. "Would you like some fried chicken?"

Mandy shook her head forcefully. "No thank you, Santa."

"Well, my dear," said Santa through a large bite of chicken thigh, "why don't you have a seat, and you can tell me what's on your mind. I hate to see you so sad." Santa paused to smile kindly at her before he drained the beer. "Ah," he said, smacking his lips as he set the platter and empty bottle on the floor, "now that was a great snack." Santa wiped his fingers on his beard and flicked a crumb off his sleeve. "I want to thank you and your family for being so thoughtful and leaving me such good food."

At this Mandy burst into tears again. "Good Lord, child! What is it? What is it? You're going to wake the whole neighborhood with wailing like that! Now you just tell old Santa what's the matter." Huffing with effort, Santa hoisted himself from the chair and crossed over to the couch, which creaked audibly with the stress of his weight.

"You ate a platter of chicken! You're gonna die! You and Momma, you're both gonna die, and then who will look after me and Tommy? We'll be all alone in the world!"

Santa was bewildered. He had experienced many children crying for many reasons, but he had never had one tell him he was going to die because he ate chicken. He tried his best to answer her logically. "Now Mandy, chicken is not poisonous, honey. I don't have any allergies to chicken. Been eating chicken all my life, actually. See? My tongue's not swelling up or anything. Go ahead, take a look." Santa thrust out his tongue for Mandy to approve, but she just kept crying into her hands and repeating, "You and Momma, you're both gonna die!"

After about the tenth iteration of this phrase Santa was losing his patience. Not only did he not have time for this, but the declared prophecy by a nine-year-old that he was going to die, ridiculous as it may have seemed, was a little unnerving. "Amanda Jo Barrett, I want you to stop crying this instant and tell me why you think eating chicken is going to cause my death."

Mandy took in a stuttered breath, wiped her eyes, and tried her best to calm down. Inhaling deeply, she launched into her explanation. "Well, last year when Daddy had his heart attack, the doctor said it was 'cause he didn't live right. Said Daddy worked too much, didn't eat right, didn't exercise. He gave Momma a good talkin' to and said that if she didn't change her ways, she'd be following Daddy straight to heaven, but Momma just laughed and said she was too old to go changing her ways now. Said there had to be some happiness for her in this life, and that with her husband dead and two children to raise on her own, was it too much to ask that with all her burdens in life she should be allowed to eat a piece of chocolate cake now and then?" Mandy gasped for air, having rushed through her confessional with the speed and anxiety of a claustrophobic escaping a cave. She sat in silence, waiting for Santa's answer, as if all were now obvious.

Santa frowned. This was more complex than he had antici-
pated. He glanced down at his watch. The illuminated dial let
him know that he was getting seriously behind schedule.
"Mandy, I'm awfully sorry about your daddy. I know you must
miss him a lot." Mandy nodded. "I have to tell you though, sweetheart, I don't quite understand what that has to do with me dying
from chicken."

"Santa, you're fat!" Mandy blurted this out with due exaspera-
tion. "You're fat, Santa! If you don't take better care of yourself
you're gonna die just like my daddy did! And then we won't have
Christmas anymore! Who will bring us our presents? Who will
make Christmas special for children all over the world? Who
will we send our letters to when no one else will listen to our
wants? You have to lose weight, Santa! You have to lose weight
and get healthy so you don't die!"

Santa sat in stunned silence. "Did you leave that rice cake on
the plate for me?"

"Yes sir."

"Ah. I see." The two figures sat in silence on the sofa, musing
in their private thoughts, the soft glow of the tree lights a gentle
reminder that it was now officially Christmas and soon would be
dawn. Santa sighed, and Mandy glanced up expectantly, total
faith showing in her eyes. "Mandy, I don't want you to worry
about me, okay? Not now, not ever. I'll be around to bring presents to your children, and their children, and their children."

"But . . ."

"Shh. Let me finish. Honey, I appreciate your being concerned
about me, I really do, it's nice to know that you care so much. But
you have to realize, I can't die. I'm a fantasy."

Mandy's eyebrows knit together. "What do you mean?"

"I'm an eternal figure. I'm built out of things like love, faith,
magic, and mystery. I exist because the universal psyche of
mankind wants me to exist."

"Sorry, Santa, but you've lost me."

"Well, let's just say that while I enjoy eating fried chicken and
pralines, they're not what sustain me; they're not what keep me

alive. I'm alive because you love me and you believe in me, you and all the children of the world. It's your faith in me, your belief that I'll show up every Christmas Eve that keeps me alive. As long as the children of the world believe in me, I'll never die."

Mandy pondered this concept. "So you're saying klestrol isn't a problem for you?"

Santa let out a hearty laugh. "That's exactly what I'm saying. Not now, not ever."

Mandy's shoulders dropped with the relief of this information. "Oh I'm so glad! But Santa, what about Momma? Can you make it so that she doesn't have to worry about klestrol either?"

"Oh." Santa closed his eyes. Why did kids always wait for Christmas Eve to have these conversations? Why couldn't she have addressed this two weeks ago when her mother brought her to visit him at the mall? "Well, you see, Mandy, it's like this."

"Never mind. I can already tell what your answer is." Her lower lip thrust itself forward in defiance. "I thought you could do anything!"

"No, not anything. Your momma's a human being, Mandy; that means she has a human body."

"That means she can die."

"Well, yes, it does. Dying is part of living when you're human. But she may not die for a long, long time."

"She's fat, Santa! She's really fat! The doctor said she was unhealthy!"

"That scares you, doesn't it?"

Mandy nodded, her eyes once again welling up with tears.

Santa was suddenly hyperaware of his own nonproblematic girth. He could imagine how unfair it must seem to a nine-year-old that he was immune to heart disease when her father had succumbed to it and her mother seemed to be well on her way. Santa exhaled slowly as he crafted his response. "Well, Mandy, your momma's a grown woman. We can't make her do anything she doesn't want to do, but we could give her a little encourage-ment, what do you say?"

"Encouragement?"

"Yes. Give her some help. We're each going to give her a gift."

"I don't have a lot of money."

"You don't need money for your gift. You'll write her a letter and tell her how much she means to you, how much you need her in your life, and why you want her to take care of herself and be healthy. Then every time she does something to try and take care of herself, you're to give her a big hug and a kiss and tell her how proud of her you are. Can you do that?"

Mandy nodded eagerly. "Sure! That's easy! I can do that!"

"Good girl. And I'll give her some walking shoes and a new cookbook. How about that?"

"That sounds perfect!" Mandy's face glowed with relief.

Santa's expression turned serious. "Mandy, you have to realize something." He looked into her trusting blue eyes. Sometimes he really hated his job. "I can't give you the gift that you really want. I can't promise you that your momma is going to take care of herself from now on."

"Oh Santa! Why wouldn't she? Doesn't she love me?"

This time it was Santa's eyes that brimmed with tears. "I'm sure she loves you more than you'll ever know, but . . . people are complicated, honey. You can't force someone to change, Mandy, and you can't force someone to take care of herself. All you can do is ask. Ask her and love her, no matter what her answer is."

Mandy sighed and curled into Santa's arm to think about this. Santa too was preoccupied. Outside, the reindeer stamped restlessly, sensing that their schedule had been dangerously curtailed. Santa couldn't bear to abandon Mandy when she was so distressed, but there remained half a world of children to be visited before daybreak. He was brooding over his options when he heard her say, "Santa?"

"Yes?"

"I'm glad you won't ever die. I want you to be around for my children so that if I do something really dumb as a mommy you can talk to them the way you talked to me." With that, Mandy leapt into Santa's lap and gave him a huge hug, burying her face in his beard where she could smell the faint aroma of fried chicken in his hair. Santa laughed with relief and tapped her on the nose.

"I'll be glad to help in any way I can. That is, if you'll make a deal with me."

"What's the deal?"

"Don't ever leave me rice cakes again, please."

Christmas at the Barriloux's

James Knudsen

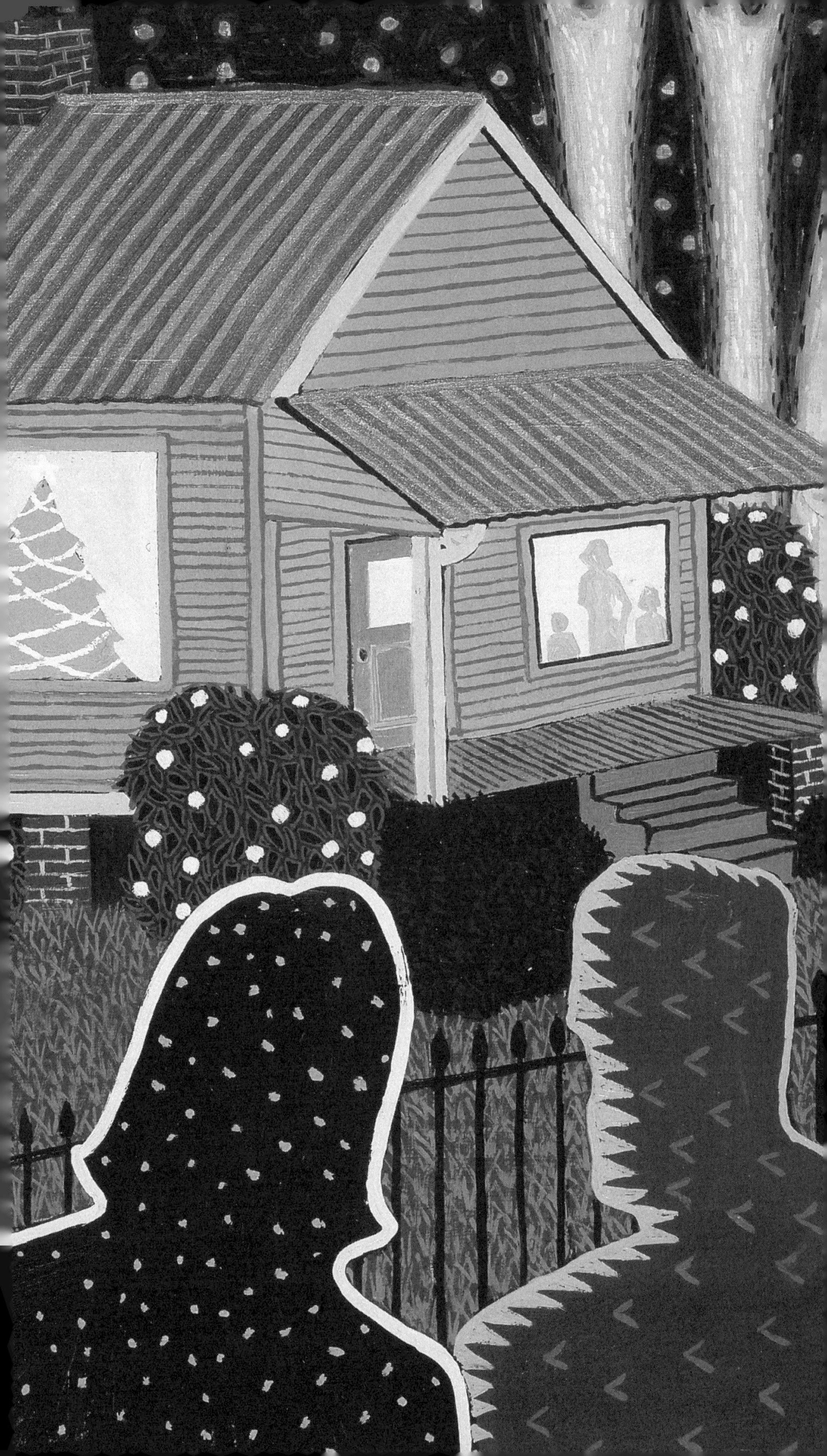

Christmas in New Orleans, for some, is celebrated by watching bonfires on the levee and Papa Noel arriving in a pirogue. For others it wouldn't be the same without a walk through the tunnel of angel hair decked with ornaments at the Fairmont Hotel or the light-draped oaks in City Park. For me, it's a time to sit by the fire with my wife and remember Christmases past. As the darkness crowds in at our windows, there is one we always relive . . .

"Hal and I will be in Alexandria until New Year's," said Caroline. "I told your wife this morning, but we just wanted to remind you."

From the look of things, she and Hal were going to be playing Santa Claus to more than a few relatives. Hal was loading shopping bags overflowing with bright red and green packages into the trunk of their car. He stopped and checked his watch. It was dusk on Christmas Eve, and they had a long drive ahead of them. "Well, have a Merry Christmas, Caroline. Don't worry, we'll watch the place for you."

"Thanks," said Caroline as she stepped from the porch. "Merry Christmas to you and Marjorie."

Before closing the front door, I took a moment to straighten the red plaid bow on our pine wreath. I was pleased that Caroline had taken time to stop by before they left. Since they'd moved in next door three months before, we'd hardly seen them, and it didn't feel right that we should be neighbors and not know the first thing about each other. The day they'd moved in, Marjorie and I had gone over to introduce ourselves, and we'd

159

always wave when we were out in the yard, but there never seemed time to really talk. The fact that Caroline and Hal were probably at least twenty years younger than Marjorie and me might make socializing awkward, but it just seemed right to make the effort.

"Who was at the door?" Marjorie stood behind me holding out an old-fashioned. We were planning to go to the early Christmas Eve service over at St. Mark's, and it was our custom to have a sip of holiday cheer before going. It was shaping up to be an uncommonly cold New Orleans Christmas, and the drink would undoubtedly warm us and make the service glow.

"Oh, it was Caroline to remind us she and Hal are going to Alexandria until after Christmas."

"You should have asked her in for a drink."

"Hal was loading the car. I doubt they'd've had time."

Marjorie sat down on the sofa across from the fireplace. A rope of pine boughs looped from the mantel that was lined with Christmas cards from our grown children and faraway friends. We stared into the lights of our tree which stood in the front window. I should have invited Caroline and Hal in for a drink, insisted on it, even if they were running late, I thought. Hadn't I been looking for an opportunity to really talk with them? I took a sip of my drink and admitted to myself that this wasn't the first time I'd passed up an opportunity, and I suddenly realized why.

The Barriloux.

The Barriloux had been the previous owners of Hal and Caroline's house, and I guess I'd always been anxious that if we got to really talking I'd end up having to tell them what had happened to the Barriloux, and I didn't want to upset or worry them about the investment they'd made in the house. Marjorie and I had been so delighted to have someone living there after all that had happened.

"This is a good drink if I do say so," said Marjorie, kicking off her shoes and stretching out across the sofa.

"Yes," I agreed. "You got the bitters just right."

• • •

We had known the Barriloux quite well, at least we thought we had. Edward Barriloux was a quiet decent type–the very picture of a young bank manager as he left for work in his navy blazers and striped ties. His wife, Kayla, had been a stay-at-home mom to their two children, Peter and Angie. Everything about the household had seemed close to idyllic. The children were well behaved and Kayla kept a beautiful home. The houses in our neighborhood are quite close together, and we would have heard or sensed if anything had been wrong. Mainly we heard the patter of children chasing each other and tickled laughter. Several times a year we'd get together with the Barriloux, a cookout or two in summer, a holiday party. Because our own children are grown and live far away, we developed a special closeness.

Last Christmas Eve, in fact, we'd been invited to their house for a Christmas party. Shortly before the party was to begin, Kayla had apparently gone out to buy another carton of eggnog, and when she returned, she had found Edward hanging from the chinning bar he'd installed in the doorway of their laundry room. He'd used a tripled-over strand of Christmas minilights. Kayla's first thought had been to protect her children from the sight of their father, but when she got to their rooms she'd found them strangled in their beds. Edward had obviously gone mad.

Totally unaware of what had happened over at the Barriloux's, my wife and I had just stepped onto our porch on our way to the party, when Kayla came smashing through their front window with a howl so raw my own vocal chords ached in sympathy. She was dead before the ambulance arrived.

By the time Hal and Caroline moved here from Houston last spring, the Barriloux tragedy was old news. With all the family members in their graves, there was no trial, no details to clear up. Like so many horrors on the news, people put it out of their minds and went on.

After the Christmas Eve service at St. Mark's, my wife and I returned home, and this time *I* made the old-fashioneds, tall ones in the glasses covered with silver and gold snowflakes we used only at this time of year.

"You forgot the bitters," said my wife after she'd tasted hers.

"You're right." I hopped up from the sofa in a burst of pre-Christmas energy and went into the kitchen. I couldn't find the bitters anywhere. "Darling," I called. "Where did you put them?"

"They're probably right in front of you," she said. "They must be. Open your eyes."

She sounded vaguely angry. I'll admit that I often misplace things and can't see the obvious, so in the interest of keeping peace, I remained silent. I searched the kitchen up and down. The bottle of bitters was nowhere to be found.

Figuring Marjorie must have carried it off without realizing it, perhaps set it by the phone or on her vanity and gotten distracted while dressing for church, I headed down the hall to our bedroom. The room was so bright I didn't notice at first that no lights were on.

The light that washed across our bed and bounced between the three panes of Marjorie's vanity mirror was coming from outside the house, and when I stepped to the window, I saw that Hal and Caroline's dining room was ablaze with what appeared to be thousands of miniature white lights. I was nearly blinded yet I stood there entranced, as if bathing in sunlight after weeks of darkness.

The sounds of children running from room to room echoed through the air. There were shouts of laughter and then a lovely woman's voice began to sing. Or maybe it was the wind. Gradually the details of the room came into focus for me; there was an amazing Christmas tree. Perfectly symmetrical and crowded with hundreds of glass ornaments of every type, looping beaded chains and tinsel.

Pine ropes dressed every doorframe and a mountain of silver and gold presents rose from the middle of the dining room table surrounded by dozens of flickering votive candles in red glass holders. It was the perfect dream of a Christmas scene. But where were Hal and Caroline? When had they returned? They should be halfway to Alexandria by now.

I turned and noticed the bottle of bitters sitting on my wife's vanity table as I'd expected. I picked it up and headed back to the living room.

"That's strange," I said. "The lights are on at the Barri . . . Hal and Caroline's."

"Must have forgotten something," Marjorie suggested.

"From the looks of things, they left a stack of presents. Seems strange they'd plug in the tree and light all those candles if they were just popping in to grab some gifts they forgot."

"They didn't even put up a tree this year," said Marjorie. "Caroline told me this morning that since they were going to Alexandria they didn't bother to decorate this year."

"But the place is ablaze," I protested. "Come look."

Marjorie gave longing glances at the bottle of bitters in my hand, her drink, and the fire flickering in the fireplace. She'd turned on the radio and Nat King Cole had just hit the part where he sings about the "toys and goodies" Santa's loaded on his sleigh. She slowly untucked her legs, slipped her shoes back on and stood up. "This better be good."

As we walked down the hallway to the bedroom, my heart beat hard, whether because I was excited about seeing the fabulous room again or out of fear that it wouldn't be there, I couldn't say.

"How many extra drinks did you fix for yourself before you got to mine?" Marjorie said smugly. Our bedroom was entirely dark. Hal and Caroline's house was entirely dark.

"Funny," I said. "They probably picked up what they forgot and dashed off again."

"But there couldn't have been a Christmas tree. Candles. All that stuff you said you saw."

"I saw it. I couldn't make up anything like that. When was I ever that creative?"

"Don't make me remind you," Marjorie teased. "Let's just say you've had some demented ideas."

"I've never *seen* things." Out of the corner of my eye, a dim spark of light made me turn toward Hal and Caroline's house, but it flashed off as soon as it came on. Had Marjorie noticed? Did I dare mention it?

Suddenly we heard a booming noise coming from outside, and we both jumped. It came again and then again. The sound was like a gigantic bass drum pounded by a huge mallet, but slightly muffled as though buried just beneath the earth.

"Where is it coming from?" Marjorie shouted.

"Hal and Caroline's." I stepped toward the window and pressed close. The booming suddenly stopped, and I realized it had been like the sound of a magnified heart, perhaps several magnified hearts beating in unison. But then there was laughter, echoing children's laughter again. Or maybe it was the wind. The lights at Hal and Caroline's snapped on again, and I turned to Marjorie in triumph only to discover that she'd left the room. I nearly screamed.

I rushed back through the kitchen and dining room, back through our cozy living room where our amber drinks on the coffee table foggily reflected the lights of our Christmas tree. The front door stood wide open. I dashed through it to find Marjorie slouched against one of the pillars on the porch as though she'd been stricken by some illness.

"Dear?" I began, trying to sound calmer than I felt.

She turned to me, her eyes wide, her hands trembling. "What's going on?"

"Hal and Caroline must've changed their minds," I said tentatively. All of a sudden the booming began again.

"It *is* coming from their house. That's what I came out to see."

"Maybe Caroline gave Hal a bass drum for Christmas," I joked. "Really, they've probably just got the stereo on too loud."

Marjorie looked at me doubtfully.

"Their plans changed. They decided to go ahead and decorate and have Christmas here." I didn't believe a thing I was saying, but the words kept tumbling out. There had to be some way to explain what was happening.

"Hal and Caroline's car is gone." Marjorie pointed to the empty space at the curb.

My mouth went dry. "Hal probably dropped Caroline off and went to the drugstore." I put my hand on Marjorie's shoulder not sure whether I was trying to reassure her or myself. "Let's go in and finish our drinks. *A Christmas Carol* with Alistair Sim is coming on."

Marjorie looked at me warily, then turned back to Hal and Caroline's house. I was glad she was finally able to see the lighted windows. Marjorie's voice wavered, "That tree looks just the way Kayla Barriloux's looked, and she just loved candles. She told me she always said a prayer for someone's soul with each one she lit. She had a candle for every person she'd been close to who died. It was like a church in there."

I stood looking at Marjorie wondering what I could say to calm her. In order to continue living in our house after the Barriloux tragedy, I'd had to work at blocking every memory of them from my mind, and now it was all flooding back to me. Those sweet children trying out their new toys Christmas morning on the front walk, waving to us across our shared side yard through their misty windows . . .

All the lights in the house suddenly went out as a car pulled into the empty place at the curb. I knew immediately that it was Hal and Caroline. The booming began again, softer at first as Caroline and then Hal got out of their car.

Marjorie moved quickly. "Caroline," she called as she headed toward our screen door and out onto the steps. "Caroline!"

I watched as Caroline practically ran toward their front porch. I had no idea what Marjorie intended to say to her, but I shared Marjorie's sense that Hal and Caroline shouldn't go into the house.

I heard the jingle of Caroline's keys. Marjorie was running now, calling out, "Stop!"

Hal looked at Marjorie in bewilderment as I began shouting too. "Hal, grab Caroline!"

He must have thought we were crazy. In the pause when he

attempted to figure out what to do, where to turn, Caroline got into the house and the door sucked shut behind her. Suddenly the lights flashed on again and the booming continued to build and build.

I stumbled and nearly fell in my rush over to Caroline and Hal's where I joined my wife and Hal in their frantic knocking and calling out to Caroline. At first I think Hal was mainly frightened of us, probably thought we'd taken leave of our senses, but when his key no longer fit the lock on the front door, he began screaming too.

The booming reached a crescendo just when Hal lifted a rocking chair from the front porch and smashed it through the front window. Suddenly the door opened and Caroline emerged onto the porch, paler than I'd ever seen her, her eyes wide with horror. Even so, she was smiling with an odd look of what I can only describe as contentment.

After bundling her off to our house and getting her settled in a comfortable chair by the fire, I made Caroline and Hal hot toddies. Hal knelt on the floor beside Caroline's chair rubbing her hands, first one and then the other until finally she was able to speak. Her voice came in a whisper, "I've just spent Christmas with the Barriloux."

Hal dropped Caroline's hands, and my wife and I exchanged glances. "It was so strange," Caroline continued. "I couldn't think about not entering the house. Something was pulling me forward. When I first stepped in the door, I went completely cold. I felt like I'd entered an ice house. We'd turned off the heat before leaving for Alexandria, so I just instinctively headed for the thermostat in the hallway by the living room, but I never made it. The lights from the dining room nearly blinded me. I could barely make out the outline of a tree. There were stacks of silver and gold wrapped presents and candles everywhere. The room just radiated, and the air was full of echoing laughter."

Hal patted Caroline's knee. She sipped her drink.

"Then suddenly I saw a woman," Caroline continued. "It was like the light of the candles passed right through her and she was beckoning me to come in. She had the most gentle smile.

When I stepped toward her, two children chasing each other dashed out from behind startling me so much that I stopped in my tracks. It was then I noticed the shadow of blood trickling from her mouth, the bruised eyes of the children. 'Welcome to my house,' she said. 'I'm Kayla Barriloux. Merry Christmas.'"

"It must have been awful," said my wife.

"It was quite beautiful in a way. The lights shining through her, the lights blossoming through the children." Caroline stopped. "I guess I'm not making much sense."

Then Caroline began to weep. I made more drinks, and we told them the story of the Barriloux and what happened last Christmas Eve. We insisted that Caroline and Hal spend the night with us. Neither needed convincing.

In the morning Marjorie and I began to talk almost in unison. Mrs. Barriloux and the children had returned to the house to celebrate the Christmas they'd missed. It was suddenly perfectly obvious even if it did require a belief in things neither of us had believed before.

I fixed a large pot of coffee, and my wife heated up a Christmas pastry dotted with red and green cherries while I found some Christmas carols on the radio and plugged in our lights. Hal and Caroline gratefully accepted this modest breakfast, but after eating it, to my surprise, were eager to go home.

"We'll go with you," I offered, "to make sure you're all right." Marjorie shot me a look that said she'd had quite enough of ghosts, thank you.

Hal's "you don't need to do that" and Caroline's "that would be wonderful" collided with each other.

"That settles it," I said. "Marjorie will watch us from the porch. She'll be ready if anything out of the ordinary happens."

Having decided, Hal, Caroline, and I proceeded directly. I studied their house as we walked and saw nothing strange. Their ivy Christmas wreath with its red velvet bow still hung neatly on their front door. All the drapes were drawn as they'd left them. The only difference was the broken front window we hadn't even thought to come back and cover the night before.

Hal inserted his key easily, and we all heard the satisfying click as the door opened. I followed him directly into the living room with Caroline, understandably, dragging a bit behind.

Aside from the broken glass on the floor by the window, nothing was amiss in the living room, and I know Hal felt as I did that the dining room must be entered quickly, without thought.

There was Hal and Caroline's mahogany table, a stack of recently received Christmas cards scattered near the center. There was no tree, no candles, no gifts, no evidence of Christmas at all.

Hal and I quickly explored the rest of the house and found nothing unusual. The place, in fact, felt strangely peaceful—utterly quiet, a faint scent of frankincense and myrrh in the air.

When we returned to the dining room, Caroline was standing by the buffet holding a cheerful rubber ball with a circus train running in a continuous line around the center. Someone, a child perhaps, had tied a red satin ribbon around it. "I found this," said Caroline. "I distinctly remember seeing it last night."

Hal and I looked at each other as Caroline dissolved into tears.

Later that day, Hal returned to bring us a bottle of Christmas wine and to thank us for all we'd done. He had some happy news too—Caroline was pregnant. They had returned home on Christmas Eve because she had been feeling carsick and as Hal put it, "She just wanted to be home."

Many Christmases have passed since then, but the Barriloux have never returned. Hal and Caroline's home is a singularly happy one. Marjorie and I have continued to spend our Christmas Eves by the fire, only leaving the house and our old-fashioneds for the candlelight service at St. Mark's, but Christmas Day we're always at Hal and Caroline's. They and their two children turn every Christmas into a fabulous celebration full of light and more than enough laughter to go around. Slowly fading from year to year under the tree sits a favorite toy. A ball decorated with a circus train that none of us can resist picking up for a peaceful squeeze.

A Color
of Christmas

Kenneth Robbins

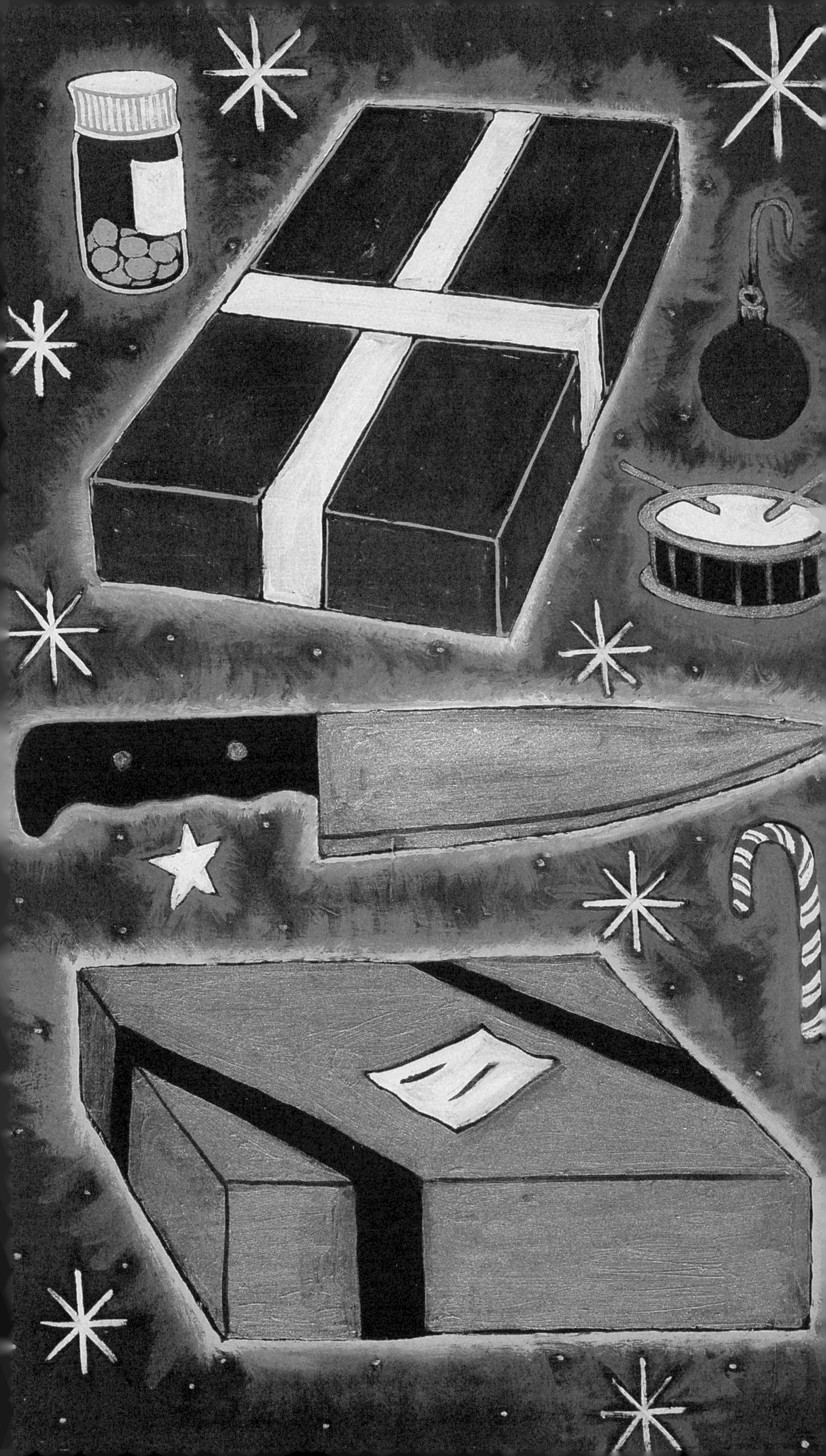

No one believed me when I told them that Mamaw was evil. They acted like it was me, not her. They were blind as bats without radar. Except Daddy. I think near the end, maybe a few days before his heart attack, Daddy understood what I'd been saying for years. Of this one thing I am certain: my daddy and Mamaw will never see one another again. He's up there, right alongside the Lord Himself while she's in the other place. I know; I put her there. And when I'm fried, I'll be there myself.

This is how I know she was evil: I carry her inside me.

I feel polluted. I am polluted. The pollution is going to stop. With me.

I grew up hating Thanksgiving and Christmas. Sometimes Easter. Those "holy" days we spent visiting Mamaw at her house or having her visit us at ours. It was those days that caused me to recognize my polluted condition. That's why I killed her on Christmas morning. It was poetic justice. My way.

Pay attention: this won't take long.

When I was eight, Mother and Daddy dropped me off at Mamaw's while they paid a visit to Papaw who was in the hospital. He was dying of some strange disease; the quack doctors didn't have a clue. He was only sixty-seven. Mamaw took me into her bedroom there in that dank and dark house of hers and sat me on the edge of her bed. It was musty. It made my bottom feel wet. I can still feel the dampness even now and I'm twenty-plus years older. Go figure.

She leaned over me and whispered, "I'm gonna show you something that's gotta be our little secret. Can you keep a secret, Mary Jane?"

"Uh huh," I said. I was eight. What else could I say?

She took a key ring from her purse and unlocked the drawer of the secretary beside her bed. The drawer squealed when she opened it. Like it was in pain. Like her touching it caused it pain. I know the feeling.

Her hand came out of the drawer, slow and silly, like it was the hand of a magician and it held the most special trick in the world. In a way it did. Mamaw was famous for her tricks. I know that now. Back then, I was stupid. I didn't know nothing.

"Guess what I've got here?" she said and asked all at the same time. "Go on, Mary Jane, guess."

"Vitamins?" I said. I'd caught a glimpse of the little bottle. It looked like one of the kinds of bottles my mother used to build her iron. Only the iron she was talking about wasn't the kind of iron I had in mind. Everything is a mystery when you're eight. Evil was a mystery too.

"Something like vitamins, I suppose," Mamaw said, enjoying her little game. "More like the opposite of vitamins."

"Uh huh," I said. I was thinking that maybe Mamaw had different kinds of vitamins, maybe steel ones. Or tin. I was pretty sure they weren't iron: they wouldn't be special then.

"Eventually, this'll get to him."

"Get to who?" I felt confused. My evil gene hadn't quite kicked in back then.

"The poor unsuspecting bastard I like an idiot said 'I do' to. One of these days, sure. They'll send him home. And when they do, I'll just keep popping these little vitamins, as you call them, into his morning coffee and his nightly tonic and pretty soon– bingo."

"Can I see?"

"No, no, sweetheart, these are for your papaw. My Christmas gift to your papaw." She put the bottle back in the secretary and slid the drawer shut, it squeaking with pain all the way, and locked it. She hooked the key on a chain around her neck and stuffed it inside her blouse. "You know why I shared with you this secret?" she asked.

"Uh uh," I said.

"One day you'll know. One day it'll be plain as the nose on my face. That makes you my very special little girl." She took me by the hand and led me from her bedroom, my butt soaking wet. Only when I went to the bathroom and pulled down my panties, they were dry as a bone. But I could still feel it, that wetness, sticking to my butt.

When I was ten, Papaw died. Heart attack, the doctors said. Clogged arteries. Lucky man, they said. He went like that–click.

You still with me? Pay attention.

When I was nine, I watched Mamaw mix a whole pound of hamburger meat around a razor blade. "For Sparkles," she said, that look on her face. Sparkles, a massive black lab with a splotch of white fur under his neck, was the neighbor's dog that hated Mamaw more than anything on the face of the earth. It hung out around Mamaw's mailbox and took after her every time she checked her mail. She'd complained, she told me, time and again, but her neighbors refused to keep Sparkles penned up. "I know how to handle canines," she said with that queer look on her face. I remember Mamaw's neighbors complaining about how Sparkles, their watchdog, had died from some mysterious internal bleeding. It wasn't a mystery to me.

I wish I could understand Mamaw's evil streak. If I could, then maybe I could understand my own. But I guess that's asking too much. We do what we do and the devil take the hindmost. I don't know how many times I heard Mamaw say that. "Let the devil take the hindmost. It's all he deserves."

Christmas when I was eleven, Mamaw asked me to help her fix the potato salad. Mother and Daddy were on the back porch, shucking the corn that Mamaw had bought at the Piggly Wiggly. They were tossing the husks over the porch railing for the raccoons to find. That's what Daddy said, over and over, "Come on, Mr. Coon, come get your supper."

In the kitchen, I chopped onions for the salad. Mamaw peeled the potatoes and put them in boiling water. After a bit, she strained the potatoes and put them in a bowl, mixing in my chopped onion, some chopped walnuts, some dill pickles, and mayonnaise. I noticed that she had set aside a small container of all the ingredients. "What's that for?" I asked.

"Your daddy. Old Max don't care for mayonnaise, so I fix him a separate helping with mustard"–that look was on her face again, the same look as the one I saw when I was eight and again when I was nine and again when I was ten–"and a few other things."

"Like what?"

"Just a touch of vitamins," she said with a chuckle. "Our secret, okay?"

I felt the hairs on the back of my neck stand on end, like the hairs on a dog's back when it gets riled. I loved my daddy more than anything, more than Mamaw, more than myself. Besides, I was eleven. I remembered Mamaw's tricking Papaw into dying of a heart attack. I wasn't about to let the same thing happen to Daddy.

I didn't know what to do. Let my daddy eat his special potato salad? Tell him what Mamaw had done? If I did that, Mamaw would kill me. I was certain of that. She would stop confiding in me and maybe start putting strange things into my food. Or putting vitamins in my Coca-Cola. One thing I knew: Daddy wasn't going to eat his potato salad, not that Christmas meal.

When Mamaw went to the porch to check on the corn husking, I dumped the poisoned potato salad into Mamaw's garbage disposal and turned it on. When she came back in, I was washing the bowl that had held Daddy's specially prepared serving.

"What ja doing?" Mamaw wanted to know.

"I was moving this to the table and it slipped from my hand. Daddy's potato salad went all over the place. I'm sorry, Mamaw, but I got it all cleaned up." I was lying to my mamaw. Yes, I had her in me. I was sinning big time by telling such a lie and I was doing it willfully, which makes it an even greater sin. I didn't care. I wasn't going to let that mean old woman do harm to my daddy.

"You're not being truthful with me," she said.

"Oh, no, ma'am. The bowl slipped and all the potato salad fell to the floor. I'm really sorry, Mamaw. I can make some more if you want."

She glared at me. Maybe that was the first time in her relationship with me that she began to realize that maybe I didn't want to be like her. That maybe, just maybe, I had a say-so in things after all.

I remember once, I guess I was sixteen at the time, when Daddy told Mother that he wasn't going to Mamaw's that year for Christmas dinner. "Every year, Thanksgiving, Christmas, it don't matter, I eat that woman's food and I'm sick as a dog for the next week. Not this year, Marjean. You can go if you want to, but I'm staying home and watching the ball game."

He stayed home every year after that. And I could see it in Mamaw's face, her disappointment. A little bit of Christmas cheer had gone out of Mamaw's life. And she wasn't about to forgive him for the loss, either.

Then that year, that final Christmas. All the shit came flushing down.

I was away at school, my final year in Tiger country. I came home as usual on the twenty-first and didn't go back to Baton Rouge until after the first of the year. I was a know-it-all senior majoring in chemistry and resented the fact that I had to go home for Christmas. A bunch of my friends had packed off to Cancún for the vacation. But me? Mother said I was needed at home. So I went home instead.

By the time I got there, Daddy had already made the biggest mistake of his life. Here, let Mamaw tell it. She told me the whole thing on Christmas morning. I taped it. Listen:

"That Max, your daddy, is truly a foolish man. You believe me, Mary Jane? More foolish than Papaw. More foolish even than your uncle Jamison, God rest his soul. Getting at your daddy was so easy, it weren't even fun. He came to me, you see, with this need of a coat. He wanted to get my daughter Marjean something really special as a Christmas gift this year. He had his mind set on a mink coat. And I said to him, 'Mink coat in the middle of Louisiana? You're stupider than I thought. What you want is a cashmere coat, Max, cashmere. You can wear cashmere in Louisiana four months out of twelve. But mink? You'll have to take Marjean to Chicago to get any wear out of that? It was so easy. Too easy. He asked me if I would help him pick something out, something I knew would make your mama feel like a million dollars. I said sure, I'd help. Sure I helped. It embarrasses me how easy it was."

She's the one belongs in Angola, not me. Now that would have been poetic justice.

We open our gifts on Christmas Eve. A family tradition. It usually just included me, Mother, Daddy, and my two pissant brothers. Hate those guys, but that's not what this confession is about.

Well, that year, Christmas Eve, Mamaw shows up for dinner. She didn't call ahead, she let nobody know. She was suddenly there, and she had that look on her face, the one I had seen much too often growing up. It meant trouble and none of us could determine what kind it was or from what direction it was to come.

All week long, Mother had puzzled over the large beautifully wrapped present to her from Daddy. It sat under the Christmas tree, taunting her. She had guessed such things as a new business suit, or a new Sunday dress, or perhaps the fancy pants suit, mix and match, she had admired in Lewis's window. With each guess throughout the week, Daddy's eyes got brighter. She, Mother, didn't have a clue, and that suited him just fine. His gift was the Christmas gift of a lifetime, the kind of gift that you give only once, it's that special.

Opening gifts at our house was a ritual. Milton, my youngest and stupidest brother, was Santa, passing gifts right and left while Mother insisted that we watch and express our awe as each present was unwrapped and admired. Each member of the family had to open a gift before the opening passed to the next, and so on until all gifts had been distributed.

Milton put the large tantalizing gift to Mother from Daddy beside her on the sofa. It was Mamaw, the only person in the family not to receive any gifts—we hadn't known she was going to be there!–who said, "Wait on that one, Marjean. I suspect it's pretty darn special." And Daddy had confirmed it, saying, "Yeah, sweetheart, let's save that one a little longer."

Finally all gifts had been enjoyed except the mystery one. Mother said, "I can't wait any longer. Here goes."

As she started to untie the ribbon, Mamaw squealed, "Wait a minute. I near forgot the present I got for you, Marjean. I want you to open it first. Milton, scoot out to my car and bring it in. It's setting on the passenger's side seat."

Daddy's face turned white. He excused himself to the kitchen where he got a beer. Marjean fussed with the package sitting on her lap, the little girl in her wanting to rip the fancy paper away and see just what her husband had gotten her this Christmas. Me? I didn't move a muscle. That look, the look of evil, was all over Mamaw's face. And I could feel my hatred for her growing beyond all bounds.

Milton came back in, a package the same shape with the same paper and the same ribbon as the one already in my mother's possession.

Mamaw took the package and held it out to Mother, saying, "You're gonna open my gift to you first, Marjean. I'm your mother. It's fitting you open my present first."

Mother did. She was so naive. She had lived with her mother much longer than me, but still, after all that time, she didn't see it, that evil glint in Mamaw's eyes. She ripped the paper away, snapped the tape that held the sides of the box together, and pulled from inside the most beautiful full-length cashmere coat I had ever seen. It glistened in the light from the Christmas tree. It had the smell of expensive all through it. Mother's eyes almost bulged from their sockets. She looked from the coat to Mamaw, back to the coat, to Daddy who had turned his back on the scene, back to Mamaw, and said, "Mother, this is–this is–incredible! I am–oh!"

She threw her arms around Mamaw's neck, hugging her with all the love a daughter can experience. I know the feeling. It's the same feeling I hold for my daddy. And as this display of unfettered joy continued with Mother putting on the coat and parading for all of us to admire, my daddy's shoulders sagged, his eyes filling with water–not tears, my daddy didn't cry! He plopped into his recliner chair, exhausted, defeated. I wanted to run to him, throw my arms around him like Mother had done Mamaw, and rip the packaging from my soul to show him just how much I loved him. But I didn't. I couldn't. Mother was all over him instead, sitting in his lap, forcing him to feel the amazing cashmere coat, kissing him as if he had done something special. To her, he had: "You told Mother how much I longed for a special coat, didn't you, sweetheart. Oh, I love you so much."

"You still got another present to open, Marjean," Mamaw said, holding out the mysterious package from Daddy.

He was out of his chair immediately, reaching for the package. "No, it's not appropriate, not now," he said.

"Oh, yes it is, Max," Mamaw insisted. "This is your special present to your charming wife. You want her to have it, surely. You want to open Max's present, don't you, Marjean?"

"Of course I do."

"No, hon, please, don't." Daddy was begging. I had never seen him beg before. It sliced me open to see him do that, especially in front of Mamaw, the one person to whom you should show no weakness.

Still wearing the cashmere coat, Mother sat on the sofa, Daddy's present on her lap. She tried to catch his eye. She wanted to flirt with him in her special way. But he wouldn't allow it. He stared instead at the winged angel on top of the Christmas tree.

The fancy ribbons, the beautiful paper, the sealed box slid to the floor as Mother, confusion, anger, disappointment, and bafflement coursing through her all at the same time, sat on the sofa with a second cashmere coat in her arms, a coat identical to the one she was already wearing.

"Max?" she said. "I don't understand."

"We'll take it back first thing Monday morning and get a refund," he said, his voice that of a defeated, deflated clown.

"No, we will not. I love it."

"Of course you do, honey," Mamaw said. "I'm so sorry, Max," she said to Daddy's back. "I must have misunderstood. I thought . . ."

Mother had slipped out of Mamaw's gift and was trying on the coat from Daddy. It was several sizes too small.

"Oh, now, would you look at that? For heaven's sake, Max," Mamaw said. Only Daddy wasn't there. He had gone to the bathroom. I heard the lock slipping into place.

"Mother, how could you!" my mother said, the horror of the situation finally finding its way into her trusting, naive brain.

"How could I what, Marjean? For heaven's sake, it was a mistake. Anybody can make a mistake."

For some reason, I couldn't keep quiet. I said, "I told you, Mother. How many times have I told you? Maybe now you'll listen."

"Told me what?" Mother asked.

"That Mamaw is evil."

Her disappointment, confusion, and anger found its target in me. Her eyes flashed hatred at me as she hissed, "I didn't send you to college to become a smart aleck. Go to your room!"

"It's true, Mother!"

"Another word and I'll send you from this house!"

I was ready to leave that house, leave and not return, but I had no place else to go and no way to get there. Instead, I charged into my bedroom, and like my daddy, locked myself in. And I prayed that night for Mamaw's death. I prayed so hard the inside of my eyeballs hurt.

Christmas morning, I woke early. I hadn't slept well at all. That shouldn't be much of a shock, seeing how we had spent our Christmas Eve. Daddy was out of the bathroom. I don't know where he was. I didn't know where anybody was. Except Mamaw.

Apparently she had spent the night on the sofa. There was a pile of sheets and blankets on the couch. On the floor were the two coat boxes, each holding the coat from the night before.

Mamaw was in the kitchen. I could hear her, singing "Bless Be the Tie That Binds," and fixing herself a cheese omelet.

"Well, look who's first out of bed this beautiful morning," she said. "You must be starved. Would you like some of this omelet?"

I did not speak. She had been slicing cheese for the eggs. The knife lay beside the chunk. I seized it by its blade, felt the edge nick the inside of my palm. I shifted the knife in my hand, getting a grip on the handle, as the thought "It's Christmas morning" ran through my head.

"That sofa of your'n is the most uncomfortablest piece of furniture I've ever experienced. I tell you, Max should spend a little of his money and buy you people something with more cushion. Next year's Christmas gift, maybe." She was laughing. "I'll even help him pick it out."

"My daddy don't need your help."

"Of course he does, sweetie," Mamaw said. "Why, that fool man can't even buy his charming wife a decent Christmas gift." That's when she told me what had happened. I switched on the tape recorder in my head, the one I had inherited from her, Mamaw's original Christmas gift to me, I suppose. I had learned in the first grade that I had this gift of perfect memory; all I had to do was click it on. Click. She told me all.

I repeated myself: "My daddy don't need your help!"

"Max? Shoot, honey, he's the stupidest dumb fool God ever–"

That's when I gave Mamaw her Christmas gift: a knife slipped in between the fourth and fifth ribs on the left side. Simple and effective and messy. And red, like a color of Christmas.

FROM

Children
of Strangers

Lyle Saxon

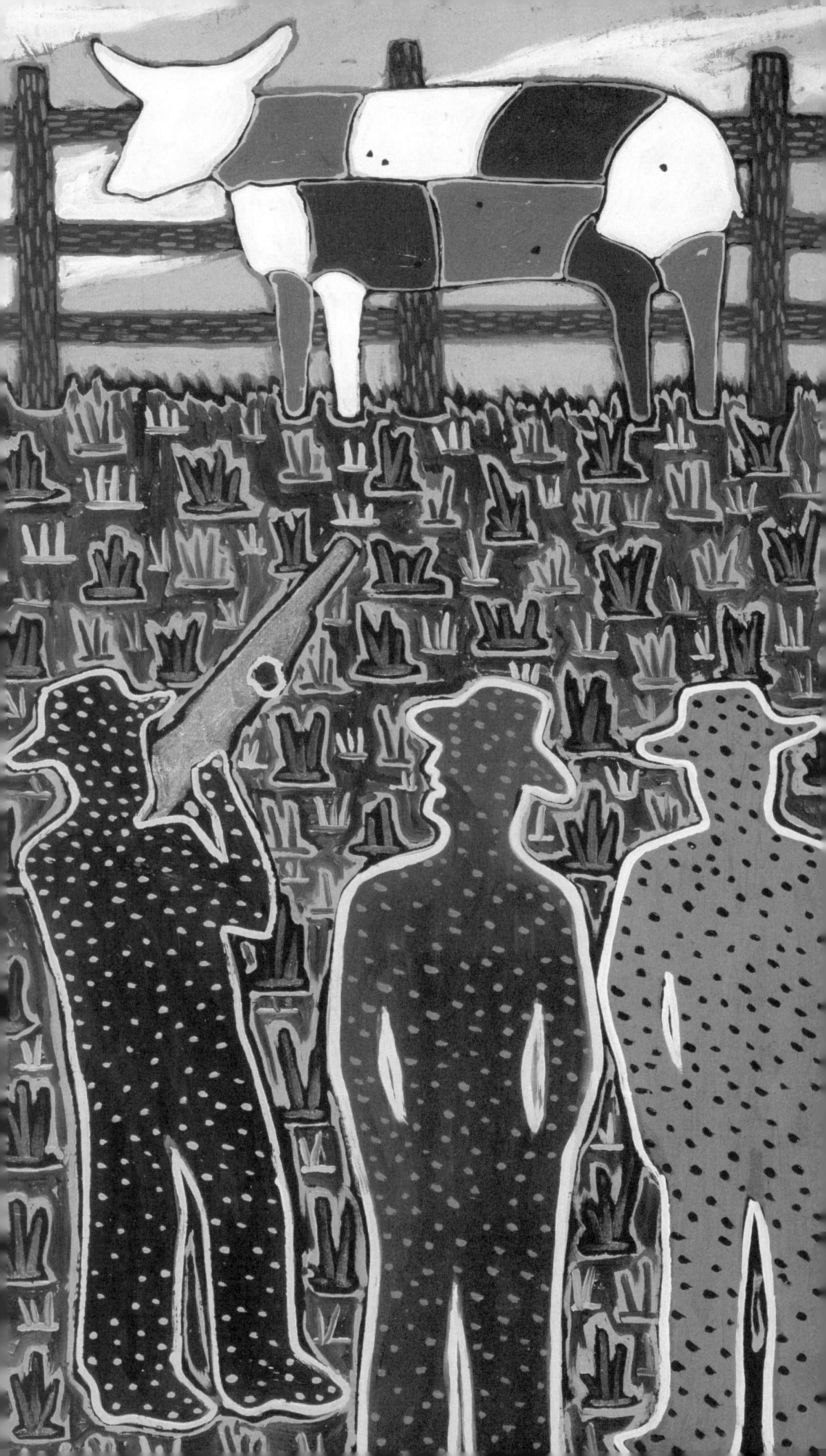

Chapter XI

The sounds of summer flowed by on the tranquil air. There were distant cries from the cotton gin, and the reverberation of heavy machinery; the whistle sounded, sharp and clear, then a change in the engine's hum as the cotton bale was compressed. Another bale was begun and the engine resumed its even vibration.

In the lanes the cotton wagons waited their turn at the gin, and white fragments of cotton bordered the dusty road where the wagons had passed . . . August.

Then warm September rain dripped from the eaves and yellow flowers bloomed along the ditches; the first yellow leaves appeared on the China trees, the first breath of autumn came with the early mornings; there was a feeling of death and decay in the midst of the lingering heat.

The pecans hung in their green husks on the trees, gathering oily nutriment, hanging there, waiting for the first frosts to detach them and let them fall upon the sodden soil, for now, after the long dry days of July and August, September's soothing rain fell into the parched furrows, going deep into the waiting soil.

Famie stood in the doorway, supporting her swollen body against the door-frame. She felt the child stir.

Numa had been gone for more than five months. She thought of him now, as she looked into the empty field where water stood between the cotton rows.

There had been so little she could say to him as he stood in the sunlight telling her good-bye. She remembered it all so well: his threadbare coat, his haunted eyes. One word from her, she knew, would keep him there, but she could not say that word. Now she almost wished that she had spoken, for today she felt friendless and desolate indeed.

Yet she was glad that Numa could not see her, for she felt that she was ugly and awkward: she did not want anyone to see her. Her grandmother, fortunately, concurred in this. She agreed that Famie should keep her secret as long as possible. It was, said Odalie, a bad business, but it was Famie's own affair.

What the old woman knew Famie could not guess, but Odalie and her sister, Madame Aubert Rocque, had discussed the matter many times. Everything was arranged for the child's birth, and Lizzie Balize, the negro midwife, had been engaged for mid-December.

Summer had passed like a fevered dream, and little by little Famie became reconciled to her lover's death. At first she would wake, crying out in the night; but now she slept dreamlessly as she used to do. Small things occupied her days, and she helped Odalie with the ironing as she had always done. There was a difference, though, for now Famie examined each article belonging to Mrs. Randolph's baby with intent eyes. Her child should have clothes like these, she decided; her child should have such clothes as white children wear.

Buying the cloth to make the clothes was another matter, for there was no money. Bizette had no luck with his cotton this year, and after his yearly account was settled at Mr. Guy's commissary there was little left. A few necessary articles were purchased, but nothing else. Old Odalie was firm in her decision that every penny must be saved. "I've known a woman to die fo' lack of five dolla's," she said, and Famie knew that it was true enough.

The girl's dark eyes clouded as she thought. Lizzie Balize was a good nurse, but suppose . . . ? There was not enough money, Famie knew, to get a doctor.

The girl sighed and turned away from the door. From the *armoire* she took a work basket and brought it to the table. There was a small blanket which she had cut from a large one, avoiding the worn-out places; it was soft from many washings, and the girl had hemmed it with pink worsted. There were some simple clothes, too, made from cotton and trimmed with lace ripped from an old dress. The things were poor enough, as she thought of the fine linen which she washed and ironed each week for Mr. Guy's wife; but even these simple garments would suffice. Later on, maybe, she could do better. Perhaps Miss Adelaide would give her something for the baby, but the girl knew that she must wait; she was ashamed for the white woman to see her now.

One day was like another: there was always the quiet river, and the brown fields stretching away. The bare cotton stalks had been plowed under and the fields lay waiting for another spring. The trees were losing their leaves, and she could see houses now that were invisible in the summer time; through the clear autumn air she watched the blue smoke rise from the chimneys at morning and evening, and she knew that women were crouching before the hearths cooking for their men.

In December the evening sky was red along the horizon and the blue mists hung in the trees and softened the sharp outline of the white church across the river; the church and the bare trees and the red sky reflected themselves in the water and made her think of a Christmas card that Sister Desiree had shown her long ago.

Famie was thinking of that picture as she crouched before the fireplace early in the morning of the day before Christmas. The coffee was dripping and the pleasant aroma filled the room. Suddenly she paused with her hand pressed against her body. She was afraid. Her sharp cry aroused Odalie and the old woman came in, tripping over her long flannel nightgown.

The coffee was forgotten as Famie was put back into the bed she had left only a few moments ago; she was surprised to feel that the covers were still warm from her body. It was not long before the pain stopped, but her breath came fast and her eyes were wide as she lay waiting for the agony to come back again.

Odalie finished dripping the coffee, dressed herself, and sent Bizette hobbling through the furrows to fetch Madame Aubert Rocque and the negro midwife, Lizzie Balize.

Chapter XII

It was twilight on Christmas Eve when Numa rode down the muddy lane toward the yellow lamplight which shone from the window of his mother's house. There was the smell of wood smoke and sizzling bacon in the frosty air. His old white horse whinnied as Numa opened the gate, and from the barn came an answering nicker from the roan mare. The boy felt his breath quicken at the familiar sight and sound and smell of home.

His mother–how old she seemed!–cried out in glad surprise when he opened the door. He held her in his arms and realized how cruel he had been to leave her alone so long; but he could not speak of it, and instead he pretended interest in the white cat which lay purring beside the fire, four spotted kittens nursing at her breast. The yellow puppy had grown into a large dog, and he came sniffing at Numa's trousers, only half recognizing him, wagging his curly tail doubtfully as though not quite sure whether he would be patted or kicked. Numa took the dog's head between his hands and looked into the animal's pale blue eyes.

He smiled at his mother. "He sho' grew up to be a nigger dog."

The old woman laughed. "He's good though," she said. "He was plenty company fo' me while yo' was gone."

At supper they were very polite to each other, talking with constraint as though they were strangers, asking each other questions, answering nicely. Numa told her how long the ride seemed: it had taken him three full days, the roads were so muddy, and the distance so great. He had only been able to make about thirty miles a day. But he had brought a present with him. Tomorrow he would give it to her.

The talk of Christmas worried his mother; she apologized that she had made no preparations for his return. How could she?

She had not known that he was coming. But there was a fine piece of pork in the smokehouse, and she would bake a cake for him.

Supper was scarcely over when there came a call from outside and old Madame Lacour cried out in astonishment. How could she have forgotten! She had promised to go to midnight Mass with her brother and his wife. They were going early in a wagon, and they had come for her. They expected to make a round of visits on the way, stopping at the homes of friends, gathering their kinfolks until the wagon was full, and then going over on the flatboat to the midnight services. In the excitement of Numa's arrival she had forgotten all about it; she was not dressed. Never mind, she would go tell them she could not go.

But Numa interrupted her. Surely she must go; he was too tired to take her; he wanted to go at once to bed. He went outside to tell his uncle and aunt to wait while his mother dressed.

They were pleased to see him, crying out in high voices. He climbed up into the wagon. They kissed him on both cheeks, and said how glad they were that he had come home. Old Amedee Lacour liked Numa and thought it a shame that he had left his mother alone for so long a time. His wife, looking like a shapeless bundle under her coat and knitted shawl, said shrilly that the girls at the last *fais-do-do* had asked her why Numa had run away. It was high time that he came home again. He should join them that night, fatigue or no fatigue, for there would be many pretty girls at Mass. Aie-yie!

She cackled with laughter.

Before long Numa's mother emerged, bundled up in coat and shawl, and Numa helped her climb over the wheel and into one of the chairs which stood in the wagon bed; she carried a blanket because she was sure that she would be cold crossing the river. Finally everything was arranged, and the boy watched the wagon go creaking down the lane and splashing through the puddles.

As he re-entered the house the old clock whirred and struck eight. Numa started guiltily. Through its glass door he could see the bottom of the clock-case, and he saw that the greasy dust lay undisturbed as he had left it.

"Nobody knows," he said aloud.

But even as he spoke there came a quick rapping behind him, and the boy turned sharply toward the uncurtained window. But it was only the yellow cur, who at the sound of Numa's voice was beating his tail on the floor.

Numa's boots sloshed through the puddles.

He told his mother that he was too tired to accompany her, and yet, the minute her back was turned, he put on his heavy boots and went out. He smiled in the darkness as he hurried.

Despite all his resolutions, he felt that he must see Famie at once. He had a present for her, and now he carried it carefully in his hand. In a store window in Opelousas he had seen it, and he had bought it for her, spending nearly his last dime in order to buy it. The thing that he carried so carefully was a small bisque statue of a bride and groom such as are sometimes used on wedding cakes. He knew that she would smile when she saw it. Perhaps she would be ready to marry him now. It seemed years since he had seen her, and no letters had passed between them.

As he left the lane and entered the path between the furrows which led to old Bizette's house, he felt so lighthearted that he could have laughed aloud. He pictured the family gathered at the hearth, and he thought of Famie's surprise when he entered with his Christmas present in his hand. As he opened the gate from the lane he heard negroes shouting in the fields and the sound of popping firecrackers from the direction of the commissary. The folks at Yucca, white and black, always set off fireworks at Christmas time.

But as he approached the house he saw at once that something was wrong. There were two horses tied to the posts of the porch, and a man sat huddled on the steps. Inside the house there were running steps, and the windows were bright behind tightly closed curtains.

And as he approached he heard a woman scream. It was

unlike anything he had ever heard before, a thin, long-drawn-out shriek of agony. The man on the steps raised his head as Numa came close; it was Bull Balize, the black son of Lizzie the nurse.

"Dey tole me not to let nobody in, not *nobody*," the negro said. "She's havin' a ha'd time."

And then, in response to Numa's quick questions, Bull told him that Famie Vidal had been in agony all day. Old Bizette sent for Lizzie Balize shortly after sun-up, and Lizzie had come at once. But something was wrong. Lizzie had tried every remedy she knew, even to putting an axe under the bed to cut the pain, and the old women had assisted her. But Famie still screamed. It made Bull sickish just to listen to it, he said.

Still uncomprehending, Numa asked: "What's the matter with her?"

"Ah don' know what a-matter wid 'er, cep'n she's havin' a mighty ha'd time havin' dat baby," the negro said.

Numa felt as though someone had slapped him across the mouth. The small figure of the bride and groom slipped from their wrappings of tissue paper and lay in the mud beside his boot.

Madame Aubert Rocque and Odalie said that Numa saved Famie's life. They thought the girl would surely die, and even black Lizzie was scared, yes! although she would not admit it. When things were at their worst, Numa had brought the doctor.

That Numa! When he heard that Famie was sick he had ridden ten miles to Cloutierville and had shown the white doctor a twenty-dollar bill. That brought him, yes, sir! The boy and the white man had driven over the dark, muddy, and dangerous roads and they arrived together at sun-up on Christmas morning. Famie was exhausted, but the doctor knew things which were beyond the skill of the midwife. The baby was born and the girl was sleeping within an hour after his arrival. It was all over . . . Numa brought a quart of fine whiskey, too, and the old women cried "Noel!" as the white man drank before leaving.

The old women talked to each other, to Numa, to Lizzie, to anyone who would listen. They said the same things over and over, adding details, laughing in relief, as they sat sipping hot toddies beside the hearth. There is a time when whiskey is good, yes, when women are tired . . . That Numa! He thought of everything. At last they went to sleep, each in her chair beside the fire. In the four-post bed Famie slept too, worn out with agony, and the child slept beside her.

Lizzie busied herself setting the house to rights, looking scornfully around her. Humph! These mulattoes were as uppity as white people, making all this fuss about a baby. And that Numa was a plum fool, bringing that doctor there and acting as though Lizzie did not know her business. Well, he wouldn't be so pleased when he saw the baby, for the child was surely not his.

"Yessuh," she said aloud, "ef'n dat chile's paw ain't a white man, my name ain't Lizzie Balize."

Chapter XIII

Christmas was gay at Yucca Plantation that year. Early in the morning Mr. Guy opened a keg of whiskey on the gallery before the commissary and gave liquor to all the negro men on the place. It was an old custom held over from slave times: his father and his grandfather had done so before him. By eight o'clock many of the negroes were reeling and rocking as they went home through the muddy cotton rows, and some of them had fallen into fence corners and lay snoring until they were hauled home by their staggering friends or by their women.

Those who imbibed more moderately tried shooting at the *papegai*–another Christmas custom.

A cow had been butchered and divided into the usual cuts, and the beef lay arranged in order on a large wooden table. The beef was all given away to the tenants and laborers; the choice cuts were prizes for marksmanship.

The *papegai* was a crude wooden cow cut from boards and

was painted red and yellow; this effigy was placed high on a pole, and the negro men took turns shooting at it with a rifle from a line forty yards away. The oldest had first shot; the younger men waited, and the boys came last of all. The men aimed at the part of the animal which they considered the best cut and which they desired most for food. They stood in line and awaited their turns, whooping applause for those whose aim was accurate, and jeering at the unsuccessful marksmen.

"Look at Papa Chawlie. He goin' tuh bust dat rump-roast!"

"Betcha he ain't!"

"Whoo-oo!"

Ping! The rifle sounded sharp on the frosty air, and there was a shout as the old man's bullet struck the *papegai* on the head instead of the tail.

"De ole man's got tuh eat brains!"

"Maybe he wants de tongue!"

Whiskey had done its work, and some of the men missed the target altogether. But in time each one hit some part of the effigy and the beef was distributed accordingly.

"There's one thing to be said for a cow," said Mr. Guy, laughing as two men disputed a coveted portion. "There are two pieces of nearly everything."

Negro women, wearing blue or red dresses and checkered head-handkerchiefs, cheered for their men, and children screamed with excitement as they set off firecrackers: for fireworks—so prized by all children—were a part of the celebration at Yucca. Each child received a pack of firecrackers, and this year each one got two Roman candles to boot. The latter were saved for night.

The negroes were merry in the muddy road beside the river: dogs barked, and horses tied to the fences reared and showed the whites of their eyes when firecrackers exploded near them. The rifle and firecrackers popped almost continuously, and the smell of gunpowder hung in the air.

At last it was over, and the men and women went homeward, the children trailing after them, and the curs following behind.

The red and blue and yellow clothes were vivid against brown earth and dark trees.

Mr. Guy, watching them from the gallery of the commissary, saw smoke begin to rise from the chimneys of the nearer cabins, and he knew that Christmas dinners were in preparation.

All this was a party for the negroes: the mulattoes took no part in it. There were many mulatto men and boys in the crowd, spectators who had come to see the fun. The old men, wearing wide black felt hats above their clear-cut faces, stood together recalling the time when *Grandpere* Augustin had similar parties for his slaves in the days before the Civil War.

When the negroes had all gone, Mr. Guy invited five of the old mulatto men inside the commissary and took them back into his office. There, beside the stove, he opened a bottle of whiskey, and filled six small glasses. It was a yearly custom. Mr. Guy recognized the difference between negroes and mulattoes; it was this little social distinction that made the mulattoes like him. Not one of them would have drunk with the negroes, nor did they expect or even desire Mr. Guy to drink publicly with any mulatto; but this little private ceremony on Christmas was a custom of long duration. It established something. Mr. Guy was a gentleman and understood things.

The clerk, who was not invited to drink, stood by eyeing the group critically. He disapproved of the whole business, and he thought that Mr. Guy spoiled the mulattoes: Just a damned race of bastards, he said to himself. It irritated him, too, that Mr. Guy felt himself so superior that he could afford to drink with a race other than his own. Back in the hills where *he* came from such things were unheard of. Men had been tarred and feathered for such carryings on. At that moment he hated Mr. Guy and his superior ways, and he hated Miss Adelaide, who never invited him into the parlor when company came. He was just a servant, like the niggers, in spite of the fact that he ate at the table with the white people.

He couldn't understand these distinctions. There were really four classes on Cane River: Mr. Guy and his kind, and then his, the clerk's kind—he knew that Miss Adelaide considered him "trash"—then there were the mulattoes who looked down upon the black people, and last, at the bottom of the heap, were the negroes themselves . . . And the negroes didn't seem to give a single damn!

"They're all damned niggers to me," he said to himself.

But as he stood watching the old men drinking with Mr. Guy, an unwelcome thought came to him: Nita looked white, but she was a nigger too. Well, what difference did it make? All women, white, yellow, or brown, were for man's pleasure. Men had to take what they could get.

Yet some of his friends, back in the hills, would call him a "nigger-lover" if they knew. The clerk felt his face flush at the thought, but he brushed the idea aside: "Jus' let 'em try it, that's all," he thought. "Besides nobody knows nothin' about it, and they won't neither."

The old men finished drinking, and put on their hats again. Then they all shook hands with Mr. Guy and wished him luck for the new year.

"Good-bye, Mister Guy."

"Good-bye, Henri."

"Good luck, Mister Ran'off."

"Good luck, Ulysse."

"Good-bye, Mister Guy."

"So long, Telesmon."

"Au revoir, Monsieur Guy."

"Au revoir, Narcisse."

"Happy New Year, Mister Guy."

"The same to you, Bizette."

Chapter XIV

Numa slept nearly all day.

His mother had prepared a dinner which she knew he liked:

pork roast, sweet potatoes, and collards, and she had baked a cake; but when she looked into his darkened room and saw him lying in the deep sleep of exhaustion, she sighed and went away without waking him. Hey law! All her preparations were for nothing. Nevertheless, Numa was a good boy, and she was so glad he had come back to her that nothing else mattered. So she put the meat and vegetables on the back of the stove to keep them warm, and set the cake away in the cupboard. She would wait and eat with him when he woke up.

In the afternoon she busied herself with the usual outdoor tasks: she fed the horses and the chickens, and milked the cow. The white cat came out of the house into the slanting sunshine and rubbed against the old woman's skirts. She poured milk into a blue bowl and talked to the cat as the animal satisfied its hunger. They were together so much that she almost believed that the cat understood what she said, and like so many lonely people, she frequently spoke aloud, addressing animals or even inanimate objects.

"*Minou*, Ah sho' ought to get rid o' yo'," she said. "Eve'body knows a white cat brings bad luck. Jus' havin' yo' in the house makes me a po' woman. Some of these days, Ah'm goin' to run yo' off and get me a yellow *minou*. That'll bring gold to me sho'. Yes, ma'am, Ah'm goin' to run yo' off from heah!"

She petted the animal as she spoke and her voice was caressing. The white cat arched her back and purred.

Numa stirred from sleep and stretched his tired body. He was stiff and sore. The ride through the night had been nearly too much for him, tired as he was from the long trip home. His head was hot and his hands were cold, and he felt as ill in mind as he did in body. Nevertheless he threw back the covers, rose, and went to the fireplace. The embers still smoldered, so he added some light wood and a handful of dried moss and the fire flickered up.

His mud-splattered clothes hung on a chair, and he picked up his trousers and felt in the pockets: there was a roll of bills, and he spread them out and counted them. Last night when he ran home and pried the false bottom from the clock-case, the money had been as he left it, but now forty dollars was gone. Twenty for the doctor and two for the whiskey, and eighteen in his pocket. Fortunately in the excitement, nobody had questioned him as to his possession of so much money; they had taken it for granted that he had earned it in his absence. Well, he would keep the eighteen dollars and use it as he pleased. But the rest of the reward must remain hidden, for if he spent it people would surely guess his secret. He pressed the false bottom back into place, hiding the money from sight. Two hundred and sixty dollars remained there.

As he put the eighteen dollars back into his pocket, his exploring hand brought out the small bisque figures of the bride and groom. They were smudged with mud, but were otherwise uninjured. The boy's mouth twisted as he looked at them. But a moment later he had poured water into the bowl on the washstand and was cleaning the ornaments carefully. Well, why not? What did it matter?

How quiet the house was. His mother must be outdoors. The small bride and groom made him smile. He would go tonight and give them to Famie, just as he had intended to do.

When he finished washing and dressing himself, he went to the window and pushed open the shutters. His mother sat on a block of wood not far away; she was stroking the white cat as it lapped milk from a blue dish. At the sound of the creaking shutter she rose and re-entered the house.

"Son?" she called.

Numa went into the kitchen and kissed her. She asked no questions as to his absence overnight, but smiled as she began to set the dinner on the table. Numa was grateful to her. Everything was going to be all right.

When they had finished and were sitting with the coffee-cups beside the fire, he gave her the present which he had brought home from Opelousas: enough cotton material for a dress. She fingered the cloth and said how pleased she was; it was exactly what she wanted, and unlike the cloth in the commissary at Yucca. Her pleasure was so genuine that he felt a warm glow of affection for her.

"An' that ain't all," he said.

She looked at him expectantly: "What yo' mean, son?"

He reached into his pocket and brought out the small roll of bills and counted out ten dollars: "Look," he said, and put the money into her hand.

Numa saw his mother's face change as she sat with the money lying on her lap. For a moment he was afraid that she was going to ask a question, but she did not. At last she said:

"Yo're good to me, Numa, and Ah thank yo' fo' it, but yo' need it yo'self. Ah'm ole, an' Ah've got eve'thing Ah need. Yo' keep it, son, and buy yo'self a suit o' clothes. Yo' lookin' plum ragged."

"Ah'll make out all right," Numa said. "Ah don' wan' no new suit now. Soon it'll be spring, and Ah'll be plowin'."

A bar of late sunlight shone through the window into the ashes of the fireplace and dimmed the pale flames which burned along the lower side of the smoldering logs. The sunlight fell upon the yellow cur sleeping between them on the hearth, and the dog whined in his sleep and his four paws quivered as through he were running.

"He's chasin' dream rabbits," the old woman said.

The boy sat thinking, wondering. Why was it so hard to speak? Why are the simplest things the hardest to say? His mother was trying to say something to him and he dreaded to hear it, yet he did not for a moment doubt her loyalty and affection. What did she know? What did she guess? He looked at her, but she sat gazing into the fire as though fascinated by the sunlight upon flame and ashes.

At last she spoke and as her meaning became clear to him, he started with surprise.

"Numa, yo' is a man now, an' yo' ought to be thinkin' 'bout gettin' married. It ain't natu'al fo' a man to stay by himse'f."

She saw the haunted look in his eyes, and put out her hand to him. "Ah know all 'bout it, son," she said.

He felt the blood rushing to his face, but he forced himself to say: "Know about what?"

"About yo an' Famie Vidal."

"But Famie . . ." He could not go on, but sat staring at his mother. Her eyes were wet and two tears ran down her cheeks; she made no effort to wipe them away.

"Odalie tol' me right after yo' went away."

"Odalie tol' . . . ?"

No, she could not go on talking that way. She could not say the words. She tried in another way to tell him.

"Numa, son . . . Ah know Famie is fo' yo' . . . Ah mean, Ah know there ain't no other woman that yo' cares about. Odalie knows it too. Odalie and Madame Aubert an' me, we talk plenty about it." A pause, and then: "Ah talk with Odalie this mornin'."

Numa's hands were clenched as he waited for her to go on. He could not meet her eyes.

"It ain't Famie's fault, son, not all of it. Famie's good. She ain't a bad one like Nita. Ah've watch' Famie growin' up . . ."

No, that was not right either. The old woman tried another way.

"It ain't the firs' time somethin' like that happened on Cane River, an' it won' be the las'."

That was all, she could say no more.

Famie lay in the big four-post bed, her dark hair spread out on the high-piled pillows, the child nursing at her breast. A red card, stuck against the lamp chimney, reflected a rosy glow upon her. In the soft light her skin was gold colored, and her eyes were large and black. To Numa, who sat in a chair beside the bed, she had never been so beautiful. Odalie had gone into the other room, leaving them together.

It was New Year's Eve, and they could hear the far-away shouts of negroes in the fields, but in the room it was quiet. The fire flickered on the hearth and the kettle on its trivet sent forth a thin plume of steam. Everything seemed warm and safe.

Beyond greeting each other they had said nothing, although she had turned back the covers so that he could see the baby, a strong, healthy boy with blue eyes. His hair was like fine down, but there was no mistaking its color; it was red.

But, someway, Numa did not care any longer about the red-haired man. He was gone and Famie was his own again. Although no words had passed between them tonight, he knew that she had turned toward him; she had taken him back.

From his pocket, he took the toy figures of the bride and groom and placed them upon the sheet. She touched them with a fingertip and smiled.

"Fo' me?" she asked. He nodded.

She understood what he meant, and put her fingers upon his lips.

A week after Easter Famie and Numa were married . . .

A
Christmas Story

Katherine Anne Porter

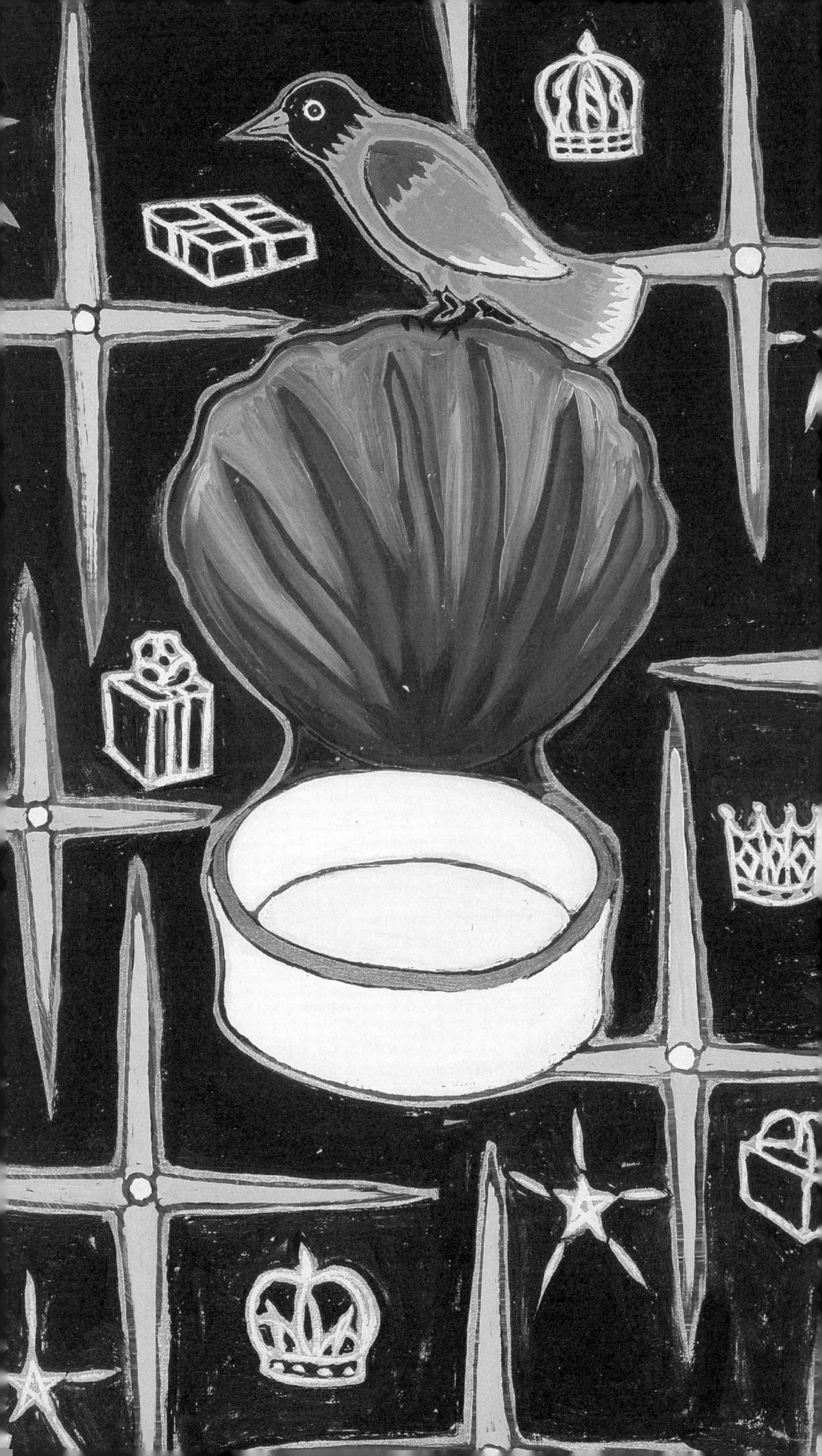

When she was five years old, my niece asked me why we celebrated Christmas. She had asked when she was three and when she was four, and each time had listened with a shining, believing face, learning the songs and gazing enchanted at the pictures which I displayed as proof of my stories. Nothing could have been more successful, so I began once more confidently to recite in effect the following:

The feast in the beginning was meant to celebrate with joy the birth of a Child, an event of such importance to this world that angels sang from the skies in human language to announce it and even, if we may believe the old painters, came down with garlands in their hands and danced on the broken roof of the cattle shed where He was born.

"Poor baby," she said, disregarding the angels, "didn't His papa and mama have a house?"

They weren't quite so poor as all that, I went on, slightly dashed, for last year the angels had been the center of interest. His papa and mama were able to pay taxes at least, but they had to leave home and go to Bethlehem to pay them, and they could have afforded a room at the inn, but the town was crowded because everybody came to pay taxes at the same time. They were quite lucky to find a manger full of clean straw to sleep in. When the baby was born, a good-hearted servant girl named Bertha came to help the mother. Bertha had no arms, but in that moment she unexpectedly grew a fine new pair of arms and hands, and the first thing she did with them was to wrap the baby in swaddling clothes. We then sang together the song about Bertha the armless servant. Thinking I saw a practical question dawning in a pure gray eye, I hurried on to the part about how all the animals—cows, calves, donkeys, sheep—

"And pigs?"

Pigs perhaps even had knelt in a ring around the baby and breathed upon Him to keep Him warm through His first hours in this world. A new star appeared and moved in a straight course toward Bethlehem for many nights to guide three kings who came from far countries to place important gifts in the straw beside Him: gold, frankincense and myrrh.

"What beautiful clothes," said the little girl, looking at the picture of Charles the Seventh of France kneeling before a meek blonde girl and a charming baby.

It was the way some people used to dress. The Child's mother, Mary, and His father, Joseph, a carpenter, were such unworthy simple souls they never once thought of taking any honor to themselves nor of turning the gifts to their own benefit.

"What became of the gifts?" asked the little girl.

Nobody knows, nobody seems to have paid much attention to them, they were never heard of again after that night. So far as we know, those were the only presents anyone ever gave to the Child while He lived. But He was not unhappy. Once He caused a cherry tree in full fruit to bend down one of its branches so His mother could more easily pick cherries. We then sang about the cherry tree until we came to the words *Then up spake old Joseph, so rude and unkind.*

"Why was he unkind?"

I thought perhaps he was just in a cross mood.

"What was he cross about?"

Dear me, what should I say now? After all, this was not my daughter, whatever would her mother answer to this? I asked her in turn what she was cross about when she was cross. She couldn't remember ever having been cross but was willing to let the subject pass. We moved on to "The Withy Tree," which tells how the Child once cast a bridge of sunbeams over a stream and crossed upon it, and played a trick on little John the Baptist, who followed Him, by removing the beams and letting John fall in the water. The Child's mother switched Him smartly for this with a branch of withy, and the Child shed loud tears and wished bad luck upon the whole race of withies for ever.

"What's a withy?" asked the little girl. I looked it up in the dictionary and discovered it meant osiers, or willows.

"Just a willow like ours?" she asked, rejecting this intrusion of the commonplace. Yes, but once, when His father was struggling with a heavy piece of timber almost beyond his strength, the Child ran and touched it with one finger and the timber rose and fell properly into place. At night His mother cradled Him and sang long slow songs about a lonely tree waiting for Him in a far place; and the Child, moved by her tears, spoke long before it was time for Him to speak and His first words were, "Don't be sad, for you shall be Queen of Heaven." And there she was in an old picture, with the airy jeweled crown being set upon her golden hair.

I thought how nearly all of these tender medieval songs and legends about this Child were concerned with trees, wood, timbers, beams, crosspieces; and even the pagan North transformed its great druidic tree festooned with human entrails into a blithe festival tree hung with gifts for the Child, and some savage old man of the woods became a rollicking saint with a big belly. But I had never talked about Santa Claus, because myself I had not liked him from the first, and did not even then approve of the boisterous way he had almost crossed out the Child from His own birthday feast.

"I like the part about the sunbeam bridge the best," said the little girl, and then she told me she had a dollar of her own and would I take her to buy a Christmas present for her mother.

We wandered from shop to shop, and I admired the way the little girl, surrounded by tons of seductive, specially manufactured holiday merchandise for children, kept her attention fixed resolutely on objects appropriate to the grown-up world. She considered seriously in turn a silver tea service, one thousand dollars; an embroidered handkerchief with lace on it, five dollars; a dressing table mirror framed in porcelain flowers, eighty-five dollars; a preposterously showy crystal flask of perfume, one hundred twenty dollars; a gadget for curling the eyelashes, seventy-five cents; a large plaque of colored glass jewelry, thirty dollars; a cigarette case of some fraudulent material, two dollars and fifty cents. She weakened, but only for a moment, before a mechanical monkey with real fur who did calisthenics on a crossbar if you wound him up, one dollar and ninety-eight cents.

The prices of these objects did not influence their relative value to her and bore no connection whatever to the dollar she carried in her hand. Our shopping had also no connection with the birthday of the Child or the legends and pictures. Her air of reserve toward the long series of bleary-eyed, shapeless old men wearing red flannel blouses and false, white-wool whiskers said all too plainly that they in no way fulfilled her notions of Christmas merriment. She shook hands with all of them politely, could not be persuaded to ask for anything from them and seemed not to question the obvious spectacle of thousands of persons everywhere buying presents instead of waiting for one of the army of Santa Clauses to bring them, as they all so profusely promised.

Christmas is what we make it and this is what we have so cynically made of it: not the feast of the Child in the straw-filled crib, nor even the homely winter bounty of the old pagan with the reindeer, but a great glittering commercial fair, glittering, gay enough with music and food and extravagance of feeling and behavior and expense, more and more on the order of the ancient Saturnalia. I have nothing against Saturnalia, it belongs to this season of the year: but how do we get so confused about the true meaning of even our simplest-appearing pastimes?

Meanwhile, for our money we found a present for the little girl's mother. It turned out to be a small green pottery shell with a colored bird perched on the rim which the little girl took for an ash tray, which it may as well have been.

"We'll wrap it up and hang it on the tree and *say* it came from Santa Claus," she said, trustfully making of me a fellow conspirator.

"You don't believe in Santa Claus any more?" I asked carefully, for we had taken her infant credulity for granted. I had already seen in her face that morning a skeptical view of my sentimental legends, she was plainly trying to sort out one thing from another in them; and I was turning over in my mind the notion of beginning again with her on other grounds, of making an attempt to draw, however faintly, some boundary lines between fact and fancy, which is not so difficult; but also further to show where truth and poetry were, if not the same being, at least twins who could wear each other's clothes. But that couldn't be done in a day nor with pedantic intention. I was perfectly prepared for the first half of her answer, but the second took me by surprise.

"No, I don't," she said, with the freedom of her natural candor, "but please don't tell my mother, for she still does."

For herself, then, she rejected the gigantic hoax which a whole powerful society had organized and was sustaining at the vastest pains and expense, and she was yet to find the grain of truth lying lost in the gaudy debris around her, but there remained her immediate human situation, and that she could deal with, or so she believed: her mother believed in Santa Claus, or she would not have said so. The little girl did not believe in what her mother had told her, she did not want her mother to know she did not believe, yet her mother's illusions must not be disturbed. In that moment of decision her infancy was gone forever, it had vanished there before my eyes.

Very thoughtfully I took the hand of my budding little diplomat, whom we had so lovingly, unconsciously prepared for her career, which no doubt would be quite a successful one; and we walked along in the bright sweet-smelling Christmas dusk, myself for once completely silenced.

CONTRIBUTORS

ROBERT OLEN BUTLER has published ten novels and two volumes of short stories, one of which, *A Good Scent from a Strange Mountain*, won the 1993 Pulitzer Prize for fiction. His stories have appeared in such publications as *The New Yorker, Esquire, The Paris Review, Harper's, GQ, Zoetrope*, and *The Sewanee Review*. They also have been chosen for inclusion in four annual editions of *The Best American Short Stories*, seven annual editions of *New Stories from the South*, and numerous college literature textbooks. A recipient of both a Guggenheim Fellowship in fiction and a National Endowment for the Arts grant, he also won the Richard and Hinda Rosenthal Foundation Award from the American Academy of Arts and Letters and a National Magazine Award for Fiction. He is the Francis Eppes Professor holding the Michael Shaara Chair in Creative Writing at Florida State University. He is married to the novelist and playwright Elizabeth Dewberry.

KELLY CHERRY was born in Baton Rouge. She is presently the Eudora Welty Professor Emerita of English and the Evjue-Bascom Professor Emerita in the Humanities at the University of Wisconsin, Madison. Her publications include six books of poetry, six books of fiction, a collection of essays, and an autobiography. Cherry's *The Society of Friends* received the Dictionary of Literary Biography Award for a distinguished volume of short stories. "About Grace" was first published in 1997 in *First Light*, Calypso Publications; it won a PEN Syndicated Fiction Award in 1990 and was broadcast over National Public Radio.

KATE CHOPIN was born Katherine O'Flaherty in 1851. Her father, Thomas O'Flaherty, left County Galway to become a prosperous merchant in St. Louis; her mother, Eliza Faris O'Flaherty, was of French Creole ancestry. Following her marriage at the age of nineteen to cotton trader Oscar Chopin, Kate relocated to New Orleans, eventually settling in Cloutierville. There the couple lived with their children until Oscar's death in 1883. Eventually Chopin returned to St. Louis and began composing stories full of local color about life in the Cane River region of Louisiana. Two volumes of short fiction, *A Night in Arcadie* and *Bayou Folk*, were greeted with critical and popular success. Her novel about a woman's quest for sexual freedom, *The Awakening*, which was published in 1899, was deemed scandalous by reviewers of the era. Chopin died in 1904.

DEBRA GRAY DE NOUX is a native of Oregon who has lived in New Orleans since 1992. She is a longtime associate publisher of Pulphouse Publishing in Eugene, Oregon. Her fiction has appeared in *Dead of Night, Night Terrors, Over My Dead Body, Peeping Tom* (England), and *Urges* (Scotland). She is the editor of the fiction anthology *Erotic New Orleans*, Pontalba Press, 2001.

O'NEIL DE NOUX, born in New Orleans, is a former homicide detective and organized crime investigator with the Jefferson Parish sheriff's office and St. Bernard Parish sheriff's office in suburban New Orleans. Among his major works are *The Big Show, Blue Orleans, Crescent City Kills,* and *LaStanza: New Orleans Police Stories.* His short fiction has been published in *Ellery Queen Mystery Magazine, Mary Higgins Clark Mystery Magazine,* and *New Mystery Magazine,* as well as in numerous publications throughout western Europe. He teaches mystery writing at the University of New Orleans and is the founding editor of two fiction magazines, *Mystery Street* and *New Orleans Stories.*

LAURA J. DULANEY, born in Charleston, South Carolina, is a southern nomad and a one-time resident of Ruston, Louisiana. She is a former teacher of English, Spanish, and drama, and is now pursuing a career in writing. Her appearance in this volume marks her publication debut.

ALICE DUNBAR-NELSON was a novelist, poet, essayist, dramatist, educator, and critic associated with the Harlem Renaissance. She was born Alice Moore on July 19, 1875, in New Orleans, the daughter of a Creole seaman and a black seamstress. Moore grew up in New Orleans and was educated at Straight University, Cornell University, the Pennsylvania School of Industrial Art, and the University of Pennsylvania. *Violets and Other Tales,* her first collection of stories, poems, and essays, was published in 1895. Shortly thereafter the author and her family relocated to the North where she met and married writer Paul Laurence Dunbar. The couple would later divorce. The rich Creole culture evoked in *The Goodness of St. Rocque and Other Stories* established her reputation as a writer of local color. In addition to her short fiction, Alice Dunbar-Nelson authored and produced several stage plays. As a critic she reviewed the works of other black writers of the time, including Langston Hughes, helping to further their careers. In 1916 she married journalist Robert Nelson, a union which lasted until her death in 1935.

PATTY FRIEDMANN, a resident of New Orleans, is the author of the critically acclaimed *The Exact Image of Mother* and the humor book *Too Smart to Be Rich.* In 1999 her novel *Eleanor Rushing* was both a Barnes & Noble "Discover Great New Writers" and a Borders "Original Voices" selection. Her next novel, *Odds,* appeared a year later. Her short stories have appeared in *Louisiana Literature, Short Story, Xavier Review,* and *Louisiana English Journal.* Her "My Turn" essay appeared in *Newsweek* in July 1999. *Secondhand Smoke,* her fourth novel, was released in September 2002 by Counterpoint Press and was a "Book Sense 76" selection.

HARNETT T. KANE was born in 1910. "Won't You Lead Us in 'Jingle Bells'?" originally appeared in *Have Pen, Will Travel,* published in 1959, a book that chronicles Kane's time spent on a book signing tour following the publication in 1958 of *The Southern Christmas*

Book. Among his other writings are *Louisiana Hayride, The Bayous of Louisiana, Deep Delta Country, Plantation Parade,* and *New Orleans Woman.* Kane died in 1984.

JAMES KNUDSEN directs the Creative Writing Workshop at the University of New Orleans, where he is a professor of English. His work has been published in *Beloit Fiction Journal, Denver Quarterly, Kansas Quarterly, Louisiana Literature, Puerto del Sol, Sonora Review,* and *Something in Common,* a collection of short stories by Louisiana writers published by LSU Press.

SOLOMON NORTHRUP was a free black man who was abducted from the North in 1841 and ended up a slave on a Louisiana plantation near the Red River. Northrup endured years of captivity before being freed; upon his release he recorded his experiences in *Twelve Years a Slave,* first published in 1853, from which his Christmas memoir is taken. His account of slave participation in holiday festivities stands in sharp contrast to one written by the wife of a plantation owner (see Ruth McEnery Stuart).

FRANCIS X. PAVY was born in Lafayette on March 2, 1954, and is a lifelong resident of Louisiana. As a child, Pavy studied art under the direction of Elemore Morgan, Jr. In college he studied music, ceramics, animation, painting, printmaking, and sculpture, graduating in 1976 with a fine arts degree in sculpture. In 1977, Pavy started working in a glass shop, making leaded and beveled glass windows and in 1982 he opened his own studio. He adopted painting as his primary medium in 1985. Pavy lives and works in Lafayette, Louisiana.

KATHERINE ANNE PORTER, essayist, short story writer, journalist, and descendent of Daniel Boone, was born in Indian Creek, Texas, but she grew up in Texas and Louisiana, residing in Lafayette and later Baton Rouge. Her first collection of short stories was *Flowering Judas,* published in 1930. Among her best-known works are

Pale Horse, Pale Rider (1939), *The Learning Tower* (1944), and her only novel, *Ship of Fools* (1962). Her *Collected Stories* (1965) was awarded the 1966 Pulitzer Prize and the National Book Award. In the 1970s she published *Collected Essays and Other Writings* (1970) and *The Never-Ending Wrong* (1977), an account of the infamous Sacco-Vanzetti trial and execution. She died in Silver Spring, Maryland, on September 18, 1980.

DOROTHY DODGE ROBBINS teaches in the English Department at Louisiana Tech University. Her essays and reviews have been published in *The Centennial Review, Critique, The Midwest Quarterly, The Southern Quarterly,* and *The Texas Review.*

KENNETH ROBBINS serves as director of the School of the Performing Arts at Louisiana Tech University. His short stories have appeared in *Briar Cliff Review, A Carolina Literary Companion, Heritage of the Great Plains, The North Dakota Quarterly,* and *St. Andrews Review,* among others. His novel, *Buttermilk Bottoms,* received both the Toni Morrison Prize for Fiction and the Associated Writing Programs Novel Award. Robbins's stage plays have been performed throughout the United States, Canada, Denmark, Ireland, and Japan. He is a former Fulbright Scholar, a Malone Fellow, and a Japan Foundation Artists Fellow.

SHERYL ST. GERMAIN was born and raised in New Orleans. Currently she is an associate professor at Iowa State University, where she teaches poetry and creative nonfiction. Her work has received several awards, including two NEA Fellowships, an NEH Fellowship, the Dobie-Paisano Fellowship, and, most recently, the William Faulkner Award for the personal essay. Her poems and essays have appeared in numerous journals, including *Calyx, New Letters, North American Review, River Styx,* and *TriQuarterly Review.* She has published five volumes of poetry, including *How Heavy the Breath of God* and *The Mask of Medusa,* and a book of translations of the work of Cajun poet Jean Arceneaux, *Je Suis Cadien.* "Trying to Sing" is from her collection of essays about growing up in New Orleans, *Swamp Songs: The Making of an Unruly Woman* (2003).

LYLE SAXON was born in 1891 in Baton Rouge. For a time he worked as a journalist in New Orleans. He was a writer in residence at the Melrose Plantation near Natchitoches during the 1920s and 1930s. There he composed his only novel, *Children of Strangers*, which drew upon both the rich heritage of the Cane River country and plantation life. He was the director of the WPA Federal Writers' Project in Louisiana, work which culminated in the 1946 publication of *Gumbo Ya-Ya: A Collection of Folk Tales*. Saxon died the same year.

GENARO KỲ LÝ SMITH earned his M.A. and M.F.A. at McNeese State University, where he studied under Pulitzer Prize–winning author Robert Olen Butler. Smith teaches creative writing, composition, and literature at Louisiana Tech University. Chapters of his first novel have appeared in *Amerasia Journal*, *turnrow*, and *Gumbo: Stories by Black Writers*. Some of his other works have been published in *The Shooting Star Review*, *The Northridge Review*, and *dis-Orient*. In 1999 he was the winner of the Zora Neale Hurston/Richard Wright fiction competition, and he was awarded the Louisiana Division of the Arts Fellowship for the year 2001–2002.

RUTH MCENERY STUART was born in Marksville in Avoyelles Parish in 1852, but grew up in New Orleans. She married Alfred Stuart in 1879 and moved with him to Arkansas, where he owned a sizable cotton plantation. When he died during their fourth year of marriage, she returned to New Orleans and began writing local color stories. Her pleasant sketches of plantation life depict kindly masters and happy slaves, an image at odds with less colorful, but more accurate, historic accounts (see Solomon Northrup). She died in 1917.